CLOSE
TO YOU

BOOKS BY KERRY WILKINSON

Standalone Novels

Ten Birthdays
Two Sisters
The Girl Who Came Back
Last Night
The Death and Life of Eleanor Parker
The Wife's Secret
A Face in the Crowd

The Jessica Daniel series

The Killer Inside (also published as *Locked In*)
Vigilante
The Woman in Black
Think of the Children
Playing with Fire
The Missing Dead (also published as *Thicker than Water*)
Behind Closed Doors
Crossing the Line
Scarred for Life
For Richer, For Poorer
Nothing But Trouble
Eye for an Eye
Silent Suspect

The Unlucky Ones

The Jessica Daniel Short Stories

January
February
March
April

Silver Blackthorn

Reckoning
Renegade
Resurgence

The Andrew Hunter series

Something Wicked
Something Hidden
Something Buried

Other

Down Among the Dead Men
No Place Like Home
Watched

CLOSE TO YOU

KERRY WILKINSON

Bookouture

Published by Bookouture in 2019

An imprint of Storyfire Ltd.
Carmelite House
50 Victoria Embankment
London EC4Y 0DZ

www.bookouture.com

ISBN: 978-1-83888-162-7
eBook ISBN: 978-1-83888-161-0

ONE

THE NOW

Sunday

There's nothing quite like a good hypocrite.

The people surrounding me, not to mention myself, will spend our day-to-day lives telling people about the benefits of moderation. A small glass of wine contains around 120 calories, so *moderation* is the key. Let's be *moderate*, people. Nothing wrong with a glass or two here or there, but let's hold back on downing half-a-bottle a night, yeah? Let's not even dream of putting away a full bottle of Asda's own £4-a-bottle white on a Friday night. That's probably 800 calories right there and all your good work will be for nothing.

All true – but none of that stops our room of 'fitness professionals' putting away the booze like a meteor strike has been pencilled in for tomorrow afternoon.

The waiter ambles around to my side of the table and reaches for my glass. His bottle is angled ready to dump another couple of hundred calories, but I place one hand over the rim and wave him away with the other.

'Not for me,' I say.

His lips twitch into something close to a smirk and then they instantly arch down again. Assuming he works at this hotel most Friday and Saturday nights through November and December, he'll have seen this over and over. Grown adults who are one step away from teenagers in a park sharing a bottle of cider.

It really is not for me, though – not tonight in any case. My relationship with alcohol is like my mother's with back-to-back episodes of her favourite soaps. A brief taste and I'm slumped in a chair, drooling for the rest of the night.

The bloke two seats away from me has no such hang-ups. He manages a leisure centre but has that hipsterish, waxy beard-look about him, as if he'd rather be running his own craft brewery. He motions the waiter over and gleefully eyes the white nectar that's emptied into his glass. When it's nearly full, he raises it in my direction: 'To us,' he declares.

I waft my almost empty glass of water towards him. 'To beards,' I reply.

He either doesn't hear me, or doesn't care, as he downs half his glass in one go. This is the problem with these sorts of awards dinners – the seating plans are thrown together like an expressionist's painting of an orgy. It's all a vague collection of limbs and there are dicks everywhere.

Even though it's a ceremony and not strictly a Christmas party, it is December – so the room is decorated with various wreathes and tinsel. There's a giant Christmas tree in the corner and twinkly lights zigzagging across the ceiling. There was turkey for dinner, but, now that's cleared away, the booze is flowing and it's time for the main event.

Well, *almost* time. I am fighting back the yawns as the comedian compère is busy making himself laugh, which at least makes it one person who's enjoying the act. Someone else on my table described him as 'old-school', which is essentially code for 'a bit sexist'. A decade back and there would've been a few racist jokes thrown in for the old-timers.

His act is drawing a mix of muted laughs, awkward silences and brainless cackling from a handful of people who've either been lobotomised or had too much to drink. When the comedian reaches for his water, he trips on the mic stand and gets the biggest laugh of the night. Life offers nothing quite as funny as a stranger falling over and then pretending it hasn't happened.

When his act is done, there's an excited hum to the room. This is the reason we've paid £80-a-head for bad food and unfunny comedy.

On the stage at the front, some bloke in a suit is messing around with the PowerPoint display that's being beamed onto the screen. He's obviously making a hash of it because that's what blokes in suits do. He jabs at a laptop, looks gormlessly to his mate off to the side, holds up both hands, and then has a hushed argument with someone else who ends up plugging in a cable. A slide finally appears, displaying 'Eighth Annual UK Fitness Professional Awards'.

It's not exactly the BAFTAs and, as I sit through a series of prizes being awarded, I start to question a few of my life choices. I've done some bad things in my time, one in particular, but I've *never* stumbled onto a stage and thanked 'God, the Queen and my Mum' for allowing my branch of Total Fitness to win gym chain of the year.

Most people here are of the eye-rolling variety. We know this is a farce, but it's also the game we play. For personal trainers like me, winning these sorts of awards means more offers of work, more appearances, better contracts, perhaps even a book deal.

I've more or less switched off when my best friend, Jane, leans over to me. She's more excited than I am: 'Is this your award?'

It takes me a second to catch what she's said but, when I look up, I realise that she's right. Jane hasn't said much all evening, although she doesn't really know anyone. I would have come with Andy, but he's busy with his scout troop. That sounds like a euphemism, but isn't – there really *is* a scout troop. I was happy to come by myself, but Jane said she'd be my plus-one and that was that. I could have mentioned a midwinter trip to the Antarctic with Piers Morgan and she'd have still volunteered to come. I think that's what happens when there's a 16-month-old at home. Any excuse for a night away. She won't say it out loud, but she's definitely missed work since giving up her job to have Norah.

The slide on the screen has changed to read 'Personal Trainer of the Year' and then 'Seven Nation Army' pulses in the background as Steven, the organiser, runs through a list of the nominees. Before today, I'd only met him via emails. He has that comic-book airline-pilot-look going on. All neat hair, stiff upper lip and moustachy.

There are five of us nominated for the award, with our photos flashing across the screen as our names are announced. 'Jason McMahon', whose head is like a cork atop a barrel, gets a big cheer from his table. The next three names get polite applause and I tense as my own face appears on the screen. It's one of the shots from my portfolio, the one that I convinced myself was a good idea after reading a *New Year, New You* article and, presumably, temporarily losing my mind.

'And finally,' Steven says, his moustache practically audible, 'after all she's been through, Morgan Persephone.'

There's a gentle wave of applause that gets louder as people realise who I am. He's pronounced my name wrong, making it rhyme with 'telephone', instead of 'per-sef-oh-knee'.

A shiver creases along my back, but not because of the mispronunciation.

After all she's been through.

Maybe they are; maybe they're not – but I can feel everyone watching as I give the watery, closed-lip smile that I've become so good at over the past couple of years. I can sense the whispers, if not hear them. People telling those next to them that my husband disappeared two years ago.

There is mercifully little time to dwell as Steven rips open the envelope like a kid with a Christmas present.

'And the winner is…'

He pauses, thinking he's Simon Cowell waiting to tell some Mariah wannabe that she's one step closer to being a little-known answer to a pub quiz question.

'…Morgan Persephone.'

Steven gets my name wrong again and there's a second or two in which I can't quite take in what he's said. It's like we're in different time zones with a slight delay.

Jane leans in and gleefully hisses, 'You won!' – and then I find myself clambering to my feet. Jane adds a quick 'Smile!', which is when I realise I'm stumbling blankly to the front, like a drunk at closing time. I wave to a pair of women I don't know on one of the front tables, largely because they're clapping and cheering. I've seen those award shows, where winners guff a load of nonsense about not expecting their victories. This isn't that. I had an inkling ever since the nominations went out in a barely noticed press release a couple of months back. I suspected I'd probably win, if for no other reason than everyone loves a good redemption story. That doesn't prepare me for the wall of noise, all from strangers. The eruption is disorientating and hard to prepare for.

I head onto the stage and Steven passes me a golden trophy that's in the shape of a treadmill. I expect it to be heavy, but the metal is plasticky and cheap. No matter – it's the title that counts. A weird thought that creeps into my mind that I'm going to need new business cards. 'Personal Trainer of the Year' sounds a lot better than 'Personal Trainer'.

Everything is a bit of a blur – but it's been like that since it all happened with David.

After all she's been through.

Sometimes it feels as if someone else is steering the ship and I'm watching myself go through life.

Not now. In this moment, I'm completely aware that nobody wants to look like the bitch who prepared a speech in advance. I run through the mental list of things to say while attempting to make it seem as off-the-cuff as possible. I remember to thank the organiser Steven; the gyms where I work and a few other industry types. To an untrained eye, it probably seems as if I know what I'm doing. That's the game, really. That's life. Nobody cares if a person *actually* knows what they're doing, as long as they look like it.

When I'm done, Steven re-takes the mic and I hustle back to my table while shaking hands like a low-level Royal opening a community centre. When I get to my seat, more people come over to offer congratulations and pass across business cards, like I'm a hooker heading to a London phone box. I know very few faces, only a handful of people from the speaking circuit.

Jane gives me a hug, but it's awkward because we're both sitting. The drunken leisure centre manager downs the rest of his wine and winks. There are more nods and waves and then, finally, Steven hushes everyone and continues onto the next category.

It's late and, despite the rush of the past few minutes, I have to stifle a yawn. I've never really got these people that can do all-nighters. I'm a drowsy mess after about 11 and, with my trophy in hand, the hotel bed is calling.

Steven runs through the nominees for Fitness Brand of the Year and, after another blast of 'Seven Nation Army', he names the winner. There's a big cheer from the table at the front and then, after a chaotic speech with half a dozen people trying to talk over one another, the ceremony is finally put out of its misery.

Jane uses the table to push herself up and is clear-eyed as she rubs my upper arm. 'You deserve this,' she says.

'It's only an industry award.'

'*Your* industry, though. It's amazing… especially after everything you've been through.'

There's that line again…

She smiles and then adds: 'Are there photos?'

'I hope not.'

Jane nods over my shoulder, to where Steven is beckoning together the winners. 'I'll keep an eye on your bag,' she says.

Suddenly, out of nowhere, I'm back to my wedding day. Back with David. I have to blink away the moment. I think of him every day – but it's never the Saturday we married; it's always what happened at the end.

Someone says, 'Where is everyone?' and then it's all, 'Stand here', 'Look there', 'Smile', 'Don't smile', 'Point there', 'Laugh', 'Roll over' – and so on. Possibly without the rolling over. There are around thirty winners in all and we're divided into various groups for the picture-taking on the stage. At the rear of the room, the staff bustle back and forth clearing the tables.

Steven continues to take photos, but Jane and others are there, too, with their phones. Nothing can happen nowadays without it being captured and sent to the cloud. Steven asks all the winners to smoosh closer together. I make sure I'm angling with my left side away from him, hiding the purple-brown scar at the base of my neck from the camera's unrelenting gaze.

He takes a few more photos and then puts his camera down. We're all ready to stop tensing our muscles when Jane calls, 'One more' and then she clicks a final photo or three.

After that, we are finally done. Everyone offers weary smiles and drifts back to their colleagues. One of the other winners asks if I want a drink to celebrate, but I'm already batting away yawns. Sex and chocolate are good – but there's nothing quite like a good sleep.

Before I can get back to the table in order to collect my bag, Steven corners me at the edge of the stage. He is wearing the looks of a man who's relieved it's all over.

'Congratulations,' he says, rubbing my arm while he does so. I'd tell him to stop, but it already feels awkward.

'Thank you.'

'I know it's been hard after everything you've been through.'

'Yes…'

I almost reach for the mark on my neck. I used to rub the scar all the time – but I've been working at stopping myself for months now. Stephen's stare flickers across it without lingering. He leaves my arm alone long enough to smooth his moustache, even though it doesn't look like a hurricane would put a hair out of place. There is a moment in which he angles forward and I wonder if he might try to kiss me. Perhaps it's ego on my part. I brace myself to flinch to the side, but he slants away at the last moment to whisper in my ear.

'I voted for you,' he says.

'Thank you.'

'You've been very brave about everything.'

He speaks as if I've done a lengthy stint in Afghanistan and am finally back in Blighty.

I don't know what to say, so give him a slim smile and a half-hearted 'thanks'.

He pats my shoulder and then disappears off to talk to someone else.

Back at the table, the leisure centre manager has disappeared, along with the remnants of the table wine.

Jane hands me my bag and we step to the side as the staff continue to clear the tables to make way for a dance floor.

'You look tired,' she says.

'This isn't really my thing,' I reply.

Jane finishes her water and passes the empty glass to one of the staff. I've only had a single glass of wine and she's not had any alcohol at all. We're a right pair of lightweights. I'm only thirty-three but can sense my teenage-self disapproving.

'I've got to head back,' Jane says, 'I don't like being away from Norah for a night… not a whole one, anyway.'

We'd spoken about this beforehand and brought two cars. I'm staying at the hotel where the awards are taking place, while Jane is driving home.

She starts to fish into her bag: 'Do you want to see the photos?'

'How do I look in them?'

'Fit.'

'Let's see then.'

She retrieves her phone from her bag and flicks through the images before passing it across. The device is one of those plus-sized ones that's closer to a TV that a phone. Give it a few years and mobiles will be the same size as the bricks that used to pass for phones in the 80s. I suppose fashion really is cyclical. I refuse to use the word 'phablet'. I'd bring back capital punishment for inventing words like that.

The thing about a photograph full of fitness professionals is that we are, by definition, fit. Almost everyone in the picture will have to stay in shape as part of the job. That brings a natural competition. Almost all the women are wearing tight, low-cut tops or dresses, while the men are in custom-cut slimming suits. Everyone is flexing their arms, either subtly or not. At one time, everyone desired the biggest muscles; now it is all about getting lean.

I glance at Jane's photo and clock myself at the side. I've got my back straight, chest puffed up, chin solid, smile fixed. Give it the old tits and teeth. Half of us are turned towards Steven's camera while the others are looking towards Jane. It's all quite the mess.

I'm about to hand the phone back when I spot a face at the very back. It doesn't belong to the group, it's not one of the winners, it's simply there. A man with very short hair, facing sideways but staring directly at the camera with piercing brown eyes. My body tenses and I can't quite take in what I'm seeing. I pinch the screen to zoom until I'm staring at the face of a ghost. He is as he was when I last saw him: wrinkles around the corners of the eyes and a knowing smirk. That's the expression I see when I can't sleep.

'Are you OK?'

I glance up to see Jane frowning in my direction. She has released her hair from its bun and the curly waves have dropped to her shoulders. She seems ready to leave.

'Yes, um…' My gaze flicks to the screen once more. 'Could you send this photo to me?'

'Sure.'

Jane takes back her phone and swipes around the screen until she says 'Done'.

The thing is, I recognise the man in the background of the photo. How could I not? It's just that it can't be him. It's not my ex-husband. It's not David.

I know that better than anyone because he didn't walk out on me. He didn't disappear two years ago and he's not a missing person. I know that for a fact because I'm the one who killed him.

TWO

THE WHY

Three years, ten months ago

Jane frowns across to the pair of blokes who are sitting in the windowsill. They're roughly our age, late-20s or early 30s, and I don't know them.

'Don't light that in here,' she says.

One of the men looks down to the cigarette he's rolling and shrugs. 'I wasn't going to.' He licks his lips and then adds a conspiratorial: 'Want one?'

'No.'

He grins and tilts his head: 'You've changed since uni.' He laughs, though Jane doesn't, and then the duo get up and head off into the garden.

'Ben's friends,' she says by way of explanation.

As they disappear, a blonde woman in yoga pants and a wool sweater ambles into the living room with her boyfriend or husband in tow. She turns in a half-circle, seemingly lost, and then smiles, waves and shrieks, 'Happy birthday!'

There are few things quite as awkward as being at the side of a conversation while not knowing who the other party is. The woman's boyfriend/husband is in the same position and we exchange knowing half-smiles.

'I *love* the new house,' she says.

'We've not got much furniture yet,' Jane replies. 'We're getting there.'

'We're still renting…' The woman delivers her retort with an obvious edge of annoyance, but then levers a wrapped present out from under her boyfriend/husband's arm and hands it over. 'That's for you,' she says. 'I can't believe you're turning thirty. I feel so old.'

'*You* feel old? You're not the one turning thirty.'

Jane opens the gift and it's a picture frame full of a scrappy piecemeal of photos. Jane looks young in all of them and she's alongside various people I don't know.

I presume this is another of Jane's old university friends. Most of the people at the house party know either her or Jane's boyfriend, Ben, in the same way.

Jane and her friend make small talk until the woman disappears off towards the kitchen, her boyfriend or husband trailing a step behind like a trained puppy at heel.

Jane runs her fingers across the pictures and then places the frame down at the side of the TV unit.

'That was Eleanor,' she says. 'I should've introduced you.'

'I wouldn't worry about it.'

I don't explicitly say that I'm not bothered about Jane's university friends, though it has to be somewhat implied. I suppose everyone has different lives depending on who they're with and where they are. It's only events like birthdays, weddings and funerals that bring it all crashing together.

It's been a steady parade of guests arriving for Jane's birthday, but, for now at least, the living room is quiet. We lean on the back of the sofa and stare towards the window at the front. We've known each other for so long that, sometimes, it doesn't need words.

Jane eventually sighs her way into a sentence: 'So…you have news?'

I glance off to the kitchen, wanting the chat but not wanting to be interrupted or overheard. 'Gary dumped me,' I say.

'I thought you were going to break it off with him anyway?'

'That makes it worse. I wasn't into him – but I wanted him to be into me.'

The grin creeps across Jane's mouth and then disappears. I laugh, anyway. We both get it.

'Then the gym is closing down,' I add. 'I lost a job and a boyfriend all within about thirty hours.'

'So… that's two things you didn't like that are both out of your life. Tomorrow's a new day and all that…' She pauses and then adds: 'Perhaps it's a chance to look at something else?'

'Like what?'

'I can ask around to see if there are any jobs going. Ben's bank is often after people to start at the bottom…'

'I don't want to work in a bank. I—'

She holds up a hand to stop me: 'I didn't mean it like that. It's just…' Jane tails off and doesn't finish the sentence properly because we both know she meant it in precisely the way it came out. She works at a design agency that is some sort of mix of public relations and brochure design. I'm not sure anyone really knows what she does, including herself. She's always been artsy and my choice of teaching exercise classes with the goal of working my way up to being a full-on personal trainer with my own studio is alien to her. We were in the same class for every year throughout school and yet there are times at which we feel like utter strangers.

Jane pushes herself away from the sofa. 'I'm going to find Ben,' she says.

'Sorry for dragging down your birthday.'

She rubs my upper arm like she always does when she wants to be reassuring: 'You haven't.'

Jane drifts away, leaving me alone in the living room with only a hum of chatter from the kitchen. Considering she and Ben are apparently still looking for furniture, their house looks largely complete to me. The living room is full of the usual things and there are no obvious gaps. She was probably talking about the little touches she considers important to *finishing* a room. The candles, the abstract prints, the books she'll never read. That's one of the differences between us, I suppose.

I head into the kitchen to get myself a drink. There are beers and wine floating around but I settle for water from the fridge.

It's all right for couples who turn up to parties and can spend the evening chatting to one another. For singles, it is a slow, bubbling panic of trying to latch onto literally anyone who is vaguely familiar. Failing that, it's anyone who seems remotely normal.

I recognise a couple of faces of people who live around the general area, but they're all friends of friends. People I might nod or wave to, rather than anyone with whom I'm pals. They'd still offer an escape, though each of them seems to be chatting and drinking with other people. I've never been one of those who can sidle up and join a conversation. It's only as I find myself back in the living room, having done a lap of the house, that I realise what should have been obvious.

My only real friend is Jane.

It's all a bit pathetic. I'm turning thirty in three months and have no job, no boyfriend and no proper friends. They've either drifted away, or gone off to get married and have kids. That's the problem with remaining in the area in which a person grew up. The competition over who's making the best of their lives is endless. Everyone started in the same place, so it's hard to blame anyone else other than ourselves for failure.

I'm on another lap, heading through the hallway, when the doorbell sounds. I'm not sure if Jane or Ben will have heard so open the door and am faced with a middle-aged man in a cardigan. He smiles awkwardly.

'Could you, uh, turn the music down a bit?'

I blink at him, largely because I'd somehow blanked out the fact there was music playing. It's only now he mentions it that I realise there's an Oasis song playing in the background. I am about to say that I'll find someone who lives here when there's a presence at my side. I glance sideways to see Ben. He's in jeans and a loose-fitting shirt with the sleeves rolled up.

'Sorry about all this,' he says, reaching for the man's hand.

The neighbour seems to have little choice in the matter and ends up shaking.

'I'm Ben. We've just moved in. It's my girlfriend's thirtieth so we were having a bit of a joint housewarming and birthday party.'

'Oh, well that's—'

'Are you from next-door? We would have invited you over but everything's happened really quickly. If you hang on a moment…'

Ben releases the other man's hand and turns quickly, disappearing along the hall towards the kitchen. Moments later, the music dims and then Ben reappears with a six-pack of Guinness in his hand.

He offers the cans to the neighbour, almost forcing them into his hand: 'Here you are, mate. Sorry about everything. What's your name, by the way?'

Ben has spoken so quickly that the man takes a second or two to take it all in. He accepts the cans and straightens his cardigan.

'Oh, this wasn't necessary. It's Cliff. My wife's Alice. She's very sensitive to loud noise, you see.' He taps his ears as if to indicate the issue and Ben tilts his head.

'Oh, that's awful. I'm so sorry. If there's ever anything we can do, just let us know.'

Cliff bobs awkwardly. I suspect he was fired up, ready for an argument and now, from nowhere, he's got a new buddy. He holds the cans up, says thanks again, and then turns and heads off back to his house.

Ben watches him leave and then closes the door, before turning to me and shrugging.

'Seems like a nice bloke,' he says.

I can't tell if he's being genuine, or if there's an edge there. That's Ben all over, though. He and Jane met at university and have been together for a decade since. He travelled from the other end of the country to come down to Kingbridge, while Jane picked the university that was a little over half an hour away from where we grew up in Gradingham. That perhaps explains the difference between them.

Ben looks to me and his eyes are like buttons: big and round and blue. It feels as if I'm frozen. He's always been able to do this to me, but it's not the kind of thing I could ever say out loud. I don't even think it's a physical thing; it's more the way he is. There's something effortless about him. As if life itself comes so naturally that he doesn't need to try.

'How's it going, Morgs?'

'It's been worse.'

'It was about time you got rid of that Gary.'

'It wasn't quite like that, but yes…'

'Keep your chin up,' he says. 'Everything will come together.'

If anyone else had said it, the words might have sounded cheesy – but there's something about Ben's phrasing that means I don't question it. Perhaps things really *will* come together.

He grins and possibly winks. It's hard to know because it's there and gone. 'I've got to go find the birthday girl,' he says. 'We'll catch up later.'

With that, he disappears up the stairs, leaving me alone in the hall. I watch him go and then move to the bottom step, sitting by myself and taking out my phone to make it seem like I'm doing something other than wallowing.

Minutes pass and then there is a clatter of footsteps and suddenly someone is sitting next to me.

'Parties not your thing, either?' the newcomer says.

I turn and it's an older man I don't know. I've never been great at judging ages but he's got that silver-fox thing going on, with short, pepper-pot hair. He's maybe a decade older than me and there's something about his shrugged indifference that is immediately appealing.

'Is it anyone's?' I reply.

'In my experience, the moment anyone invites you to a party, you start thinking of ways to possibly get out of it.'

I laugh and shuffle sideways on the step so that I can lean on the wall and get a better look at him.

'How do you know Jane?' I ask.

'I don't really. I'm an old friend of Ben's from university. We were in the football team. A few of us came together for a bit of a reunion.'

As if to emphasise the point, he raises his can of Boddington's to someone who passes us on the way up the stairs.

'What about you?' he asks. 'How do you know Jane?'

'From school. I think we were six or seven when we first met.'

He pouts a lip and nods. 'I think you win,' he says, offering his hand. 'David,' he adds.

'Morgan.'

'Nice to meet you.'

THREE

THE NOW

Here's the thing with being a killer: for the most part, it doesn't change a person from appearing 'normal'. Murderers still have unexpected items in the bagging area and get stuck in traffic jams. We're still against racism and sexism. We support gay marriage and love Attenborough documentaries. We're not monsters. We go to work and lose hours looking at videos of dogs on the Internet when we're supposed to be doing other things. Taking the life of another human doesn't stop the world from turning. Day becomes night becomes day.

Everyone else has spent two years thinking David disappeared. What I did to him only changed me in the sense that I know murder is something of which I'm capable. Serial killers can be glorified, but I've never had the urge to repeat the act. I suspect most people who've killed are like me. We live in plain sight. We're neighbours and friends; colleagues and relatives – it's just that our secrets run somewhat deeper than most.

My phone buzzes as the photo arrives from Jane. I pinch the screen and zoom to take in the features of my dead husband.

Is it him?

It *looks* like him – but the photo is pixelated on my screen. I pinch in and out but can't be certain. David didn't have any distinguishing features like tattoos, deformed ears, or a big nose.

The man in the picture has the same greying hair and rigidly straight back as my David.

He's only visible from the chest up, but it looks like he's wearing a navy-blue suit. David did used to own one, though most of his clothes ended up at the charity shop.

I look up from the phone, scanning the room for anyone in a blue suit.

'Are you sure you're OK?'

'Fine,' I answer, too quickly. I assume she never noticed the figure at the back of her photo. Why would she? She'd have no need to be scanning the other people in the picture.

'I've got to get going,' Jane says, dangling her car keys from her ring finger. 'Congratulations on the win. I'm so pleased for you.' She leans in and kisses me on the cheek and then hoists her bag higher on her shoulder. 'We'll catch up soon,' she adds.

Having been ready for sleep, it now feels like I've downed a quadruple espresso. My head is buzzing and it's as if I can suddenly see more clearly. People are starting to drift away from the main room; heading to bed, or out to their cars to drive home. Others are crowding around the bar, while the DJ at the back is busy talking over the music. A few of the more inebriated are already on the dance floor, flapping around like epileptic farm animals.

I do a lap of the room, looking for anyone in a blue suit. There are a couple of men – but none who look like my former husband. David didn't have any brothers or cousins that I know of. I stop to look at the image once more, but it's hard to know either way. Jane's phone has a bigger screen than mine.

I can barely watch a television show in which there's not someone who looks a bit like someone else I sort of know. If I'm ever watching something new, I spend half the show trying to figure out what I've seen the lead actor in before, and the other half wondering who the rest of the cast look like. It's not beyond the realms of possibility that there's someone who *looks* like David.

The award in my hand means that various people are stopping me every few paces, largely to say congratulations – although it's hard to miss the head tilts and sympathetic smiles. The story goes that David disappeared two years ago and it's as if everyone expects me to be constantly on the brink of a breakdown.

I do a second lap of the room and, after seeing nobody who looks like David, I head towards the reception area of the hotel. There are plush crimson carpets and more people milling around. Someone is lugging a suitcase to the front desk, though there is no one in a blue suit.

I'm not sure what else to do and find myself in the elevator, pressing the button for the upstairs floor to head to my room. A man eyes my trophy and nods an acknowledgement.

When I get upstairs, I spend the usual amount of time trying to get into my room. The keycard fails to work on the first two attempts and, as I'm about to start cursing everyone involved in the hotel industry, I realise it's because I'm using it the wrong way around.

Inside, and I clip on the chain and thunk down the lock. I sit on the bed and stare at Jane's photo. The resemblance to David is uncanny. He might not have had any significant distinguishing features – but he had a solid jaw and thick brows that framed his dark eyes and always seemed to give him an authority. I tell myself it's not him – that I, more than anyone, know it can't be.

I'm still staring at the photo when the phone buzzes and makes me jump. It's from Andy.

How did it go?

I begin a reply, but my fingers are trembling too much to type properly. It doesn't help that autocorrect is up to its usual standards of changing words like 'sleepy' into 'slutty'. That would be an entirely different kind of reply, so I call him instead.

Andy sounds surprised when he answers: 'You sound more coherent than I thought you might,' he says.

'I've not been drinking.'

'I thought you'd either be partying or sleeping. How did you do?'

'I won.'

There's a slight delay and I wonder whether the line has cut out, but then he replies: 'You don't sound too excited about it...?'

I'm not sure how to answer but manage: 'It's been a long day, that's all. I think I need some sleep. Shall we catch up after your class tomorrow?'

'Sure.'

Andy's not the type to hold grudges or start arguments – but I can't quite tell from his voice whether he's annoyed.

'I'm looking forward to Saturday,' he adds.

'Me, too.' I wait and then add: 'Good night.'

He chirps 'I love you' and there's a split second in which I consider saying it back. I have said the words to him before, but it doesn't feel right now. Things seem different. I quickly press the red button to hang up instead. He'll think that I didn't hear him.

Another yawn purges through me and the clock says that it's almost midnight. The past hour has charged by.

I don't know what to do. In many ways, nothing is different. I came to these awards as planned, I won, and now the night is over. Everything is the same and yet nothing is. I look at the photo once more, where David's face is peering out from the back of the winners. I zoom in and out, I fiddle with the brightness and contrast, but there's no denying it's him or someone who looks uncannily *like* him.

I down my phone and then rest the trophy on the nightstand. After that, I wriggle out of my dress, before having a wash in the bathroom. It's not long before I'm drawn back to the photo. I can't leave it alone. It's not David and yet, somehow, it is. He's frozen in the moment; neither smiling or frowning, his gaze angled towards Jane as if he knows precisely where the camera is.

When I look at the clock again, it's a few minutes after one. Another hour has zipped by, as if I've blinked forward in time.

There's a bump from the corridor and I hurry across the room until I'm pressing my eye to the spyhole. The hallway is bloated from the fisheye glass, though the only thing of interest is a messy tray of room service left on the floor outside the opposite door.

I return to the bed and sit, then lie, then sit, then stand. Nothing is comfortable.

I slept next to David for long enough – I married him, I killed him – and yet, two years on, he's seemingly here again. Is it a twin? A brother? A cousin? It's not as if he didn't lie about his family once. More than once.

As I lie on the bed and stare at the dimpled bumps of plaster on the ceiling, I can only think of the night it all happened. There was so much I never knew about my husband and now, I suppose, there might be one more thing.

FOUR

THE WHY

Three years, nine months ago

David pulls out my chair and waits for me to sit before tucking me in under the table. He texted me three times after we went our separate ways that first night – and, after two weeks of messaging back and forth, we're finally on a proper date.

The waiter comes across and David says something in Italian to him. Or I assume it is Italian – it's not as if I understand. The waiter takes my coat and then disappears off without a word to me.

'What did you say?' I ask.

'I was asking about wine. I've heard they've got a good cellar here.'

'Oh…'

'Are you a wine drinker?'

'I'm not much of a drinker at all, really.'

He nods knowingly: 'Of course. I should've realised, what with your job and everything.'

David reaches for the table water and pours some into my empty glass. He's in jeans and a sports jacket, which, for most people, would look like some sort of middle-aged cry for help. For him, it works. There's a sophistication about him. As I thought when I first saw him, he is almost exactly a decade older than me. That sort of age difference has never done anything for me before – but I figured there was no harm in going out to dinner together. It's not as if I'm getting any younger – and, besides, there are so many dickheads out there that it's rare to stumble across someone I actually like.

I don't bother correcting him about the fact that I've never really been able to handle my alcohol. If he wants to think it's because of my job, then fair enough.

The Italian place he chose for us to eat is one that I've walked past for years without ever really noticing it. I checked the prices once and decided it wasn't for me. I'm not saying Domino's is the pinnacle of culinary excellence – but I *am* saying a pizza shouldn't cost £20. The inside is all faux Mediterranean, with the walls covered with prints of olive groves and sprawling, sun-drenched shores. If that doesn't set enough of a mood, there are plastic grapes hanging from fake trees in the entranceway, plus glass jars filled with pasta lining the walls.

I'm still eyeing the menu when I sense David watching me around the large card that serves as a menu.

'Did you go to university?' he asks.

I suddenly feel self-conscious, wondering if this is something that might matter to him.

'No,' I reply.

'It's all a bit overrated anyway,' he replies. 'Some of the best people I know are self-taught and self-made.'

'I'm trying to get into personal training,' I say. 'I've done the courses and am running a few classes at some of the local gyms.'

I don't mention that my main gym is closing.

'What's your end goal?' he asks.

'My own studio.'

He nods approvingly: 'I like people who dream big. Have you always worked in fitness?'

'I've done a few things – waitressing, a bit of secretarial stuff. Nothing that took…'

David nods along, but I wonder if he's thinking what I am: that it's embarrassing to be almost thirty and have so little to show for it. Whenever meeting a new person, the first questions are always about name and occupation. It's how we all judge one another. How we judge ourselves, I suppose.

'I've been doing this for about four years,' I add quickly. 'I had to get a few qualifications and I was covering maternity at a gym in Kingbridge. It's spiralled from there.'

I'm not sure why, but I care what David thinks. I want him to approve. Jane has been pushing me for a long time to get what she would see as a 'proper' job. I don't think she'd still be with Ben if it wasn't for the fact that he worked in a bank. Things like that matter to her.

'It's very impressive,' he says. 'I admire people who branch out to take control of their lives.'

He stares at me with such earnestness that I have to hoist the menu higher and hide behind it. I'm not used to this sort of praise.

The waiter relieves the embarrassment by appearing back at the side of the table and asking if we're ready. We each order and then David asks if I'd mind him choosing wine for us to share. I say it's fine and then he opts for something he says he's certain I'll like. I'm not sure how or why he's come to this conclusion but am fine to go with it.

When the waiter heads off, he takes our menus with him, leaving me nothing to hide behind.

'What about you?' I ask, trying to get the conversation away from me. 'What do you do?'

'I trade collectibles.'

'I'm not sure I know what that means.'

He presses back and puffs out his chest. There's pride in talking about something he enjoys explaining. 'It's a family thing. My dad used to do it and I picked it up from him. I buy items like vinyl, books, comics, prints – that sort of thing – and then sell them to buyers around the continent, or in the US.'

Things are starting to click into place. I'd wondered why he was away for work since I met him at Jane's party but didn't want to ask.

'That sounds fun,' I say.

'It can be.'

'Do you travel a lot?'

'Sometimes. It depends on circumstances. I can go months without having to leave home and then need to be on the road for weeks at a time. There are all sorts of conventions. If you know what you're looking for, you can make a good living.'

My mind wanders, knowing that Jane won't approve of David's job.

'How did you end up in Kingbridge?' I ask.

'I came for university. I'm from near Margate, but Dad died while I was on my course, so I never really left.'

'Sorry to hear that.'

He waves it away in the way people do when they don't want to talk about something.

I'm not ready to let him turn the conversation back to me, so quickly add: 'You told me you knew Ben through football at uni – but you're a bit, um…?'

David smiles and interrupts before I can finish the thought: 'You can say older.'

'Sorry…'

'You're right. I went to university a bit later in life than most. One of the ways I tried to fit in was to get involved with the football team. I used to be a bit nippy in my time. Not a bad winger. I once scored four in a cup final when I was still at school.'

'You must've been good.'

He shrugs humbly, although, if he was *that* modest, he wouldn't have mentioned it in the first place.

'I was scouted by the county,' he says. 'Had trials with Gillingham and Brighton, but things didn't work out. Even with university, I was always putting off going into the same business as Dad. I think I was always destined to do this.'

The waiter returns with a bottle of wine and there's the cartoon routine of him pouring a bit, David tasting and giving a barely-there nod, and then the waiter pouring it into both of our glasses. They exchange another word or ten in Italian and then we're alone once more.

David raises his glass: 'To entrepreneurs,' he says. 'We're both doing our own thing.'

I'm not sure that's true, but we clink glasses anyway and I have a sip. I half expect David to ask me what I can taste. People bang on about peat and floral aftertastes, but wine tastes of wine to me. It's not complicated. Luckily, David says nothing of the sort.

It's not long before the food arrives. David tells me how he once came across an early Superman *Action Comics* issue that he bought for a pound and sold for 'six-figures'. Then there was some early Ferrari memorabilia that he picked up from a flea market in Italy that he sold for 'the cost of a car itself'.

We spend most of the time talking about David, which is fine as it takes the focus away from me. Conversation comes easily and, though there's more than a hint of the grandiose about his boasts, it's not the worst trait. If I'd bought something for a pound and sold it for six-figures, I'd be telling people, too. His last name is 'Persephone', which he insists does not rhyme with 'telephone'. He brings it up without prompting, but says the name with pride, as if it's Windsor, or something like that. A moniker of which to be honoured. Perhaps it's why he says it, like it's a tactic or something, but I find myself running the name Morgan Persephone through my mind. I can already hear people mispronouncing it and having to correct them.

In a blink, the evening passes. We share a tiramisu and then I realise the restaurant is largely empty. The staff are hanging around

with little to do. It doesn't take a psychic to realise that they're
ready to go home.

The waiter brings the bill unprompted, presenting it in a smart
leather booklet as if it's a treasured first edition. The type of thing
David might buy cheaply and sell on.

David reaches for the bill, but I'm not the sort to give too much
ground and passively allow him to pay. Our fingers brush and it
feels like that jolt of knowing the correct answer to a question.

There is a brief moment in which we both freeze and I know
he feels it, too. It's only a second, perhaps not even that, and then
he slides the bill away.

'I've got this,' he says.

'You don't have to.'

'It's fine.'

He reaches into the inside pocket of his jacket and then checks
the other side. His brow creases and then he tries the two outer
pockets on his jacket, before he stands and checks his jeans.

'I can't find my wallet,' he says. 'I had it when I left the house.'

He pats all his pockets once more and then takes off the jacket
and tries again.

'All my cards were in there,' he adds. 'I'm so sorry about this.'

I assure him it's fine, though the waiter has noticed there's
a problem and comes across to ask what's wrong. David asks if
anyone's handed in a wallet, though there is no such luck.

'I'll pay,' I say, digging out my purse from my bag.

David starts to argue, but it's not as if we have much choice.
'There was that thing about pickpockets in the news the other
day…' he adds.

He's still patting his pockets, not concealing that spark of panic
when something valuable is lost.

'I'll pay you back,' David says.

I tap my PIN into the card machine and wait for it to process.
'You can pay next time,' I reply.

There's a momentary gap and then he gets it: 'There'll be a next time…?'

The machine starts to spit out a receipt as I remove my card with a smile: 'I have to get my money's worth somehow.'

FIVE

THE NOW

Monday

I'm still awake at quarter past two in the morning when the text arrives from Jane.

Got home safely! Congrats on the win! Sleepy time now! Zzzzzzzzzz

I put down my phone and twist over in the hotel bed, facing the other side of the room. The lights are off but there's a disrupting hint of white creeping under the door from the corridor. It's an itch that can't be scratched. I can somehow see it even with my eyes closed. I roll back the other way but my feet are caught up in the covers and there's an orangey glow from the street light creeping around the curtains. More distractions. There's no way I can sleep here.

I reply to Jane:

Think I'm going to drive back too. Can't sleep here

I flick on the bedside lamp and then cram everything into my small suitcase. The trophy won't fit, so I end up carrying it down to reception, along with my case. The party has seemingly fizzled out and the reception area is empty except for a weary-looking woman behind the desk. She's tapping something into her phone but quickly puts it down when she notices me.

'Can I help?' she asks.

'I'd like to check out.'

I expect there to be weirdness, but I suppose she's seen far stranger things than a guest checking out at 2.30 a.m. I hand over the room key and get the bill, before heading out towards the car park. I pass the door to the suite in which our awards party was held, and there is a phalanx of unfortunate sods cleaning up after us. The lights continue to twinkle above them, like the scene on a particularly bleak Christmas card.

Outside, and the tarmac of the car park is covered with a glistening sheen of frost. The trees that ring the hotel are glazed white and the air bites like a snarling wolf.

Winter could not care less about how quickly I want to get home.

My windscreen is covered with a layer of ice and, after getting into the car, I turn the heaters up to full and sit with my fingers on the vent, waiting for the glass to clear.

All the while, I think of David with his secrets; and now David in the photo. There is no logic to it and yet, I suppose, ever since I killed him, I've been expecting another of David's surprises. I couldn't have suspected something like this but, among the confusion, there is a degree of inevitability.

Killing David was never going to be the end of his legacy.

The fans have cleared a clear oval in the centre of the windscreen and I ease my way off the car park. It's only a couple of minutes until I'm swallowed by the darkness of the unlit country lanes. It's the type of night where the cold is so all-encompassing that it scratches at a person's soul; where the darkened, frozen tendrils slither unseen until warmth is a distant dream.

I turn on the radio to distract from the night. Because things aren't desolate enough, the presenter is doing a phone-in about the best type of cheese, which is intercut with Christmas music. There's a time and a place for Cliff Richard – birthday parties for dementia sufferers, or Guantanamo Bay – but it's definitely not empty back roads in the dead of night.

The country lanes lead me to deserted A-roads, where there are a handful of headlights. I'm on autopilot and my mind meanders, wondering why other people are out at this unholy hour.

It's almost two and a half hours until I arrive home. It's admirable that the radio presenter somehow managed to drag out a discussion about cheese to last the entirety of the journey. It's a degree or two warmer in Gradingham than at the hotel, but the trees and bushes are still peppered with white. I switch off the engine and sit in the car as the windows immediately begin to steam. The winners' photo is still open on my phone, but, as I zoom in on it, things feel different. Perhaps it's the change of location, or maybe it is the mindlessness of the radio, but the picture of David doesn't feel as shocking as it did when I first saw it. It will simply be someone who looked like my ex-husband, nothing to worry about. A coincidence of circumstance as opposed to anything more. I try to put it out of my mind as I turn onto my street.

Some might think it strange – but I've always liked the sound of my address. It's hardly apt for the weather, but 1 Sunshine Row has an appeal that belies the basic look of the red-brick block.

I yawn as I unlock my front door and sleep suddenly feels close once more. There's nothing quite like my own bed. Like a friend who'll always be there.

As soon as I step inside, the hairs stand up on the back of my neck. It's instinct, like the sense of being watched, or that flash of panic a moment before something terrible happens.

I turn on the light and stand on the welcome mat, taking in the room ahead of me. It is a two-bedroom apartment. There is no hall and the door opens directly into the open-plan living room and kitchen. There are few places to hide and, at first glance, everything feels normal. The television is on the stand where I last saw it. The router is at its side, with green and orange lights blinking. There is still a cluttered pile of mail next to the microwave; with a porridge-coated bowl in the sink and a carton of almond milk on the side that I must've forgotten to return to the fridge.

'Hello…?'

There's no reply and I stand by the door waiting and listening. Nothing, except my imagination.

I step across to the kitchenette, ready to drop my keys into the ceramic Tigger head that's a constant feature of my day. Keys go in; keys come out. If it wasn't for that, they would end up lost in coat pockets, bags, or who knows where. I found it at a collectors' market when I was with David. It cost a fiver – but value isn't only measured with money. It is worth so much more than that, though there are only two people who have ever known its true symbolism. There's me – and there's David.

As I go to drop my keys into Tigger's head, I stop with my hand outstretched towards the counter. When I left for the hotel, I took my keys from the ceramic head. Now, hours later, the counter is inexplicably empty.

SIX

THE WHY

Three years, eight months ago

I'm sitting on the step of my flat when the battered Transit pulls in. The rims are rusty and the exhaust spews a dark, noxious cloud into the alley at the back of where I live. Over time, currencies come and go. People will trade rocks for metals; potatoes for beans. Gold is only valuable because someone decided they liked how shiny it is. Anything can have value – yet there is *always* a time in a person's life where he or she needs a van.

Ben clambers down from the driver's seat as Jane trails around from the passenger side. He borrowed the vehicle from one of his mates, which is, as best I can tell, the way most people get hold of a van. Ben opens the back and then reaches in and picks out a large cardboard box.

'It's not as heavy as it looks,' he insists.

It would sound more authentic if he wasn't rocking from foot to foot, while alternating his grip as if clinging onto a banana skin soaked in washing-up liquid.

Ben rests the box on the lip of the van's bumper and looks towards me. My flat opens into what is, essentially, a dead-end alley. The apartment above mine has a door that opens onto the road at the front, but nobody lives there. I don't know who owns it and have always assumed it's an investor, or something like that.

'Where do you want it?' Ben adds.

I hold open my front door. 'In the living room,' I reply.

He lifts the box, then lowers it. 'Are you sure?'

'I figured David can move things around when it's all inside.'

Ben bites his lip and it's only then that I realise I've misunderstood what he was asking. He wasn't questioning if I was sure about where to put the box…

Either way, the moment is lost and he crouch-walks inside as a grinning Jane watches on.

'He kept claiming it was awkward, rather than heavy,' she says.

'Where's David?' I ask.

Jane turns towards the parking spaces on the road and then ends up looking back to me: 'Isn't he here? I figured he was inside. He left before us.'

I check my phone, but there are no missed calls or messages. 'I've not heard from him,' I say.

We stare at one another blankly for a moment. The journey from David's place in Kingbridge is only a 20-mile drive to mine in Gradingham. It's one road and almost impossible to get lost, even if he didn't know where he was going.

'Perhaps he had to stop for petrol…?' I say.

Jane stares at me for a second too long, but then seemingly catches herself and turns away as Ben re-emerges empty-handed from my flat. The three of us head to the back of the van and take out more of David's belongings. Ben hoists down another box that he insists isn't heavy, while Jane picks up a rucksack that's locked with a small padlock. I grab a duffel bag that is soft and probably filled with clothes.

We carry everything into my flat and put it down on the floor of the living room, next to the first box.

Ben straightens himself and massages his neck: 'I need a smoke,' he says. He takes a step towards the door and then adds: 'Maybe David will be here by the time I'm done.'

There's an obvious punch of annoyance and, though I don't necessarily blame him, it's very out of character.

With Ben outside, Jane and I are left perching on a pair of stools next to the kitchen counter. She makes a point of turning around to take in the space, asking where David's things are going to go without actually doing it.

'I didn't know Ben was smoking again,' I say.

'He's not... not really. He only has the odd one when he's had a stressful day or week.'

I think about pushing it, asking what's led to this particular slip, but I'm not sure I'd get an answer. It's never a good idea with Jane to even imply that everything with her and Ben isn't pure paradise.

Jane takes the impasse to glance around once more. We've known one another since we sat side by side in primary school. We've had numerous silly teenage arguments but always made up quickly. We've shared clothes and gossip; we obsessed about boys and bands. We've grown up together. It's like I can read her mind and I'm certain it's the same for her. We don't always need words.

'I know what I'm doing,' I say.

Jane doesn't bother to deny that this is what she was thinking. 'I'm not saying you don't,' she says.

'David's landlord is selling up,' I add. 'It's not his fault. I offered to let him move in. It was my choice. He didn't ask.'

That's largely true. We'd moved onto seeing each other most nights, even if it was only for a movie and a glass of wine or two on the sofa. He'd mentioned that he might have to move away after his landlord sold and it was clear at what he was hinting. He kept coming back to it before I finally caved. He didn't *ask* specifically, but he might as well have done. I had to ask myself whether I wanted him to leave.

'You don't have to justify anything to me,' Jane replies. 'But it's a big step. You only met at my birthday six weeks ago.'

The fact that she knows this apparently off the top of her head says plenty.

'Didn't you and Ben move in together during your second year at uni?' I ask.

'That was different,' she says.

'Was it? I thought you moved in together to save money and share costs…?'

Jane bites at her nail and then turns and rubs my upper arm. There are so many times that I want to tell her to stop, but it's gone on for so long that I figure it's too late now. I suspect it's more reassuring for her than it ever is for me.

'You're right,' she says. 'I just want you to be happy.'

'David makes me happy.'

Well, happy enough.

She presses her lips together and I know she isn't convinced. I wonder if there's an element of jealousy. Ever since university, she's had Ben. They've been a duo and I've been the single friend hanging around. It's different now.

I'm not in the mood to argue. Our fallings out are always around insignificant things, never anything important. I don't get the chance to reply anyway, because the sound of raised voices drifts through the open front door. Jane and I exchange a bemused look and then we head out to the front, where Ben and David are at the back of the van. Ben has a cigarette in one hand and is jabbing a finger at David with the other.

'That's a lie,' Ben shouts. 'You know it is.'

'Just shut your mouth.'

'I'll do whatever I—' Ben cuts himself off as he notices us in the doorway.

'Everything all right?' I ask.

Ben and David exchange a look that I can't read – and then Ben tosses his cigarette onto the ground and crushes it with his foot.

'Let's get this stuff inside,' he says.

Without another word, Ben grabs a box from the van and carries it towards the flat. Jane and I step out of the way to allow him to pass. David crosses back to his car, which he's parked at an angle at the front of the van. I follow him over, watching as he removes a satchel from the back seat. There's a bobblehead of some footballer on the shelf at the back, though I have no idea who it is.

'Probably didn't need the van,' he says. 'I don't have as much stuff as I thought.'

I nod towards the flat, from which Ben is yet to reappear. Jane has disappeared inside, too. 'What was that about?' I ask.

He digs into the satchel with his back to me: 'What?'

'The argument with you and Ben.'

David turns and shrugs. 'Not much. We're not going to let him spoil our day, are we?' He starts to move past me and then stops, waiting until I'm at his side. 'Number one, Sunshine Row,' he says. 'I like the sound of that.'

SEVEN

THE NOW

This is the equivalent of when somebody starts a sentence with, 'We need to talk'. The truth is that people never need to make a formal announcement about having to talk. If they need a chat, they get on with it. Pre-proclamations mean trouble – and so does the missing Tigger pot.

Everyone who sees it assumes I'm a fan of Winnie The Pooh, but it's nothing to do with it. When I bought it for £5, I was with David and he thought it might be worth more than the price. There was no way I could have known that such a seemingly insignificant piece of clay would change my life. It's probably the reason I glued it back together after it was broken – I couldn't bear to throw it away. It's why it sits on my counter, housing my keys. The last thing I see before I leave the flat and the first thing I see when I return.

But now it's gone.

I check the photo on my phone once more, zooming in on David's face. I'm filled with the same feeling I get when I wonder if I've remembered to lock the front door. I suspect everyone has it at some point. I'll leave as normal and set off on my journey and then, ten minutes later, for seemingly no reason, a thought will worm its way into my mind that I forgot to lock the door. Even if I remember specifically putting my key in the lock, the voice will continue to insist that I did that yesterday. That I definitely forgot to secure things today.

And now I'm wondering if David can be alive.

I *know* I killed him. I *saw* his lifeless eyes. I got rid of the body.

Yet, not only is he in the back of a photo of what most would assume is my proudest moment; but the object that will forever bind our fates has disappeared.

I scratch away the chills that ripple along my arms and then find myself rubbing the scar on my neck before catching myself. I decide that it can only be me who gets a grip on this madness.

I search along both sides of the counter, wondering if I might have knocked it off and somehow not noticed.

Nothing.

I then check the drawers and cupboards, wondering if I moved it and somehow forgot. I look in the oven and the fridge and then move into the living room. I try underneath the sofa cushions and then underneath the sofa itself. After that, I flick through the racks of CDs and then try the cabinet underneath the television.

Nothing.

I look in the bathroom and the spare room. I try my own bedroom, checking the wardrobe and then going through my drawers. I have my head under the bed when I'm sure I hear a creak from the living room. I hurry to the doorway and stare across to the sofa and then the kitchenette on the other side of the room.

There's nobody there.

'Hello?'

There is silence except for the echo of my own voice, which I realise could be in my imagination, too.

I find myself staring at the tissue box on the coffee table, wondering if it was on its side when I left. Then there's my shoes next to the bed. Weren't they straight, rather than askew? I can't remember.

The Tigger pot is nowhere to be seen, but, not only that, there is no sign of anyone breaking in. The door was locked; the windows are closed and secure.

It's almost half past five in the morning and nearly an entire day since I last slept. Yawn is building upon yawn, with tears of exhaustion running down my cheeks.

I can't bring myself to unpack my night bag, though there is one final thing to check. I go through my top drawer next to the bed, pushing aside the obligatory underwear until I find my passport at the back. I flick through the pages, looking at the stamps and then settling on my own face. Nobody takes a good passport photo. The range of expressions go from 'a bit like a corpse', to 'potentially deranged'. Mine was renewed a little after I got married. It was less than three years back, though it feels like an age. I was so different then. Perhaps others can't see it, but I can. There was an optimism and hope about me during our wedding. It was the marriage itself that took that from me.

Underneath the passport is a little over £100 in cash, which is exactly what I remember having there.

I've been out of the apartment for less than a day. Could David have been in, taken the clay pot, and then driven to the conference, milled around, and then... what? Anyone *could*, I suppose. The timings are possible if someone could get themselves in and out – however unlikely that seems.

I tell myself that things will figure themselves out in the morning. *Later* in the morning. The pot will show up in an obvious place and I'll not be able to believe I missed it. David's mysterious twin will turn out to be some hotel worker who was caught at the perfect angle in the perfect light that makes him look like my former husband. I'm tired, that's all.

I'm undressed and in bed when I poke my head out and check underneath for a final bit of reassurance. There is nothing there except shoes and empty boxes which once contained things like my phone.

As soon as I've laid down, the digits from the clock burn bright through the darkness. I'm transported back to the hotel room, knowing I won't be able to sleep.

When I was younger, I'd always rest on my left side, facing the outside of the bed. After David moved in, we figured out that he did the same. I told him he could have that side of the bed and subsequently taught myself to sleep on my right arm. It now feels strange to sleep facing any other way.

I close my eyes, cuddling the pillow into my ear and, the next thing I know, the digits on the clock are telling me that it's a few minutes after eight. It takes a groggy few seconds for me to realise that I've slept for two and a half hours. It's hardly a good night's sleep, but it will do for now.

It takes a few seconds more for me to notice the trophy on my side table and then everything that happened last night comes bubbling back to the surface like a dodgy kebab. I'm not supposed to be home; I'm supposed to be in a hotel. There was the phone photo of David, the missing pot from my kitchen.

I pull myself out of bed and amble bare-footed into the living room. I glance towards the kitchen, but my keys still sit on the bare counter. I've not pulled the curtains and light is spilling across the living room. I head to the window and stand, staring out to where the sky is blue. It's going to be another cold, clear day. I turn to face the room but instantly spin back. Something feels wrong, though I can't quite figure out what. There's a partially collapsed wall to the side of my apartment, with a pile of bricks on the ground. I'm not sure why, but it started to fall down a couple of years back. I find myself staring at it, wondering what feels wrong. It's like seeing a pensioner in skinny jeans.

I can't come up with anything, so turn back to the room and head to the fridge, where I pour a glass of water from the filter.

It's cold and smooth and I can feel it clearing my thoughts. I can hardly call the police to report a missing pot – especially not when there's no sign of anyone having broken in. I finish the first glass, so pour another, enjoying the fuzziness clearing. I'm going to go to the gym and run off a bit of the anxiety. I have some of my best ideas when my body is occupied and my mind is allowed to wander.

My gym bag is at the bottom of my wardrobe, so I grab that, slip into a tracksuit and then grab my house and car keys from the counter.

It's when I get outside that I realise what's wrong. It should have been obvious when I was looking through the window. The problem wasn't the collapsed wall; it was what's supposed to be in front of it. My car *should* be parked outside my door – except that it isn't.

At some point since I arrived home from the hotel three hours ago, it has disappeared.

EIGHT

I head around the corner of the block and look along both sides of the road. I'll sometimes park my car at the front because it's easier than trying to reverse between the various bins that people leave out. There are intermittent gaps in the cars from where residents have gone to work, but mine isn't there. It won't be – because I *know* I parked outside my front door.

Back at the crumbling wall, I look for signs of broken glass, or some other indication that somebody smashed their way into my vehicle. I don't know if things like hotwiring are possible with modern cars. What I *do* know is that the keys are in my hand.

Except there is a second set.

I hurry back inside, heading to the top drawer of the dresser at the side of my bed. I checked the obvious things – my passport and the cash – but it hadn't crossed my mind to look for the other things I keep there.

I take everything out of the drawer, piling my underwear on the bed next to my passport and the money. My chest starts to tighten as I stare at the now empty drawer. I look in the one underneath, but there's no spare car key there. I know where it was – and I know that it's gone.

There's no doubt now. The Tigger pot was a piece of clay with little monetary value. There was a chance it might have shown up in the coming days and I'd have remembered moving it. My car is another issue entirely.

I've dialled two nines when I stop and query whether a stolen car counts as an emergency. There are those lists every year of people who dialled 999 because they'd lost their umbrellas, or something similar. I call 101 instead and wait on hold for a minute until a handler asks why I'm calling.

'I think my car's been stolen,' I say.

I hear a tap of a keyboard and then she checks my address and the registration plate. My mind instantly turns into an abyss in which I can barely remember any details about the vehicle. The colour, make, model, year and especially the plate number are up for grabs. I find a photo on my phone and describe that.

When she has the details, the handler moves onto the specifics: 'Where did you park the car?' she asks.

'Right outside my house.'

'Is that a road, or…?'

'Sort of a private driveway.'

'OK… and have you checked along the street, just in case…?'

It's a fair question. I have visions of people calling the police because they're on the wrong floor of the Tesco multi-storey – and their car is a level below.

'I've looked,' I reply. 'It's nowhere around here. I know where I left it anyway.'

'Are there any signs of breakage around where the vehicle was parked?'

'There's no glass – but my spare set of keys are missing from my apartment.'

The handler says, 'I see' as I hear the gentle clatter of a keyboard and then she replies with: 'Are you saying you've been burgled – or could someone else have access to the keys?'

'How do you mean?'

'Like a family member, something like that?'

'I live on my own. The spare keys are kept at the back of one of my drawers. I've not checked on them in a while. I've not needed to.'

'When did you last know the keys were there?'

'A few weeks ago, maybe? I'm not sure.'

'And does anybody else know where you keep the spare keys?'

'I don't think so.'

There is a final clack of the keyboard and then: 'OK. An officer can visit you this evening. You—'

'This evening?'

'That's the earliest I can get anyone to you.'

'I thought someone would come now…?'

'I'm afraid that there's nobody available.' She says it with a twinge of a person who's gone through this before. I've heard stories about there being no budgets and no officers. I guess a person only notices when something happens to them directly.

We arrange for the officer to come around at nine to take a statement and then I hang up.

I've not been entirely truthful. David knew where I kept my spare car keys. He also had a set of keys for the apartment. After I killed him, I didn't really think to check where he had them. There are far deeper things going on in a person's mind after an event like that.

A few days afterwards, when it finally dawned on me, I assumed his keys were in a pocket, or something similar. There seemed little point in getting the locks changed, because it wasn't as if he was coming back. It might have looked strange to the neighbours, too, if my husband had seemingly disappeared and then I promptly got a locksmith over to make sure he couldn't get back in.

Because of that, my next call is to an emergency locksmith. He says he'll be right over and then I'm left sitting on the front step, staring at the gap where my car used to be. I check the road for a second time, figuring it would be typical if it was outside the front door after all. I'll have to call the non-emergency number again to make clear that my car is outside my flat after all and that, yes, I will go for an eye exam.

It's almost a relief when it's nowhere to be seen.

Almost.

The locksmith arrives twenty minutes later and pulls onto the spot where my car should be. He has brawny shoulders, a bit of a belly, dirty fingernails and hairy arms. The type of bloke who looks like he could probably install a bit of drywall.

There is minimal fuss as he gets on with the job. I wait on the kerb outside as he drills out the old locks and then hammers in a new one with measured brutality. I spy some of the neighbours' curtains flickering and don't blame them, though it might be helpful if a couple of them were being nosey when my car was being stolen. I fiddle with my phone, zooming in on Jane's photo and then swiping away to skim through my Twitter feed. It's hard to remember what people used to do before phones came along. Sit alone on benches and kerbs like complete lunatics?

'That's it, love,' the locksmith says after a while.

I head back to my door as he clears away the debris with a handheld vacuum. He hands me three shiny keys and then presses onto the bonnet of his van as he scribbles out an invoice. I can hardly complain – and I'm certain he's not ripping me off – but the price is up there with motorway service stations for relation to the real world.

He must see it in my face: 'You did say you wanted it as an emergency,' he says.

'It's fine,' I reply, 'I'll do a bank transfer by the end of the day. I'd pay cash but…' I tail off and pat my pockets as if to indicate something he probably hears most days. I always feel bad about homeless people. They sit around asking for change but who carries around coins nowadays? It's all tap-tap-tap, with either phones or cards.

I wait in the doorway as the locksmith heads off and then try all three of the new keys. The lock is smoother than the previous one and, when I get inside, I do another lap of the flat, checking for either my car keys, or the pot from the counter. By the time I'm back where I'm started, it's at the point where I am struggling to deny what's in front of me any longer. Aside from David being back, what other explanation is there? He was in the photo. Someone got into my flat – and it was only he who had keys.

I'm in the living room, gazing aimlessly out towards the spot where my car should be parked, when a police vehicle pulls in. An officer clambers out from either side and they put their hats on in unison. One is a good head taller than the other, as if they've been paired together purely for someone else's amusement.

I get to the front door before they do and the taller of the two jolts back with alarm when I open it a moment before he was about to knock.

'I thought you were coming over tonight?' I say.

The officer blinks and glances to his colleague before turning back to me. 'Sorry?'

There's that horrible moment in which it feels like everyone in an awkward situation is looking to everyone else. It's quickly apparent to all of us that they're here for a different reason.

'Are you Morgan Persephone?' he asks, rhyming my name with 'telephone'.

'Per-sef-oh-knee,' I say.

'Morgan Per-sef-oh-knee…?'

'Right.'

'And you drive a black Volkswagen Golf…?'

'Yes. Have you found it?'

They exchange another momentary glance and I know in that half-second that something terrible has happened.

'We have found it,' the officer says. 'It was involved in a collision with a pedestrian.'

My stomach gurgles noisily; a clingy child desperately wanting attention. It feels like everything's stopped and I find myself parroting along.

'A pedestrian?'

The officer clamps his lips together grimly. 'I think it might be better if you come to the station.'

'The station?'

His expression doesn't move and it takes a good two or three seconds for me to figure it out. When I do, it seems so obvious.

'You think I was driving...?'

NINE

I've never been breathalysed before. It's one of those things I've seen on TV; something that could only ever happen to somebody else.

I'm still outside my flat when the officer asks whether I've recently cleaned my teeth or used mouthwash. When I say I haven't, he removes a plastic tube from a sealed bag and inserts it into a small black box. He talks me through the process, as if I've never figured out how to breathe before, and then I end up blowing into the tube until there's nothing left in my lungs. He pulls the device away and stares at the front. I know I only had one drink early in the evening at the awards last night and yet there's still a part of me that is terrified I'll somehow test positive. It's hard to believe there was ever a time when having a few drinks and then driving home was the norm.

'Does it matter that I've not eaten?' I ask.

'No.'

The officer is offering his best poker face. If there's some sort of error, I'll be tarnished, regardless of my innocence. What would be the point in arguing with science?

It feels like an age until he peers up and says, 'All clear.'

I start to sigh with relief and only catch myself afterwards when I realise it could seem like I was pleased to be getting away with something.

*

Police interview rooms on television always seem so much brighter and bigger than the one in which I am now sitting. I was expecting that at least one of the walls would be a mirror with someone on the other side, but there's none of that. Instead, it's four concrete walls, a heavy door and a pair of cameras fixed to the wall. The lighting is like something from a grungy 70s movie, leaving everything with a browny hue, as if I'm living in a sepia photograph.

I've already been through my story once, but I don't need to be a detective to understand why they have issues. I assumed the officers who came out to breathalyse me would be doing the interviewing, but I've not seen them since they brought me here.

Sergeant Kidman does most of the speaking. She's a little older than me, though not by much. She's got one of those faces as if she lost an argument with a wall at some point: a cross between a dumpling and an axe. I can easily imagine her arguing with a supermarket cashier over an out-of-date coupon.

'I don't think I understand why you left the hotel in the middle of the night,' she says.

There's a table between us, so at least TV police shows don't lie about everything.

'Is the victim all right?' I ask.

Sergeant Kidman looks to the officer next to her. I can't remember his rank but his last name is Robinson. He's barely said a word.

'I'm not sure yet,' Kidman says.

'Are they… um…?' I tail off, not quite able to put it into words. I've not been told whether the pedestrian hit by my car was a man or woman. I know almost nothing about what happened.

'Are they what?' Kidman asks.

'Dead.'

She pauses, letting me squirm, though I try to sit still.

'I'm not sure yet,' she adds.

'Can you tell me anything about what happened?'

'I'm sure we'll come to that, Ms Persephone. For now, I'd like to talk about everything that led up to it.'

She pronounces my name right, which almost nobody does, and I wonder how much she knows about me. After David supposedly disappeared, I had little option other than to go along with the appeals for his return. Plenty has been written about me in the past couple of years and it's not like I've got one of those names that can be confused with some physicist who lives in Durban. If people Google my name, it is me who shows up.

'What do you want to know?' I ask.

'Why did you leave the hotel in the middle of the night?'

'The bed was uncomfortable,' I reply.

'Did you mention this to anyone at the hotel?'

'No. I just left.'

'It seems strange that you'd pay for a hotel and then leave at half past two in the morning.'

'That's what happened. I thought I'd sleep better at home.'

'You're saying that, at sometime between two and half past two this morning, you decided a hotel bed was too uncomfortable and drove two and a half hours home to get some sleep?'

She makes it sound as if I'd decided to pop to the Moon to buy a KitKat.

'That's right,' I say.

I'm trying to sound confident because it's all I have. I can hardly tell her that I was spooked because I thought I saw my former husband in a photograph. My *dead* former husband.

It's as if she can read my mind when she replies with: 'Was there any other reason you left the hotel?'

'No.'

'If you'll excuse me for pushing the point, it's just that not many people check out of a hotel they've paid for at two-thirty in the morning.'

'I wouldn't know what other people do…'

There's a tiny amount of satisfaction as she leans back in her seat and I get the sense that she knows she's getting nothing more from me on this.

One of the things I came to learn in the weeks after I killed David was that I'm an incredible liar. I suppose everyone has their talents – perhaps acting or singing; playing football, or the ability to wear Burberry and not look like stained wallpaper. One of mine is that I can look a person dead in the eye and come out with the most outlandish nonsense while not flinching. Confidence is everything. I've wondered since what that makes me; whether there's something wrong. About a year ago, I read that, if a true psychopath has the ability to question if they're a psycho, then they are definitely not. I'll take that, I suppose – but I'm still one hell of a liar.

'Were you with anyone?' Kidman asks.

'When?'

'When you checked out of the hotel?'

'No.'

'What about in the car?'

'No.'

'At home?'

'After the awards, I went to bed and I was by myself until the locksmith turned up at my flat.'

Kidman makes a point of turning to her colleague and muttering, 'We can get CCTV from the hotel to check that.'

If I was lying about that part then I might have reason to worry – but that side of my story will check out.

'Did you drive straight home?' she asks.

'Yes.'

'Which route did you take?'

It's a simple question, but I end up stumbling over it, getting the name of the A-road wrong and then correcting myself. I might be a good liar, but I don't pay attention to road signs. Kidman seems uninterested by these details in any case.

'How much did you drink at the awards dinner?' she asks.

'I passed the breathalyser test.'

'That's not what I asked.'

'I had a small glass of wine at the very beginning. It was a welcome drink that everyone got when they walked in.'

'What time was this?'

'Perhaps seven o'clock?'

Kidman makes a note of this on a pad and then leaves a gap. It took me a while to realise how often police do this. They create an uncomfortable silence which the person they're speaking to feels obliged to fill. At first, I'd keep talking, but then I learned to shut up and wait for whatever was next. On this occasion, I don't mind playing a little dumber than I am.

'I'm not very good with alcohol,' I add. 'I've never been a big drinker.'

Kidman nods along, though doesn't write anything. She's twiddles a pen between her thumb and forefinger – and perhaps it's that which sends me back to my living room after what happened with David. That was the last time I was interviewed properly by the police. It was far less formal then, with an officer named Sparks asking the questions. He was an old, grey-haired guy and I got the sense he was winding down to retirement. It was as I was making tea on the exact spot that David died when I convinced myself that I could get through it all.

'What time did you arrive home?' Kidman asks.

'It was about five. I don't know exactly.'

'And you drove straight home?'

'Right.'

'You didn't stop anywhere on the way down…?'

'No.'

'What music did you listen to while you were driving?'

My instinct is to shoot back with, 'Who said I was listening to music?' – but there's no need to be aggressive. My car was stolen and I'm the victim here.

'I was listening to the radio,' I say. 'I can't remember the station but the DJ was talking about cheese. That's all I remember.'

It gets a raised eyebrow but little more.

'The problem I have with this,' Kidman says, 'is that your car ended up four miles from your flat.'

'I told you that it was stolen.'

'It was four miles from your flat and whoever was driving hit a pedestrian.'

'It was stolen – and I was asleep. As soon as I woke up and saw the car was gone, I reported it.'

Kidman nods along and scratches at her earlobe. There's a frizzy strand of hair that she tucks tight and then, after a glance to her mute colleague, it's finally his turn to speak. I remember now that he's a constable, so a lower rank. The lack of wrinkles mean he's probably younger than me, though he has a shaven head that makes it look like he's gone bald. It's all a bit contradictory.

'If you still have one set of car keys,' he says, 'how could someone have got the other set?'

'That's what I asked when I called you,' I reply. 'There was a spare set at the back of my underwear drawer.'

'But you said there was no sign of a break-in.'

'There isn't.'

'Does anybody else have keys to your flat?'

It's impossible not to think of David.

'No…' I say. 'Well, my ex-husband does. He went missing about two years ago.'

Robinson looks to his superior and it's obvious from the momentary recognition that they both already know this.

This time, it is Kidman who picks things up. She presses forward on the desk and interlinks her fingers: 'Did you change the locks after your husband disappeared?'

'No. Why would I have done?'

'Some people might have felt more secure knowing they were the only person who had keys to their home…?'

'He was my husband – it's not like I was scared of him.'

At least I don't need to lie about that.

'Have you seen your husband recently?'

I stare back at Kidman, matching her gaze. I can't quite figure out if it's as I suspected – that she thinks I was driving – or if she believes David might be back.

'Of course not,' I reply. 'They told me it was seven years before they could issue a death certificate. I could apply for a divorce, but there doesn't seem much point.'

'Do you think he's dead?'

I open my mouth and then immediately close it. I thought I was being clever but, instead, I was the one who brought this up. I take a breath and try to come up with something better than the only words in my mind.

'I don't know,' I say.

It's not great. Yesterday, I would have said it was a lie. In almost all respects, I still believe it is – except that there's a niggly seed of doubt.

Fortunately, Kidman nods along and seems to accept this: 'Does anyone other than your ex-husband have keys?' she asks.

'No.'

'Have you ever lent your keys to anyone?'

I start to say 'no' and then I remember: 'My friend, Jane, got me a cleaner for my birthday last year,' I reply. 'I think it was a bit of a joke because my place was messy. I was out taking classes at the gym and left the keys for a few hours. When I got back, my friend was there and let me in. I can't think of another time.'

It's hard not to feel awkward. I have something to hide in respect to David – but I definitely wasn't driving my car when it apparently hit a pedestrian. I'm lying, though not about the thing they might suspect me of.

I can see how it all sounds: I left a party early in the morning and, hours later, my car hit a pedestrian. If I'd failed the breathalyser test, I'd have already been charged. My mind starts wandering to things like CCTV. They surely can't have footage of the crash, or anything around it, else they'd know I wasn't driving. I opted to go without a solicitor, because I wanted to appear as open and honest as I could. I'm now wondering if that was a mistake. Unless I've misread things, they believe I hit the pedestrian, rushed home on foot, and then called to report my car stolen.

Kidman seems unbothered by my cleaner story and moves on: 'Has anyone else been in your flat who might have taken the spare keys?'

'Only my boyfriend, Andy. He wouldn't have taken the keys, though.'

She takes his details anyway – and I figure I'll have to let him know they might be in contact. In everything that's happened, I've not thought about him since we were on the phone last night.

'Anyone else?'

'My friend, Jane, comes over fairly regularly, but she—'

'Jane is the person who was with you at the awards dinner?' Kidman asks.

'Right.'

'She also left early?'

'Yes.'

She takes Jane's details and, from nowhere, it feels like my entire life is up for grabs. My friends will be getting calls to see if anyone can vouch for me. Either that, or there will be implicit accusations, as if I've accused them of stealing my keys and car.

Kidman picks up her pad and drums her fingers on the page before looking over it to take me in. 'What I don't understand is how it all comes together,' she says. 'You say your friend and boyfriend couldn't have taken the keys; you say your husband is missing. There's no sign of anyone breaking into your flat – so how do you explain your car being found in a ditch four miles away from where you claim you left it?'

'I don't *claim* I left it anywhere. I *parked* it outside my house. It was stolen.'

'How?'

'I don't know. Hotwired? Something like that.'

'I don't think your car can be "hotwired".' She makes air quotes and I sense a disdain that I don't believe is in my mind.

'I don't know what to tell you,' I say. 'I noticed my car was missing and I called you.'

'Is that so?' she says.

'That's so.'

TEN

THE WHY

Three years, eight months ago

Considering I'm aiming for a career in the fitness industry, there's definitely something off about the fact that I sweat like a 1970s BBC presenter when they hear a siren. Some people can run as if they're being chased by bear and have to get ahead of their slowest friend – and still finish dry. With me, it's like I'm halfway through a waterboarding.

I can't stop eyeing the puddle of sweat at the side of the spinning bike, wondering if anyone else will notice and realise how disgusting I am. I shout that it's time for the final climb and then push high out of the saddle to do it myself. The woman directly in front of me is on her first session and was gasping after the first climb almost twenty minutes ago. She is now pressed on the handlebars panting for air. I try to catch her eye to ask silently is she's OK, but she doesn't look up. I end up half watching her, while calling for everyone else to pedal. I could really do without someone having a heart attack during one of my classes. That puts a bit of a blemish on a CV.

'Nearly there,' I call.

The leisure centre's 'spin studio' is more of a backroom that's hidden along a warren of corridors somewhere near the boiler. I think it used to be a squash court. The alleged air conditioning spits out as much hot air as an uninformed listener on a radio phone-in. The air is clogged and humid and there's no escape. Hot yoga is starting to become a thing and I guess the facilities are turning hot spinning into a pioneering offshoot.

'And dial it down three notches,' I shout.

There's a collective gasp of relief as everyone sits back on their saddles. The woman struggling in front of me sways slightly as she fiddles with the bike's resistance dial.

'Let's keep bringing it down,' I add. 'One more notch.'

Another minute and we're done. People clamber off their bikes and start to wipe off the saddles, while I use one towel to mop the floor around me, and another to dry myself. Most give brief waves as they head back to the changing rooms and the new woman at the front insists she'll be back. Another enthusiastically declares that she's off to Turkey for a couple of weeks and will see me when she gets back.

I wait until everyone's left and then check around to make sure nobody's left anything. I'm ready to leave myself when I notice a woman leaning on the door frame. She's in gym gear and there's a sheen of sweat around her neck. I think she was on one of the bikes at the back, wearing a large headband that she's now removed. I can't be certain. She's not one of the regulars, although there's something vaguely familiar about her.

'You're Morgan, right?' she says.

'Yes…'

I wait for her to add something and, when she doesn't, I continue: 'It was hot in here today, wasn't it?'

'I'm Yasmine,' the woman says. It could be a simple introduction – a pair of women swapping names – but she speaks with such self-assurance that it's clear she expects me to know who she is. I try to remember whether I know any Yasmines, let alone her, but I can't think of anyone.

'Sorry,' I say, 'Did you want to sign up for a package of classes…? They're doing ten per cent off if you book more than six in one go…'

'You know David, don't you?' she replies. 'David Persephone.'

'Yes…'

'He's not told you about me, has he?'

Yasmine stands with her arms folded across her front, her features firm and unimpressed. Perhaps it says more about me than it does David, but my first thought is that she must be an ex-girlfriend. We've not gone through a full list of everyone we've ever been with – and I don't think he's mentioned a Yasmine anyway.

'Should he have?' I ask.

She glares at me like the way a stewardess looks at a hen party on a plane. It's as if she's wondering how to deal with me when she opens her mouth and says, 'It's just…'

She doesn't get any further because there's a whine of the intercom speaker overhead. Whatever's being said is far too echoey for me to decipher but, when I look back to Yasmine, she is striding her way out of the studio. I wait for a moment, wondering if she'll turn to give me some sort of clue as to what's going on. It's only when the doors bang at the far end of the corridor that I realise she isn't coming back.

There's no phone signal at the back of the leisure centre, so I have to hurry through the warren-like passages towards reception. There's no sign of Yasmine, who is either an extremely fast walker, or she's disappeared into one of the changing rooms.

I wait underneath the overhang outside the front doors, watching as the rain pours off the roof and thunders to the ground. It's damp and clammy and my phone screen is unresponsive as I try to scroll through for David's number. Not that it matters because, when I do finally manage to call him, there is no answer. I try a second time, though there's no response. He did say there would be times he was unavailable – and every call we've shared has been at a time he suggested. I shouldn't be surprised that I can't reach him, I suppose.

My first attempt at a text message – 'Who the hell is Yasmine?' – is quickly deleted. I'm not sure yet if there's any reason to be angry. That might be something for later.

I type out 'Something weird happened. Call me', but delete that, too. I'm not one of those Facebook attention seekers who'll post something cryptic simply to get a slew of 'U OK hun?' responses.

I settle for something that I hope is breezy and whimsical. Something a sane, functioning human being would go for.

Hi! All's fine here. Hope your trip is going well with loads of bargains! PS: Who's Yasmine?

ELEVEN

THE NOW

The custody officer bats away a yawn and seems ready for a nap when she hands me some papers and tells me that I shouldn't be planning any holidays.

'I'm supposed to be moving in with my boyfriend this weekend,' I reply.

'I don't see why that would be a problem,' she replies. 'As long as we know your address.'

She talks me through how I'm supposed to return to the station in a month to either be re-bailed or exonerated. 'It might happen sooner than that,' she adds.

I tell her that someone was supposed to be visiting later to take a statement about my stolen car. It's all a bit redundant now, so she makes a note and says I can contact the non-emergency number if there's anything I want to add.

It's only as I'm leaving the station that I realise the implication. If whoever was hit by my car ends up dying, it could be a manslaughter charge. Suddenly, it feels like a bad idea to have spoken to the police without a solicitor. Perhaps karma does exist? I've apparently got away with something I *did* do and yet I could be in severe trouble for something I didn't.

As soon as I'm outside, the wall of cold hits me like a brick. After the breathalyser test, I didn't have the clarity of thought to grab anything like a hat or gloves. I've only taken a few steps across the car park when it feels as if I've buried my face in the freezer. I have no easy way to get home. Kingbridge Police Station is twelve or thirteen miles away from where I live in Gradingham. I suppose I'm fit enough to run it – but the country lanes will be covered with frost – plus, even if I wanted to, I'm not in any gear that's particularly suitable for such a long run. It would take too long to walk and, though there must be buses, I have no idea about the schedule. I could try for a taxi – but my purse is sitting on the counter at home.

Hours have passed in a blink and it's now a little after two in the afternoon. I'm not sure what else to do, so I start walking towards the golden arches a couple of streets over. They'll have free Wi-Fi there.

As I walk, I call Jane. I only manage the word 'hi' and she must hear it from my tone. We've had enough of these conversations over the years – and she's always been the first person I contact when something is up.

'What's wrong?' Jane replies.

'Can you come and get me?' I ask.

'Of course. What's happened? Are you at the hotel?'

I stop for a second, confused until I realise that she has no way of knowing for sure that I arrived home from the hotel. The last time we were in contact, she'd texted to say she was home safely.

'I'm near the police station in Kingbridge,' I reply.

There's a longer pause this time and I can hear the hesitation from the other end of the line. 'The police?'

'I can wait at the McDonald's,' I add, skirting the obvious. 'Do you know the one?'

'Why have you been with the police?'

'It's sort of… complicated. Can you come?'

'Sure. I've got Norah and she's not a fan of her car seat, but I'll be there as quickly as I can.'

Jane says goodbye and then she's gone.

I cross a couple of roads and traipse across the McDonald's car park. There is a lone vehicle parked off to the side, with a woman in the driving seat staring aimlessly across the tarmac while munching into a burger. I can imagine her car and this hideaway being her last sanctuary of tranquillity before the madness of the school run, or whatever else she has to do.

It's relatively quiet inside, though none of the staff members bother about me as I sit in the corner with a coffee and log onto the Wi-Fi. I search for details of the incident involving my car. There are a few stories and social media posts about how the centre of Gradingham was shut down through the morning after a pedestrian was hit. Other than that, details are sparse. It's hard to put that to one side, though the red dot of email notifications is also burning accusingly at my lack of attention.

A few of the people with whom I swapped business cards last night have emailed, largely saying things like, 'Just checking in to say congratulations on the win'. There's somebody who's organising a fitness conference in Edinburgh next year who's wondering if I'm interested in hosting a session. There's the usual marketing emails from companies I've used once and now think I want to buy something from them twice a week for the rest of eternity. After that, there's a note from the organiser, Steven, which is a general message of congratulations. I figure I'll deal with everything later, but then have another idea and reply to him, asking if he can send me any photos from the previous night. There might a shot of the man in the blue suit from a different angle, or in altered light, that makes it clear it isn't David. If I can make myself certain it's definitely someone else, I can focus on trying to figure out who stole my car – and how.

Someone in a grey uniform comes across and starts sweeping up around me. He asks if I want him to clear away my empty coffee cup, but I keep hold of it, if only so that it's not completely obvious that I'm freeloading the Wi-Fi and heat. I suppose loitering is part of the fast-food business model. The main difference is that it would usually be teenagers hanging around inside to get away from the cold.

I see Jane's black 4x4 pull into the car park after almost fifty minutes. She parks and ducks momentarily out of sight to grab her phone, but by then I'm already halfway across the car park. She waves when she spots me and I clamber up into the back, behind the passenger seat, as if she's a chauffeur.

Norah is strapped into the carrier that's belted into the passenger seat and Jane reaches across to wipe something from her daughter's face.

'Traffic's a nightmare,' Jane says as she turns to me. 'There was some sort of hit-and-run in Gradingham this morning. They've shut down the road for investigation work. It's total chaos.'

'That's sort of why I'm here,' I reply. 'It was my car.'

Jane has turned back to the windscreen, but she stops and our eyes meet in the mirror. Her brows have dipped inwards.

'What do you mean?'

'Someone stole my car overnight.'

'From the hotel…?'

'I drove back not long after getting your text. I couldn't sleep.'

Jane has her hands at a textbook two and ten on the wheel. Someone who's used to driving carefully with her young daughter at her side. She's started to reach for the handbrake but stops in mid-air as it sinks in. She doesn't turn as she speaks.

'The police think you did it…?' There's a glimmer of doubt in her voice, as if she's really saying: 'Tell me you didn't do it…?'

Norah is babbling to herself in the front seat and then, from the stream of infant consciousness, produces the word 'tree'. It breaks the impasse as Jane twists against her seat belt to look at her daughter and then me.

'She likes the word "tree",' Jane says. 'I think she's going to be a botanist.'

'Or a lumberjack.'

That gets a smile. 'Not a lumberjack.'

'I got home and went to sleep,' I say. 'When I woke up, my car was gone. I called in to report it and then the police turned up and breathalysed me.'

Her eyes go wide: '*Really?*'

'I passed. I only had that one glass early on last night. They might contact you at some point. I had to tell them who I was with at the awards dinner.'

She pouts a lip and the momentary glimpse to Norah tells me that she doesn't particularly want to get involved in whatever I've caught myself up in. I don't think I blame her.

'Is the road still closed?' I ask.

'There was a load of signs up when I was trying to get here, so I think so. I had to take that back road that goes past the rugby club, near Little Bush Woods.'

'Can you take me to the crash?'

There's a momentary hesitation, but then Jane reaches for the handbrake. 'Sure.'

The scene of the crash is simultaneously better and worse than I imagined. There's almost a comedy to it in that whoever was driving my car smashed it into the lamp post adjacent to the 'Welcome To Gradingham' sign. Underneath, it still reads 'Thank you for driving carefully', which now comes across as somewhat sarcastic.

The lamp post has doubled in half and there's a small white tent on the grass verge, where, presumably, the poor pedestrian ended up. There are no pavements out here, yet locals are used to walking the country lanes to get to some of the houses that sit a little outside the village boundaries. I've done it myself – more or less everyone who lives in the area will have done the same at some point.

My car is also in the verge, though it is almost entirely shielded from view by a series of screens. There are three police cars parked opposite the crash scene, with barriers across the road. A uniformed officer is standing to the side, whirring his finger in a circle to encourage us to turn around. Instead, Jane parks on the side of the road, where there are already a couple of other vehicles. In a village where very little happens, this is up there with a new Nintendo console for entertainment. The officer is trying to convince people there's nothing to see, while kids who have dumped their bikes on the ground are taking photos on their phones. The 'Thank you for driving carefully' juxtaposition will be a meme within the hour – if it isn't already. It might be funny if it wasn't my car and I wasn't the person accused of a hit and run. Not to mention the victim…

'I'll wait,' Jane says, seemingly reading my mind once more.

I let myself out of the car and approach the makeshift barrier. The crash scene has suddenly become Gradingham's top tourist attraction. When the only competition is the duck pond, it's not much of a surprise.

As well as the officer at the barrier, who has seemingly given up on trying to turn people away, there are more watching on as three people in white paper suits disappear behind the sheet that's covering half of my car. There are skid marks on the road, with rubber marks from where the car veered off to the side.

There's blood, too.

A splash of deep crimson has stained the grass at the top of the verge, before disappearing down the slope, out of sight.

The number plate at the back is covered by the sheet, but the purple heart that hangs from the mirror is clear enough. There's no question it's my car.

'You have to move back.'

I look up – and the officer who was guarding the barrier has been joined by a second. The newcomer has his arms spread wide in front of the kids and is beckoning them away.

'Why?' one of the kids ask. I'd guess he's about thirteen or fourteen.

'Because I said so.'

'So?'

'This is a crime scene. Can't have anyone interfering with the investigation.'

'You're on the other side. How do we know *you're* not interfering?'

The officer rolls his eyes as if he's heard all this backtalk before. I can imagine my mother saying that it wasn't like this in her day. Kids would get a clip round the ear, and all that. 'Never did me any harm,' she'd say.

'Just move away,' the officer repeats.

'What happened?' the boy asks.

'What do you *think* happened?'

'Is anyone dead?'

I look to the blood and the bent sign. If the pedestrian was hit in anything close to a direct way, then I can't see how someone would survive. The speed limit going out of the village is fifty mph and this isn't the type of road where people drive at twenty – let alone in a stolen car. I'm not sure why they didn't before, but things suddenly feel very serious.

'On your way,' the officer says.

The kids finally get the message and head over to their bikes. A few seconds later and they're cycling back towards the village.

The officer turns to me and sighs. There's a freshness to his features and he doesn't have any of the harshness of Sergeant Kidman from the interview room.

'You've got to go, too,' he says.

'I am, it's just…'

I think about telling him it's my car but can't see how any good will come of it. He's not going to let me pass – and I'm sure it won't look good that I'm here. Instead, I turn and head back to Jane's car, before getting into the back.

'Do you want to go?' she asks.

'Yes.'

'Is it definitely your car?'

'Yes.'

She starts the vehicle once more and swings around in a U-turn.

'They say whoever was hit is in intensive care,' she says, momentarily catching my eye in the mirror.

I have to look away: 'Are there any other details?'

'Someone in the Facebook comments said it's a man from their road, but that's about it.'

She drives in relative silence for a minute or two. It's only Norah who doesn't notice how awkward things have become. She babbles away happily to herself.

It's another minute or so until Jane breaks the impasse with a breezy-sounding: 'Any news after winning the award?'

It feels like such a long time ago that I was on stage.

'Like what?' I ask.

'I didn't know if you might've had any job offers...?'

'There might be an event in Edinburgh next year. I've got to email the guy back.'

'That's great news!'

'Right...'

It's hard to feel enthused with everything else going on. I wonder if I should bring up what I saw in the back of her photo – though it's difficult to know how to broach it. *Hey, you remember my ex-husband...*? I want to ask her about it – but, at the same time, if she didn't notice David, or the person who *looks* like David, I don't particularly want to draw her attention to it.

There is another gap and then: 'It's been ages since you visited,' Jane says. 'I've not seen Andy in a while, either. Why don't you come over this week…?'

I have the instant panic of trying to come up with an excuse for not going. My idea of a good evening has generally always involved having my feet up in front of a television. Ever since what happened with David, I've become even less likely to take people up on their offers to do things. The less I have to talk about him or myself, the smaller the chance of accidentally letting something slip. Jane is perhaps the only person with whom I'd be close enough that my guard could drop and the truth might pop out.

'What nights are you working?' she asks.

It's only the question that jolts my memory. 'Tonight,' I reply. 'I've got a spin class at six.'

'Are you free Wednesday?'

'I'm not sure. With us moving in together on Saturday, I've still got packing to do. I've hardly done anything yet.'

'You must have one evening free, though…? You'll be busier when you're actually moving in.'

'I'll check with Andy and see what he says.'

I'm hoping he'll be busy all week because I'm not sure I can risk simply not asking him. I have big lies to cover up and one thing I've learned is that there's no point in piling smaller ones on top.

'Do you want me to drop you off at home?' Jane asks. 'Or the studio?'

I don't have a mode of transport for now, so tell her the studio. I've got the spinning class there in a few hours and can't be bothered trying to figure out a way to get across the village in these temperatures.

It's not a long drive, though the day is already starting to darken as we pull into the car park at the back. Natural light is at a premium at this time of year.

When we come to a stop, I thank Jane for picking me up and she turns in her seat, smiling awkwardly.

'Can I ask a favour?' she says.

It's hard for me to begrudge that, especially as she's just picked me up and driven me back to the village. I do know that, whatever she asks, I'm going to have to say 'yes'.

'Of course,' I say.

'I'm getting that mole removed on Thursday afternoon,' Jane says.

'The one on your neck?'

'Right. It was supposed to be a four-month waiting list, but they had a cancellation. The only thing is that Ben can't get out of work and, um…' She tails off but glances to Norah at her side.

I almost can't believe the words as they come out of my mouth, though I suppose one good turn deserves another, far worse, favour.

'I can take Norah,' I say, regretting it before I've even finished. I'd rather spend time on the doorstep with a Jehovah's Witness than have to babysit a sixteen-month-old. Ask to borrow someone's brand-new car and they'll look at you as if you want a kidney – but the same person will be delighted to thrust their actual offspring onto literally anyone else with barely a blink.

'That's fab of you,' Jane replies. 'We can talk details later in the week. Maybe Wednesday night…?'

'I'll let you know once I've talked to Andy.'

Jane blows me a kiss and then I get out of the car and head for the back door of the fitness studio.

If karma *is* a thing, then it has a strange way of manifesting itself. After what happened with David, life has delivered me everything I wanted. When we met, I told him that I wanted my own studio and here, three years on, I have precisely that. It's barely a couple of miles from my flat and so successful that I have to turn down personal training clients as I can't fit everyone in. I've gone from grotty sauna-like conditions at the back of decaying council-run leisure centres to a custom-built place of my own. Not only that but I'm part of the conference tour scene. I get invited to various events once or twice a month on average, where I either host mass fitness sessions or give talks about the industry. I suspect that anyone who ends up on a speaking circuit knows deep down that it's money for old rope – telling people what they want to hear – but I'm not complaining. If someone wants to pay me to spout the same old drivel over and over, then I'm all for it.

My building has studios on two floors and I've taken to renting out the space to other trainers to use with their own clients. My office is on the top floor, hidden away in a corner, largely so I can avoid everyone else, under the pretence of having work to do. I breeze through the space and head up the stairs, before unlocking my office door and letting myself in. Once inside, I check my emails, wondering if Steven might have got back to me with any more photos. He hasn't, so I trawl through the Facebook profiles of some of the people I know from last night. There are all sorts of pictures posted, though none I can see with the man in the blue suit.

In among that, I keep an eye on the local news feeds, looking for any update on the hit-and-run victim. The police seem to be coy on releasing the person's identity and status, which I suspect is a bad sign. If it was something minor, the road wouldn't still be closed. They will be collecting evidence in case the victim dies and the investigation becomes far more serious.

It feels like minutes since I arrived and yet, when I look to the clock, it's already quarter to six. I lock my office door and change into my cycling gear, with the studio-branded orange top. I head down the stairs to the spin studio, though it's hard to think of much other than the day's events.

Cool air is blowing through the studio as I take a seat and start working the spin bike. Assuming there is no group before mine, I always start pedalling a good ten minutes before the class begins.

I keep the resistance low as my class files in, armed with towels and water. Almost everyone says 'hi' as they take their respective spots and get themselves ready. After everything that's happened in the past day or so, it's good to feel my legs turning once more. It's a form of serendipity. Some people find exercise stressful, but it's always been the opposite for me. I can switch off and let the world pass me by.

At a minute to six, the room is almost full, so I turn up the volume of the music and tell everyone the level at which to set their resistance dial. It's going to be a fast one today: fewer hills but a quicker pace. It's more for me than anyone else in the class. I feel like this needs to be one that hurts.

I am so focused on pedalling as quickly as I can that I almost don't see the latecomer. I've not seen her in more than a year – and she's never been to my studio – but she takes the spare bike on the front row off to the right. I look up and do a double take – but she's ready for me anyway, staring defiantly across as she clips herself onto the pedals.

Yasmine.

TWELVE

THE WHY

Three years, eight months ago

David continues to sit on the sofa while he scrolls through something on his phone.

'Why didn't you tell me you had a sister?' I say from the kitchen.

He doesn't glance sideways as he keeps thumbing at the screen. 'I thought I had,' he says.

'You don't forget a sister,' I say.

'I suppose you never asked…'

The pan of rice is bubbling away and I lean on the counter as I stare across to him, waiting for him to turn. I wonder if we're going to argue for the first time. We've had something of a honeymoon period since he moved in and this is the closest we've come to falling out. He told me he'd explain all about Yasmine on his return and, now he's here, he has barely got off his phone.

'How could I ask about a sister I didn't know existed?' I say.

David sighs and turns to look across at me. 'Yasmine's my older sister,' he says with a shrug. 'She moved to Kingbridge with me when I came across to go to uni.'

'I don't understand how, if she's your sister – and you lived with her – she never came up in conversation. She knew about me.'

'Back then, she couldn't afford a place of her own and was still living with our parents. When I went back to university as a mature student, she moved in for a while as she got herself together.'

In the couple of months we've known one another, David and I have talked about our pasts. I know he comes from a village on the Kent coast, although the name fell from my mind almost as soon as he told me. I try to remember the specific conversations. I definitely mentioned I was an only child and I suppose that, because he didn't say much in response, I assumed he was, too. I guess it's true what they say about what assuming does.

'We don't really get on,' David continues. 'When we were living together, it was too close. It pushed us apart. She didn't want to go back to our parents, but couldn't afford to get her own place. I didn't want to kick her out, so we ended up living in this sort of mutual… well, "hatred" is a strong word, but "dislike", I suppose. Even though it was years ago, we never really made up. I don't talk about her because I don't see her.'

'But she knew who I was…'

David reaches for the remote control and flicks on the TV. He starts to switch between channels. He seems completely uninterested in the conversation.

'I don't know why it's a big deal,' he says.

'It's not a big deal – but a total stranger came up to me and knew who I was. It turns out she's your sister, even though I've never heard of her.'

'I ran into her a week or so ago,' he replies. 'Just before I went away. We don't get on, but it's not like we're enemies. We said hello, that sort of thing. She's living with a boyfriend now. I said I'd moved in with someone wonderful – a trainer who hosted exercise classes. I figured that was it. I didn't know that she'd visit you. I have no idea why she did.'

'Wonderful' sounds like deliberate overkill but it's hard to ignore the surge in my stomach. Nobody's ever described me like that before.

The boiling water has almost disappeared, so I turn off the heat and drain the pan. That done, I take the chicken from the oven and serve that and the rice onto a plate, before joining David on the sofa. He takes his food and starts to eat with a fork, while still channel-surfing with the other hand.

'Do you have any other brothers or sisters I should know about?' I ask. Any anger I might have had is fading fast.

'No – it's just Yasmine and me. Our parents died before I met you, so it's literally just me and her.' He has a mouthful and then puts his fork down on the plate. 'We should probably be closer – but she has her life and I have mine. What will be will be, and all that.'

I don't know how to reply. It's not that I have any reason to disbelieve him but something doesn't feel quite right.

He pauses and then adds: 'You're my family now.'

David stares across to me with such focus that it's as if I can feel his loneliness. We've not really spoken about it properly but we stumbled across one another at a time where I think we both needed it.

'Will it help if I talk to her?' he adds.

'What about?'

'To ask why she came to your class?'

'Just leave it,' I say. 'If she comes back, I can talk to her then. If she wants to be in contact with you, I suppose she will.'

He nods and has another bite of food. 'Whatever you want,' he says, before turning to me and smiling. 'Anything for you.'

THIRTEEN

THE NOW

The customers who take my classes have usually pre-paid for blocks of ten. That means the same faces appear over and over. It creates a group in which everyone knows who I am, as well as a community who can compete with and support one another. That doesn't mean there isn't the odd newcomer – though it is the exception, rather than the norm.

Yasmine clips into her bike as if she's been here dozens of times before. As soon as our eyes meet for the first time, she turns away and stares at the front. I can hardly abandon the session, so find myself going along with it all. Much of the script and structure for the spin class is already in my head. The choice of music dictates when we should go faster or slower. A large part of it is going through the motions, while keeping half an eye on everyone – which is probably why I find it so relaxing.

It's the opposite this time, however. I can't stop glancing off towards Yasmine, who steadfastly refuses to look at me. She's in lycra and seems trimmer and fitter than when I last saw her. Her hair is definitely longer and is tied back into a face-tugging ponytail.

I make my first mistake at the initial song change, thinking the pace is about to go up instead of dropping. The woman directly in front of me peeps up from her hunched cycling position, noticing that the tempo isn't tied to the music. Others do, too, so I call for everyone to dial down the resistance and try to act as if it never happened.

By the time the class is thirty minutes in, I've messed up the pacing three times; got two different people's names wrong, and somehow unclipped myself from the bike, slamming my ankle into the pedal. It's as if I'm a novice once more, going back to the days when I was nervously taking my first classes and overthinking everything.

All the while, Yasmine has studiously avoided looking anywhere other than the screen in front of her that's displaying the stats about her speed and distance.

When we get to the end, I realise that I've barely noticed the pool of sweat around my bike. I do my usual trick of mopping the floor with a towel to get rid of the worst of it, but, by the time I look back up, Yasmine is already on her way to the door. Even though people are still warming down, I hurry after her – and there's a moment of déjà vu as I remember our first meeting. There was a spin studio then and a chase along corridors.

This time, I catch her outside the studio on the edge of the car park. I reach for her shoulder and she spins to face me. We're underneath a street light that's pouring a dim orange glow down towards the path. Up close, there are a concentric collection of wrinkles around her eyes. Although she was older than David, she always looked younger – but much of that youth has disappeared since I last saw her. She'll be closer to fifty than forty, so I suppose it's little surprise. Age is the one thing we can never escape.

I suddenly realise that I don't know what to say.

'What do you want?' Yasmine asks.

'What are you doing here?' I reply.

'What do you mean?'

'You've come to my studio; my class. It can't be an accident…?'

She shrugs dismissively; something that certainly runs in her family. David was always a master at scorning subjects about which he didn't want to talk.

'I joined on the phone,' she says. 'Someone took my details earlier. It's a free country, isn't it?'

'But why here? Why now?'

Another shrug: 'What does it matter? I wanted to get back into training after having Eden. You should be flattered that I chose here. I saw you in the news all last week – someone posted it on my Facebook. Some award thing you were up for…'

I spoke to someone from the local paper and a photographer came to take some pictures. He kept trying to get me to lean over for a down-top shot – but I was too far ahead of him to go for anything like that. I was also named in a couple of the trade publications. Everything ended up online, so Yasmine might well have read about me. I also know that she gave birth around a year and a half ago. Probably around the time I last saw her.

It's all plausible… and yet, combined with everything else that's been happening, it doesn't feel right. David reappears in a photo, someone steals my car – and then David's sister, who never seemed to like me, walks back into my life, all within twenty-four hours.

'Is that it?' Yasmine asks.

'Eden's your daughter?' I reply, not entirely certain.

'Do you care?'

'She's my niece.'

Yasmine snorts, shakes her head and then spins and walks away without another word. I watch her go, not following because I have no idea what to add.

When I get back inside, I almost miss Andy sitting near the front desk. He's wrapped up in his wool coat that he got from a charity shop. Sometimes, he never seems to stop talking about the bargain he found. I'm probably imagining it, but the retail price seems to get higher with every telling, while the amount he paid gets lower. If it goes on much longer, it will end up with the woman behind the till paying him to take the coat away.

He stands as I spot him: 'Where'd you get to?' he asks.

'What do you mean?'

'You rushed right past me on the way out.'

It's only now that I remember I'm supposed to be meeting him after my class. There's still a towel in my hand and I dab at my forehead. I'm saved from having to give him a proper answer because a couple more people from my class exit through the barriers and say goodbye on their way out.

Andy loosens his scarf and fiddles with his watch. In contrast to the age difference between David and me; Andy is a year younger than I am. He is baby-faced to the point that he sometimes gets ID'd in pubs. It wouldn't be quite so annoying if I was ever asked to prove my age. Instead, I'm constantly waved through by people younger than me who definitely do not view me as one of their own.

'How's the packing going?' Andy asks.

'Oh, right… um…'

'You look upset.'

'Did you hear about the hit-and-run?'

'Of course. Everyone's been talking about it in the shop today.'

'It was my car,' I say. 'Someone stole it after I got back from the hotel. I was interviewed by the police.'

His smile dims and fades until even he can't do anything other than frown. He knows the implication instantly: 'They think you were driving?'

'I've been bailed pending further investigation.'

He stares, eyes widening until he manages: 'I don't think I understand…'

'I drove back from the hotel overnight because I couldn't sleep. After I parked and went to bed, someone stole the car. I phoned up to report it, but whoever took it had already hit someone by then.'

I know that this is a long way out of Andy's comfort zone. He's the type of person to see the good in everyone. He believes in rehabilitation instead of punishment. He'd make a terrible politician because, as the public demanded fire and brimstone, he'd try to placate them with a journal-published report about the value of community reintegration versus prison costs. It's who he is.

'Did you talk to a lawyer?' he asks.

'No... I just... told the truth. I thought...'

Andy nods, but there's disappointment in his eyes; like his newly trained puppy has done a wee on the living room carpet. 'You should probably get a solicitor,' he says.

'I will.'

I've sometimes wondered why Andy and I are together. I certainly like him, though I often think it might be because he's my shield. Nobody is going to look at me as a murderer while my boyfriend is busy giving up his time for a scout troop.

'I think I need a quiet night by myself,' I say.

This seemingly comes as no surprise as Andy tightens his scarf.

'I'm looking forward to Saturday, though,' I add.

'Me, too,' he replies. 'I've cleared a whole room if you want to convert it into a walk-in wardrobe. We can put some shelves and rails up – or there's a company in Kingbridge that do that sort of thing for you. They specialise in maximising storage space. It's up to you. Your room, your space.'

'Thank you.'

He pulls me closer and puts his arms around my back. I wrest into the crook of his neck and can feel his heart beating, steady and predictable, just like the way he is.

'I want it to be *our* house,' he whispers. 'Not mine...'

Andy inherited his parents' four-bedroom house a few years ago. I suppose it's the only way anyone under the age of about forty can afford anything bigger than a box in a doorway. He's been rattling around in the space by himself ever since. I've stayed over there semi-regularly; certainly more often than he sleeps at mine.

It was his suggestion for me to move in with him. He encouraged me not to sell my flat, saying I could rent it out as we 'see how it goes'. There was a big part of me that agreed, simply to be rid of Sunshine Row and what happened there. I'm still married, so I suppose there's some sort of technical adultery in there. The usual village nutballs need have something to gossip about.

Andy releases me and steps away: 'You'll have to show me your trophy another time,' he says.

It takes a second for me to realise he means my win from last night. It feels like an age ago. 'Sure,' I reply.

'Are there photos?'

There's definitely *one*…

'I'm waiting for the organiser to email me,' I say.

'We'll get it printed out and framed.'

'Right…'

'Jane texted and said you were thinking about doing something with the four of us on Wednesday night. I'm free if you are…?'

I suppose this is one social invitation I can't get out of. I had a feeling Jane might contact Andy directly. He gets on with everyone and hands out his phone number like dodgy blokes in anoraks give away sweets to kids.

'I've been wanting to catch up with Ben for ages,' Andy adds. 'See how his football's going.'

'I'll try to sort out a time,' I say.

We look to one another, with apparently neither of us quite sure what to say now. We've always had awkward goodbyes. They've never been of the 'No, you hang up' – variety, more a rush to leave first.

'What are you going to do for a car?' Andy asks.

'I'm not sure. Jane gave me a lift here. Everything happened so quickly that I've not thought it through yet.'

'You can take mine if you want? I've got the van for work, so can get around in that.'

'Oh…'

Before I can give a proper response, Andy has dug into his pockets and handed the keys over.

'You're insured for any car, aren't you?' he asks.

'Yes.'

'It's in the car park,' he adds.

'Don't you want a lift home?'

He pats his flat stomach: 'I need the exercise!'

'Oh… OK.'

'I'll see you Wednesday night, then…?'

'Right.'

He pecks me on the cheek, gives a wave to one of the other trainers, and then spins on his heels and heads out the door. This is typical of our relationship. We've never been the type of couple to live in one another's pockets, or put on over-the-top displays of public affection. After David, I like that. We spend more nights apart than together, which is why moving in is such a big change.

I feel myself starting to shiver with the mix of the opening and closing front door and my sweaty T-shirt. There is a private shower in the staff area at the top of the stairs, but I have the urge to shower at home and barricade myself away from the rest of the world.

I head for the stairs, ready to grab a hoody from the upstairs office when my phone beeps. It's a text from an unknown 07 mobile number and I almost delete it without bothering with the content. It'll only be some company telling me I'm eligible for compensation over some injury I've never had.

Except it isn't that. The message is far simpler and far more chilling:

Miss me? X

FOURTEEN

I stare at my phone, reading the message over and over, as if expecting something more substantial to appear. I move away from the steps, back towards reception, and turn to look at everyone who's left. There's only Jess behind the counter – and she's busy talking on the phone.

Who is this?

The reply comes almost instantly:

Nice top. You always looked good in orange.

I shiver, spinning the entire way around, although not seeing anyone I'd missed. Jess is making notes from whoever she's talking to and, as far as I can see, there is nobody else in reception. I hurry to the glass doors at the front and step outside, feeling the chill as I stare out into the darkness.

There's nobody there.

WHO IS THIS?

There is no instant reply this time. I hurry inside and up the stairs, phone in hand, willing it to buzz but simultaneously hoping it doesn't. When I get into my office, I lock the door behind me and sit in a darkness that's broken only by the glowing light from my phone.

Could it be Yasmine? She knew I was wearing orange. She can't know the truth, but I suppose it was her pregnancy that was the beginning of the end for David and me. I'm not trying to absolve myself from the blame – I know what I did – but everything might have played out differently had it not been for her.

It was only after David's disappearance… David's *death*… that I found out precisely where she lived in Kingbridge. Her house is relatively close to the police station where I was questioned earlier. Despite what she said about seeing me in the news, she's chosen to drive all the way to Gradingham for a spin class – *my* class – when she could've signed up for one much closer to her home.

I call the number that texted me, but it rings and rings without reply or a voicemail message. I think about sending another message, though realise it will achieve little. Whoever sent it knows who I am already – and, if he or she wanted to reveal their identity, I'd already know.

I change out of the orange studio shirt and then put on a winter coat and cap before leaving the studio. I could be anyone.

Andy's BMW is parked perfectly in the car park, as if he got out and measured the gap on either side between the car and the lines to ensure he was in the centre of the space. I spend a few minutes trying to readjust the mirrors and getting the seat in the right place. The car is so big. Usually, 'BMW' and 'wanker' would go hand-in-hand, which is why it felt strange when Andy bought one. I suppose I've joined the club now, at least temporarily.

I deliberately avoid the road on which my car is – or was – buried in a verge, instead following the country lanes around the edge of the village until I hit the main road. It's a steady drive to Kingbridge, although Andy's car feels like a surging behemoth that constantly wants to move faster than I'm willing to go. Like trying to wrestle a sleeping bag back into one of those impossibly small pouches.

It's as I pass McDonald's that I start to feel a little lost. Yasmine lives on a newish estate towards the back of the police station, but it's a labyrinth of dead-ends and unhelpful signs. I can feel more curtains twitching as I drive into the third cul-de-sac and have to turn around at the end. The pitchforks will be on standby as someone with too much time on their hands gets ready to kick off because a stranger has parked outside their house.

It's on my next pass along one of the main connecting roads that, almost inconceivably, I spot Yasmine walking a dog. I was looking for a familiar house – but here she is herself, bundled up in an unbuckled coat over the same yoga pants and bright shoes she had on at the studio. Her hair is high in a ponytail and I'm so surprised to see her that I almost swerve towards her without thinking. I manage to catch myself and continue driving past, watching as Yasmine tugs at the dog's lead, oblivious that I'm so close.

I end up parking at the end of a row of cars and watch in the mirror as she waits for her dog to sniff a lamp post.

I wait until Yasmine passes and then get out from the car as quietly as I can. I pull the hood up over my head and start to follow her.

Things would be easier if it wasn't for Yasmine's dog stopping at almost every bush, lamp post, wall or patch of grass for a sniff and a wee. The animal seems to have an infinite bladder and Yasmine doesn't appear to be in much of a hurry as she pauses each time until he or she is ready to move on.

It's dark and the paths are largely deserted, so I find myself ducking behind hedges and hovering behind cars. To an untrained observer, I must look like some sort of flasher waiting for a moment – though Yasmine doesn't ever look behind.

After a while, she turns into an alley. I have to hurry to close the gap, not wanting to lose her when she gets to the other end. It's only as I turn into the alley myself that I realise it isn't a passage at all. There's a small green that's hidden by the surrounding bushes and Yasmine is sitting on a bench underneath a street light. Her dog is off weeing on the fence as I almost walk into the bench. I angle backwards, narrowly stopping myself from toppling over.

It makes no difference as Yasmine is on the phone, oblivious to how close we are. I can't back off now, so continue onto the grass, my head down, trying to maintain a gentle pace.

'…really got it coming to her,' Yasmine says to whoever is on the other end of the phone call.

I try to slow without making it obvious I'm doing so – but I am already a couple of steps past her.

'I know,' Yasmine continues with a laugh. 'I wish I'd seen the look on her face.'

FIFTEEN

THE WHY

Three years, seven months ago

David holds Mum's hand as we head along the path towards her bungalow.

'I can see where your daughter gets her looks from,' he says.

She laughs in a way I don't think I've heard in years. Whenever she had a new outfit, she'd ask Dad how she looked. He'd always say that she'd look great in a bin bag and she'd chuckle to herself. It never seemed to get tired but, then, neither did they. As a couple, they had the sort of relationship that I'm not sure exists any more. They were devoted to one another and, possibly until now, that laugh was reserved only for my father.

Now it is David with whom she is smitten. It's extraordinary how he wanders into people's lives, including mine, and enchants them.

'People always say she looks like me,' Mum says.

'There's definitely a resemblance.'

We get to the door and Mum fumbles in a pocket for her key. The wind blusters across us as a couple of seconds becomes ten and things start to feel awkward. After Dad died, my mother sold up and moved to this retirement bungalow on the coast. Poynton-on-Sea is perhaps the place she was always happiest. Her, Dad and

I would come here for a holiday every summer and, even though it's only twenty miles from Gradingham, it felt like another world.

Mum now has the key, but she's struggling to fit it into the lock. David hovers at her side and I wonder if he somehow knows that offering to help will instantly change her opinion of him. Patience is what she wants and patience is what she gets.

Waves slam into the cliffs below. When the tide is out, there is a sprawling beach on which I used to play as a girl. I've often wondered if I've ever been as happy as I used to be back then.

Mum finally gets the key into the lock. She stands slightly taller with relief and then shoves the door inwards as if nothing was wrong.

Her bungalow smells of burnt toast, but there's no point in mentioning it because she'll claim I'm imagining things. She closes the door behind David and me and then beckons us towards the sofa. David asks if he needs to take off his shoes, but she replies with 'Of course not, love.'

The sofa is second-hand because almost everything she's ever owned once belonged to someone else. It has a faded floral print and is as uncomfortable as I remember; as if any foam filling has been replaced with Lego bricks.

David turns between us somewhat theatrically: 'I bet you were a heartbreaker back in the day,' he says.

Mum touches her permed bob. 'I did have a few boys courting me.'

He gets to his feet. 'Would you like a cup of tea, Mrs Noble?' he asks.

'It's Wilma,' she replies. Mum motions to stand, but once she's down, that's it for a couple of hours.

'Let me,' David says and Mum settles once more.

'Everything's in the cupboard by the door,' she says. 'I'll have a splash of milk. No sugar for me.'

'All the smartest people have their tea that way.'

David leaves us momentarily and I have my usual few seconds of panic when I'm left alone with my mother. It always feels as if she's a blink away from forgetting who I am.

'How's the flat?' she asks. It is perhaps her favourite topic of conversation when it comes to me. When she sold her house and bought this, she gave me some of what was left to put down the deposit on my flat. Probably because of that, I think she sees my place as partly hers.

'It's fine,' I say.

'Have you picked up your clothes since I was last there?'

I want to say that I'm an adult and can leave my clothes where I want – but it's not worth it.

There's a snap as the hob is lit. Mum has never got on with electric kettles. I suppose it's the ease of use that annoys her, though I've never asked.

'He's quite the catch,' Mum says.

'David?'

'Who else? Better than the other boys you've brought home.'

'Hardly "boys"…'

'Where'd you find him? Not on that Tinder thing, was it?'

I start to reply and then realise what she's said. 'How do you know about Tinder?' I ask.

'I'm not as out of touch as you think, young lady.'

Before I can reply, David reappears in the doorway. It's like he's a natural at meeting parents because he apparently knows exactly how to push Mum's buttons. I suppose that's a surprise in the sense that his own parents have died. It's not long before he's set her off and she's telling stories about being a teenager in the sixties.

One of her prized stories, the one I've heard probably more than any other, is the time she saw John Lennon. That's it. She *saw* him. She never watched the Beatles in concert and she never actually *met* him; she spied Lennon from across the road. But the way she tells it, she was the fifth Beatle.

'I always wished I'd got his autograph,' she says. 'He seemed like such a nice young man. I should have crossed the road and said hello.' She tails off and then adds a new bit: 'Course, it's all selfies nowadays.'

David laughs and plays along. 'If you'd done that, Yoko wouldn't have got a look-in!'

'Oh, you…'

It's as if Mum is flirting as she giggles and bats a hand towards him. I'm almost embarrassed, but then days like this are better than the ones where she shrieks that I'm trying to rob her.

After David brings in the teas, Mum continues to talk him through her teenage memories. In her telling, the culture we know today is a direct consequence of her tastes from the time. David must know it's nonsense, but he nods along like a dutiful boyfriend trying to impress a girlfriend's mother.

Mum talks her way through almost forty-five minutes, which is probably the most coherent I've seen her in years. It's only when David's phone rings that the flow is interrupted. He checks the screen and holds it up.

'I'm so sorry,' he says. 'I really have to take this. It's business. I won't be long.'

Mum tells him not to worry and then David disappears out the front door. With him gone, Mum twists in her seat to ensure he's out of earshot. She bites her lip for a moment but I know what's coming.

'You're not going to blow this, are you?' she asks.

'What makes you think I will?'

'I'm just saying. Men like David don't come along very often. Once I found your father, I made sure I kept him.'

I turn away from her, watching David's shadow as he strides back and forth outside the window. It was time for him to meet her, I suppose, given that we're living together. I think the speed of it all is starting to catch up with me. We only met three months ago – and here we are.

'You don't know him, Mum,' I say.

'You're the one who moved in with him after a month.'

'It wasn't a month.'

'Close enough.'

She has a point, and yet she doesn't. Sometimes people get swept up into things and it overtakes everything else because it feels right. With David's landlord selling up, it seemed like a natural thing that, if he had to find somewhere new to live, it might as well be with me. It's worked for both of us. I think I needed his encouragement – and it can't be a coincidence that things are finally beginning to happen with my career since he came into my life.

That doesn't mean I believe I've made a mistake by moving in with David, simply that things were different when Mum was young.

I don't reply, so, after a moment, she continues: 'Anyway, I'm just saying—'

'I know what you're saying, Mum. Can we not talk about it, please?'

Mum straightens in her seat, annoyed. I wonder if she'll remember this conversation tomorrow. She's only seventy, but Dad's death took more from her than she'll ever admit. This is her own bungalow but there's someone who checks on her every day and makes sure she's eating. It's not full-on home help and it's not residential care – but it is a half-step.

'What does he do?' Mum asks.

'I told you,' I say, before catching myself. In Mum's world, all pieces of information are new and she definitely doesn't forget things.

'You've not told me anything,' she snaps.

David is still pacing back and forth outside the window and there's no chance of him saving me in the short term.

'He buys and sells things,' I say.

Her face falls slightly and her tone sharpens: 'Like a market trader?'

'No, Mum, *not* like a market trader. It's high-quality stuff. He buys and sells rare vinyl and books, things like that. He scours the country for collectibles and then sells them on for a profit.'

Mum examines me for a moment before deciding that this is acceptable. 'He must have a good eye,' she says. 'Does he make good money?'

'I'm not answering that, Mum.'

She shrugs indignantly: 'Well, you'll need something. It's not as if you've got a big career plan. When your looks go, what've you got left?'

I stare at her, but she's refusing to meet my gaze. I think about not answering, but that will only make it worse.

'We support each other,' I say. 'He's been passing around my personal training cards, plus checking out new gyms when he travels. He knows what I'm trying to achieve – and I *do* have a career plan, actually.'

Mum harrumphs to make it clear that she believes precisely none of this. Next, she'll be telling me how she had to walk ten miles uphill through a snowstorm and then hurl herself off a cliff to get to school on time. Obviously, she would do that both ways. I'm not sure where the cliffs are in Gradingham…

Mercifully, the front door clicks and then David reappears in the living room. He crosses to where I am on the sofa and reaches into his pockets before passing over an oblong box. It's wrapped with silver paper, with a golden bow on top.

'I know it's your thirtieth on Tuesday,' he says, 'but I figured I'd give you your present a bit early.'

It's obvious that he's done this to gain favour with Mum, though I'm not sure if that's a good or bad thing. For now, I'll take the distraction.

'Go on,' he says as I run my fingers across the join in the paper.

The gift is heavier than it looks and the paper is sealed down with at least a double wrap of tape. It takes me a while to find a join and, when I finally get the paper off, it reveals a crimson plastic box. David is watching my mother as I open the lid to reveal a sparkling silver watch.

'Ooooh,' Mum says. 'That looks expensive.'

I have no idea about watches but have to agree. I think I read somewhere that the value of things like watches and jewellery can often be measured by weight. The heavier something is, the more likely it is to be worth something. I'm not sure how that could apply to a strip of lead painted gold, but it sounds good.

'Are you sure you can afford this?' I ask, turning to David. It's not a problem as such, but he's still not contributing much to our finances. Or, more to the point, *my* finances.

He's beaming with pride: 'Of course. I stumbled across a proper trove of records the other week.'

He stretches across and straps the watch to my wrist before I can say anything about it. I've never worn a watch with any regularity before – and I'm not sure it's for me.

Mum instantly reaches for me to get a better look.

'Your father used to love a good watch,' she says, before turning to David. 'Some of my friends have record collections. I can have a word if you want. Perhaps you can go and see if there's anything worth your while…?'

I start to interrupt but David talks over me: 'That sounds amazing, Mrs Noble.'

'It told you, love – it's Wilma.' She glances to my watch again and then adds: 'Do you have your own family?'

'My mum died when I was young, but Dad ran a collecting business, which I guess is where I get it from.'

Mum nods along: 'You're an only child?'

David glances momentarily towards me: 'I have an older sister. She's a bit protective of me, though we tend to do our own things.'

'Oh, that's lovely. What's her name?'

I've not seen Yasmine since that time at the gym – and we've not talked of her. With that, I can't take much more of these happy families so stand somewhat abruptly and announce that I need the toilet. I head along the hall into the bathroom and then lock the door behind me. I can hear the soft muttering of David and Mum, though can't make out the words. I sit for a minute or do with my eyes closed, wanting to leave. I'm not even sure why. This is one of my mother's better days – except there's something about her being nice to someone else that will always rankle. I'm not sure I'll ever get past the feeling that she likes literally anyone more than she likes me.

I'm not ready to return to the living room, so take off the watch and examine the back. It only takes a brief Google search to find the model David's given me. I have to check the top five links to make sure there hasn't been a mistake somewhere.

The watch is worth £3,000.

SIXTEEN

THE NOW

Tuesday

Nothing happening is worse than something happening.

Well, maybe.

I haven't had any further texts overnight from the unknown number. Google throws up no matches for it and I decide against messaging or calling. I try searching for Yasmine's name online, but there's little information about her – and her Facebook page shows me only her name and a photo. It's rather annoying when people know how to turn on their privacy settings. I probably should have called the number when I was following Yasmine – but it didn't occur to me at the time.

It's been a day and a half since seeing David in that photo at the awards. A day since my car was stolen. I woke up this morning expecting something to happen – more cryptic texts, or contact from the police. Instead, there is nothing. I potter around, making myself coffee and indulging with a couple of slices of toast. There's still no sign of the Tigger pot and so, after that, there's little to do other than work.

The windscreen on Andy's car is frosty, but the heating deals with that in barely twenty seconds. If this was my car, I'd be impatiently outside with a bucket of hot water in an attempt to get things moving. That does make me think that whoever took my car must have done so not long after I parked it. If it had been left for long, it would have been an icebox.

It is only a short distance to the studio, but I drive as carefully as if I'm taking my test and there's a mardy middle-aged singleton at my side. It's partly because Andy's car still feels like it's trying to drive itself, but mainly because it would terrible if I had an actual crash while denying being involved in another.

By the time I let myself into the studio, one of the other trainers – Mel – is busy laying out the mats for her yoga session. It's clear that almost nobody yet knows about my car being involved in the crash because we go through the usual small talk. One of the other trainers is off to Bermuda for Christmas, so we go back and forth about how strange the festive season will be if it's warm. People start to arrive and Mel sets her whale music going, which is always my cue to move on.

I head up to my office and open the slats of the blinds enough that I can see out, while nobody should be able to look in. It gives me a view of almost the entire lower level, including the entrance and reception, and I spend a couple of minutes watching as more people arrive. I'm not sure what I'm looking for but, whatever it is, it's not outside my window.

My desk is full of pads and pens, even though I rarely use them. Almost everything is done digitally, but I end up writing myself a list:

Someone who looks like David?

A brother?

I start to write David's name and get as far as the capital-D before stopping myself. Even entertaining such a thought feels like a step to madness. Neither of the other two explanations feel particularly solid, either. David didn't tell me about Yasmine at the beginning – but it's not as if he concealed her identity for the whole time we were together. It was weeks, not years… although I have wondered if he'd have ever told me if I hadn't brought it up.

I remember some of the things from David's death two years ago with perfect clarity and yet, like anything, memories fade. Truth blurs with fiction and I've told so many fictions since what happened that I sometimes find myself believing the lies. I repeated them so often in the immediate aftermath that I sometimes lie awake at night trying to figure out what was real and what wasn't.

But I *do* remember how I killed him and what I did directly afterwards. I felt uneasily calm, perhaps as composed as I've ever been. It's only now that I wonder whether it was an illusion and my mind is playing with itself. Perhaps I was never that collected and everything that happened did so in a crushing panic? Somehow, in among all that, I failed to notice that David was never dead…

That's my fear – that the truth I've been telling myself for two years was never the truth to begin with. That's why nothing happening is worse than something happening.

I'm scratching the scar on my neck again – and everything that has happened has seemingly left me slipping into old habits once more. I watch the lower floor for a while longer and then turn back to my list, though I still can't bring myself to add David's name to the bottom.

After getting through a few bits of admin, I take Andy's advice and call a solicitor's office. It's the same one I spoke with when I was trying to figure out whether it was worth divorcing David. The person who answers the phone must know who I am as she puts me through to 'one of the partners' – Mr Patrick – almost immediately.

I tell him what happened, half expecting him to reply that he can't help. I'm braced for the worst, but he's calm and seemingly unruffled. Mr Patrick has one of those voices that's as smooth as a Creme Egg left in a windowsill on a summer's day.

'I think what you're missing is that the police have to *prove* you were driving,' he says. 'It's not the other way around. You don't have to prove that you weren't.'

'I wasn't,' I reply.

'And I'm sure they are rapidly coming to that conclusion.'

He tells me to leave it with him for now but to get in contact if I hear anything more from the police. I instantly feel better after hanging up. It's obvious, of course. The one thing everybody knows about a justice system is that people are innocent until proven guilty – and so it's clear that the police have to prove it was me driving. If they had any evidence of that – which they can't because I wasn't – then I would have already been charged.

I turn back to my computer and again look for details from the crash. In the time I've been speaking to the solicitor, a news story has appeared that names the pedestrian who was hit. 'Trevor Barnwell, 52, from Gradingham' was struck in the early hours of yesterday morning. It says that police are investigating the circumstances, but, other than that, there are few more details than before.

I spend the rest of the morning getting on with the smaller jobs I usually put off. I pay the cleaning bill and send out a couple of invoices, before a text arrives from Andy, who asks how I'm doing. When I say that I'm working as normal, he asks if I want to go for a meal that evening. I'm tempted to say no, if only because I'm in the mood to barricade myself away from the world. Instead, I end up agreeing because at least it will be *something* that's happening.

It's only after all of that that I remember to check the membership system. It takes me seconds to find Yasmine. As she said, she signed up over the phone yesterday. The timing is curious, but I'm not sure what else to read into it.

Although we call it a 'membership system', it's not quite true. We don't sell memberships because there's no on-site gym – we sell blocks of classes. Yasmine's address is listed, which, if I'd checked in the first place, would have stopped me from having to drive aimlessly around her estate. If I'd done that, though, I'd have missed her walking along the streets.

Her phone number is also on file – although it doesn't match the unknown 07 one that's been texting me. I'm not sure if that means anything. There's an email address, too – and everything seems as it should. I'm still not sure what to make of what I overheard from her call last night. It's not as if I can do much in any case. I can hardly follow her everywhere.

I take a few minutes to watch what's going on below, where one of the physical therapists has arrived. He has a roll of towels tucked under his arm and spends a minute or two chatting to Jess on reception, before heading off to one of the smaller side rooms. There are two more classes in the afternoon, with two more trainers. This somehow ended up being the business plan in that I've gone from *actually* doing what I wanted to taking money from other people who are now doing it.

I turn back to the computer screen but can't face the mundanity of it any longer. I never grew up wanting to put numbers into spreadsheets or fill in the blanks for invoices. I'm not sure anyone did. Instead, I change into the running gear I keep in the cabinet. I hesitate when it comes to the orange studio top but opt for it anyway.

It's a warmer day outside today, though not by much. My breath spirals ahead of me as I start jogging along the pavement that leads towards the centre of Gradingham. The hedges that line the path gradually turn into low walls and houses set back from the road.

Gradingham has its moments during all four seasons. In the spring, the fields that surround it bloom with a golden yellow and, on sunny days, it feels as if the whole village is glowing. The summer means emerald green fields under endless blue skies. There are fêtes and beer gardens; with weekly barbecues at the cricket club. Autumn brings a rainbow blanket as the leaves change colour seemingly day to day. Even winter, with its glacial verges and biting cold, has its charm. When it snows, or the frost is particularly thick, these stone-clad buildings are coated in postcard-perfect white. I've lived here all my life and, I suppose, the window is narrowing for me to ever leave.

The houses turn into the High Street and I run along the deserted path before crossing the road at the end and heading back the way I've come.

With a job in fitness, everyone assumes that trainers enjoy activities like this. There is a degree of truth to that – but running is still horrible. Sometimes I crave a chip butty like anyone else and would rather have my feet up in a comfy chair.

I'm thinking of chips as I arrive back at the studio. My watch says I've done a fraction over 10km and I head upstairs to have a shower. In the time that has taken, I've received no further texts, calls or emails.

I waste another hour doing little but wondering if this is it from now on. Instead of any sort of conclusion to who was in the photo, or who took my car, I'll live with this needle of paranoia.

I am working my way through a stack of receipts when an email arrives from Steven, the awards organiser. He has sent me a link to a website that is hosting a series of photos from the night. I skim through a badly written report and the list of winners to get to the pictures. Most of them are of individuals or small groups posing somewhat awkwardly. I'm in four – two of which are from when I was on stage getting the award; the other two were taken when I was looking the other way in a group shot. I go through each image looking for the man in the blue suit who looks like David.

He's not there.

Almost all of the photos were taken in the early part of the evening, so it's not necessarily a surprise. If he was only in the room for the moment the winners' group photo was taken, then he wouldn't be in any of the others.

I focus on the final ones in the set – but Steven's photo was taken at a different angle than Jane's. Some of the winners are looking to this picture-taker, while others – including me – are staring at someone else who had a camera. It's all a bit of a mess – and there's no sign of anyone who looks like David in the back. It's only when I'm comparing his pictures to the one Jane sent me that I remember the circumstances. We were all ready to step away when she stopped us for one final shot. It was that one in which the man in the blue suit appeared.

I'm still scanning through the photos when my phone rings and the word 'MUM' flashes across the screen. It's rare that she calls me – and almost all our phone conversations happen at pre-determined times. I'll go into them with a literal list of things to mention because, without that, I'll be stuck with a lecture about how my life is going nowhere and that things haven't been the same since David left. That's if she remembers David has gone.

I wince as I press the button to answer. It is never good news when she calls unexpectedly.

'Hi, Mum…'

'You'll never guess who's got cancer.'

I stumble over a reply. As opening gambits go, it's strong.

'Sorry…?' I say.

'Go on: guess.'

'Mum, I—'

'Iris. I just heard. Lung cancer. Never smoked a cigarette in her life. Still, we all breathed it in back then. She's only two years older than me. Makes you think, doesn't it?'

I don't get a chance to 'think' because she's off. There's no time for me to tell her that I have no idea who Iris is because she's busy explaining in intricate detail about how chemotherapy might or might not work and how Iris has been given three months to live. There's a sort of glee to her telling, as if one of her friends having cancer is an indication that Mum herself has lived a good life because she hasn't got it. Even if I could get a word in, I wouldn't know what to say. I've learned with experience that the best way to handle these types of conversation is to let Mum talk herself out. Give it five minutes and she'll move onto the weather.

That's why I'm only half listening when all the hairs on my arm stand up.

'Anyway, it was nice for David to pop in. I'll never know why you got rid of him. Still, I suppose that's the modern way, isn't it? I just think that—'

'You saw David…?'

Mum stops speaking and I can imagine her frowning with annoyance at being interrupted.

'What?' she says.

'You said that you saw David…?'

There's a pause and then: 'Who?'

'David.'

'Who?'

I stop and take a breath. Mum is at her most coherent when she's allowed to process things at her own pace. Interruptions not only annoy her but they make her lose any train of thought.

'You said that David popped in,' I say slowly.

There's another gap and I'm worried I've lost her. I wait and then hear her clucking her tongue.

'He came by yesterday,' she says.

'Are you sure?'

'I might be old, Morgan, but I'm not senile. He popped in yesterday. I'll never know why you got rid of him. Still, I suppose that's the modern way, isn't it? I just—'

'Mum.'

'What?'

'I'm coming over.'

SEVENTEEN

THE WHY

Three years, five months ago

Edinburgh's cobbled streets are covered with a slick of damp as the grey wash hovers ominously above. It feels like it might rain, although the woman at the hotel said that it's always like that.

'Never go out without a coat,' she said.

'Even in July?' I asked.

'*Especially* in July.'

There was sun this morning, but the darkness and chill of the day makes that feel like something of a dream.

David grips my hand a little firmer as he leads me through an arch which brings us out onto more cobbles. We don't speak because we don't need to. There's something intrinsically old-time romantic about wandering hand-in-hand through these ancient streets. This is the sort of thing I pictured about being in a relationship. I check the watch that he gave me for my birthday and it tells me that it's almost three in the afternoon. It feels a long way from the village in which I grew up, yet there is nowhere in the world I'd rather be.

It takes us almost half an hour to walk to the exhibition centre. David seems to know what he's doing as he leads us around to one of the doors at the side. There's a big sign for the 'International

Collectors' Fair' and David flashes a pass to a man on the gate, who waves us through. Inside, it smells of crisp, frayed paper; like walking into a musty bookshop. There are long rows of stalls that stretch from one side of the hall to the other. People are crowding along the aisles, shuffling forward like penguins huddling for warmth.

We stop on a platform overlooking the scene and David leans forward on his forearms as I slot in at his side.

'I found some gems from your mum's friends,' he says. 'I've already got some interested buyers in Sweden. I might have to fly out there in a week or so.'

'I've heard Sweden's really expensive,' I reply.

'Most of Scandinavia is. They earn more, so it doesn't matter to them. It's only when you visit that everything seems to cost a lot.'

'How much will you make?'

'Enough to make it worthwhile.'

David seems to be scanning the stalls for something, so I continue waiting at his side, watching the masses below. It's only then that I realise how few women there are. There are men of all ages, shapes and sizes – although they are almost all white. This business feels very focused.

With David saying his haul is 'enough to make it worthwhile', I wonder if I should finally bring up rent. He's been living with me for three months now and I've never quite got around to asking him to contribute to our living arrangements. Perhaps not even rent, but food or a share of the bills – that sort of thing. On average, he's probably gone for a day a week at various fairs, though I'm not always sure. Until he brought me here, I was beginning to think that he was, essentially, unemployed. I never brought it up, but he might have picked up on it, which is why we're in Edinburgh – and why he has been paying for everything.

So far, we've spent a whole day wandering the streets, which was topped off with afternoon tea and a whisky-tasting that somehow left me both light- and heavy-headed. I slept well last night.

David is still scanning the floor, where the long rows seem to be split into sections. There are records in one area and books in another, while I can also see magazines, comics, newspapers, figurines, street signs, football programmes and toys. There is even a stall below us selling the sort of bobblehead that's in the back of David's car.

'Is this the type of place you sell?' I ask.

David hums a little, turning from side to side. 'Not really. It's small fry here. People come to be cheapskates. The big money is in importing. If you can get something in bulk from somewhere like Bulgaria or Romania, there might be some first editions in there.' He licks his lips and then adds: 'I might be on to something in Slovakia. Got a supplier who reckons he's come across a load of records from the sixties and seventies. All smuggled stuff from back when it was behind the Iron Curtain. Perfect condition, he says. He mentioned some Bowies, but that's probably only scratching the surface.'

I'm not sure how to reply. It's the first he's mentioned of it and, if it's true that big events like this are a waste of time, then I'm not sure why we're here.

'The problem is having the money upfront,' David says.

He lets it hang for a while and only continues when it's clear I don't know how to reply.

'A lot of my money is tied up in stock,' he adds.

He has mentioned this before, although I've never been quite clear where David's stock actually is. He told me he's got records and books in storage that are waiting for the right buyer. When I asked how long it might take to sell, he shrugged and said that's the business.

'It's true what they say,' he adds. 'It takes money to make money – but the banks don't want to know.' With barely a breath, he nods below: 'Shall we go for a wander?'

I follow him down the stairs and we join the hordes of people who are ambling along the aisles. I never realised quite how much there was to collect. So much of what is on display looks as if it came straight from the landfill. There's a stall where someone is offloading rack upon rack of metal signs. It looks like they're from the fifties and sixties, with many advertising cigarettes in a way that seems so strange nowadays. I can understand collecting something like records – they can be listened to and there's something artistic about the sleeves. I can't see the point in anyone amassing signs.

David notices me staring and clamps a hand on my shoulder as he laughs. 'It's not what *you'd* buy – it's what *someone else* will buy.'

We continue on, looping around to another aisle where there are rows of stalls selling toys. There are walls of action figures that I remember from my youth. Star Wars, Thundercats, He-Man and She-Ra, and Ninja Turtles are the ones I spot first – but there are many more. I was never that interested in anything specifically marketed for girls, which is perhaps why it's a surprise to see the sheer breadth of colourful My Little Ponies on the next stall.

'Takes you back, doesn't it?' David says.

The final stall has mainly Disney plushes. I step inside, partly to get away from the masses, and instantly baulk at the prices. There's a palm-sized Mickey Mouse soft toy for which the seller is asking £300. David flits through the price labels and seems unsurprised by it all.

'Do you sell soft toys?' I ask.

'Not regularly. They sometimes show up in a bulk buy.'

'I can't believe this costs £300.'

David points to the £450 tag attached to a Pooh Bear.

'Do people pay that?' I ask.

'How do you think people like me make money? You can buy a hundred things in a job lot and it only takes one sale to cover the cost. Anything else is profit.'

He has explained this before, but it's now I see it myself that it feels like something that can – and does – make money.

We're about to leave the stall when I spot a small, clay Tigger pot next to the counter. It's the odd item out in a stall of soft toys. When I was a girl, I read the Winnie The Pooh books and Tigger was always my favourite. Pooh always seemed to be so depressed and then Tigger would bounce around and make things better. That's how I remember it, anyway.

'Do you like it?' David asks.

'I think my mum used to have one. I might've played with it when I was a kid. I remember filling it with buttons.' I swirl a hand, trying to find the recollection. 'I sort of remember it, but I don't. I must've been really young.

David turns to the girl behind the counter: 'How much?' he asks.

She spies the pot in my hand and pouts a lip. 'Twenty?'

'There's a chip at the bottom. How about five for cash?'

The girl doesn't bother to check the damage, which I hadn't noticed. She mutters, 'OK' and then I hand her a note.

We continue walking around the fair and David shows a little interest in one of the record stalls, though he doesn't buy anything. It takes us around ninety minutes in total until we're back where we started at the platform overlooking the hall. I assume we're going to leave, but David stops and leans once more. I join him because I'm not sure what else to do.

'Have you thought about it?' he asks.

I stare sideways at him, wondering if I missed a sentence among the hubbub: 'Thought about what?'

'The seed money for the Slovakia thing…'

I don't know how I missed it before, but it now seems obvious that he was asking for money when he brought it up earlier. I wait for him to look at me, though he is focused only on the floor below.

'I can't lend you what I don't have,' I say.

'But *you* could get a loan,' David replies. 'Say it's for a car, or whatever. Once I've got the stock, I'll be able to get your money back straight away. Like that Pooh Bear thing down there.' He wafts a hand in the direction of the toy stall.

'But that Pooh hadn't sold,' I reply. 'You can put a price tag on anything – but if it's unsold, then it doesn't matter.'

David shakes his head. 'You're not seeing it.'

'I can't go and ask for a car loan and then give the money to you instead.'

He bites his lip and nods slowly before suddenly spinning on his heels. 'Shall we go?' he says.

'Are you sure that's all right?' I ask.

He continues nodding, too quickly. 'Of course,' he replies. 'Let's go.'

EIGHTEEN

THE NOW

I've pulled up the handbrake of Andy's car when I spot Veronica hurrying along the pavement. She has a satchel over her shoulder and is wearing a pair of bright white trainers, with thick dark tights.

Mum's bungalow is among a collection of thirty or so that are occupied by people who are of, ahem, 'advancing years'. Mum doesn't like the term 'elderly', let alone 'old'. It's a gated community, where cars have to either be buzzed in or stop to type a code into a metal speaker box. The security detail is slightly compromised by the fact that anyone can simply open the pedestrian gate and walk in, though it gives a veneer of sanctuary, which is probably the most important thing.

Veronica visits six days a week to make sure everyone is healthy and has what they need. She's a mix of warden and companion, with a large aspect of babysitter thrown in. She is also the most patient person I've ever met and does a job for which there is not enough money in the world to tempt me.

As I get out of the car, she stops and offers an impressed smile.

'Nice…' she says.

'It's not mine,' I reply. 'I'm borrowing it for a few days.'

She hoists her satchel higher and smiles politely, ready to get back to whatever she was doing.

'Were you here yesterday?' I ask.

'On and off.'

'Did you see anyone new around?'

Veronica shakes her head. 'I don't think so. It's pretty quiet around here in December.'

She pulls her cardigan tighter as if to emphasise her point. While she's doing that, I unlock my phone and find the photo Jane took the other evening. I deleted all the old ones of David and I have no idea what happened to the wedding photos. I certainly don't have them. I zoom in on the face of the man who looks like David and turn it around for Veronica to see.

'I don't suppose you've seen him around, have you?'

She squints and then slowly shakes her head. 'I don't think so… is there anything to worry about?'

I put the phone back in my bag. 'Not at all.'

Veronica eyes me for a moment, but I can't explain much more than that. She wasn't working here when David was around. She probably knows my husband disappeared – everyone seems to – but I don't want to get into it today.

'Bit chilly out,' I say, which is enough to break our impasse.

Veronica pulls her satchel higher again, agrees with me, and then heads off towards the furthest of the bungalows.

I let myself into Mum's, though she barely looks up as I enter the living room. She's in her chair, arms folded, watching an auction show on TV.

'Look at this,' she says. 'He's trying to get £200 for that flowerpot. No chance.'

I go through the basics – filling the kettle and setting it on the stove before cleaning away the cups and plates Mum's left in the sink. Veronica does it some days, but it's not really her job. When the kettle starts whistling, I make a pair of teas and then head back into the living room. Mum takes hers without a word and sips from the top before putting the cup on the side table.

'Do you want another pillow?' I ask.

'I'm not an invalid.' She takes a breath and then nods at the screen. 'I told you he'd never get £200.'

I sit on the sofa and shuffle around, trying to get comfortable. I only stop when Mum tuts loudly in my direction and it feels like I'm a scolded six-year-old again.

'Mum…' I say.

She doesn't turn from the screen.

'You said you saw David…'

She snaps her reply: 'Who?'

'David. My ex-husband.'

Mum's attention switches to me momentarily but only for a second until she looks back to the screen.

The thing is, she's not been diagnosed with anything like dementia or Alzheimer's. First, she would refuse to go to the doctor; second, she wouldn't acknowledge any diagnosis anyway. Third, she can sometimes be frighteningly clear about things that actually *did* happen in the past. Finally, there's a horrible part of me that doesn't want to push for any sort of confirmation because I don't want to know.

Sometimes, she will talk about things from a decade ago as if it's happening now. Once, she spoke as if Dad was still alive and he was in the other room. She can forget that she now lives in Poynton-on-Sea instead of Gradingham, where she spent her previous fifty or so years. She thinks she's on holiday and talks about looking forward to getting home. And then, twenty minutes later, she'll have forgotten we ever had the conversation.

There's obviously something not right – and it's getting worse. That doesn't mean that I know what to do. Her own stubbornness will win over anything I could suggest.

She doesn't speak for a good thirty seconds as she watches the TV – and then, from nowhere, she says: 'David…?', making it sound like a question. It is as if she doesn't know the name, like it could be a character on television about whom she is unsure.

I show her the photo on my phone from the other night. She takes it from me, her hands shaking as she tries to grip the screen.

'I hate these things,' she says.

'Do you remember David?' I ask.

She squints over her glasses at the photo: 'Course I do.'

'Was he here, Mum?'

'He made me a nice cup of tea.'

The hairs rise on the back of my neck. It feels as if there is someone behind me, blowing a gentle breeze.

'When?'

The delay is interminable. On the television, someone in a red shirt is running along a street, waving a lamp at someone else in a red shirt. Mum is captivated by it, her gaze unflinching.

'Oh, y'know…' she says.

I wait to see if there's anything more, but that's all she has. This is the type of response she gives when she doesn't know the answer but will absolutely refuse to admit she is unsure. I won't get a better reply.

For a while, we sit and watch the television together. We'd do this when I was young, but, back then, it was something like *Art Attack* or *Fun House*. I was an ITV girl.

The auction show ends and then, amazingly, another begins. I wonder if this is all that exists on daytime TV. Mum gives a running commentary on everything that's on screen. Everyone is an 'idiot', 'stupid', 'ugly' or wearing something 'hideous'. She doesn't seem to have a good word to say about anyone.

I don't interrupt because it will be met by an indignant silence. Sometimes it is nice to hear her voice, regardless of what she's saying.

It's only after we've been sitting for twenty minutes that I spot what's sitting next to the TV. I get up and pick up the small frame and return to the sofa. Mum doesn't move and it takes me a short while to figure out what it is. It's a strip of white cardboard that's scuffed and a little battered, which has been framed by dark cherry wood. As best I can see, it is a ticket for a New York Mets' baseball game from 1979. It takes me a good minute to understand what the black squiggle across the centre actually represents.

I hold it up, waiting until Mum turns slightly towards me.

'Where did you get this?' I ask.

'Get what?'

I don't want to pass it over in case she drops it. My fingers are shaking as I hold it up for her to see.

'This ticket, Mum. Where did you get it?'

'I've had that for ages.'

'You haven't. I was here two weeks ago and it wasn't here.'

She crosses her arms and turns back to the TV. I wouldn't usually push an issue like this, but it's too important.

'Where did it come from?' I ask again.

The frown lines deepen around the rim of her eyes. 'Just put it down.'

I move until I'm standing in front of the television, blocking her view. 'Did David give this to you?'

With a speed I've not seen her produce in years, Mum reaches forward and snatches away the frame. 'It's mine!'

She holds the frame to her chest, cradling it like she's clutching a newborn.

It wasn't that hard to figure out once I realised what the scrawl on the ticket actually was. The 'J' at the beginning was as clear as could be.

It was the one thing she told David she always wanted.

The one thing she always said she regretted not getting.

The one thing she craved.

John Lennon's autograph.

NINETEEN

THE WHY

Three years, three months ago

I'm so tired that I almost fall through the front door. I go to hang my coat on the hook, but there is already a row of jackets there, as if David is breeding them. I move a couple of his so that they're on the same peg, and then hang my own. After that, I head to the kitchen and drop my keys into the Tigger pot, before opening the fridge. I left some chicken in there last night – an Asda rotisserie job – but that is gone. So is what was left of the apple juice I'd bought myself.

David is in the living room, his feet up on the coffee table as he simultaneously taps away on his phone and watches TV. It's the exact same position I left him in this morning. He barely turns as he mutters 'All right' in my direction.

'Did you eat the chicken?' I ask.

'Yeah.'

'I was going to have it for my tea.'

'Sorry…'

He doesn't sound particularly remorseful and I have to content myself with a glass of water for now.

I check the fridge again and then turn back to David. 'Did you have the bibimbap as well?' I ask.

'The what?'

'The rice bowl.'

'That was lunch,' he replies. 'It was really nice. I was wondering what it was.'

It's probably because I slam the fridge door, but David finally realises there's something wrong. He puts his phone down and crosses to the kitchen.

'Everything all right?' he asks.

'I've just done three classes in a row – and you've eaten all my food!'

'I didn't know.'

'You've been in all day. You could've gone shopping.'

He presses back onto the counter and, though I can see he's trying to look somewhat sorry, it doesn't stop the smile slipping onto his face. He's like a child who's just been told off.

'I have news,' he says.

'What?'

David reaches into his jeans pocket and takes out a wad of banknotes that he places on the counter.

'There's five-hundred there for you,' he says.

I look from him to the money and back again. 'Why?'

'I figured a sort of rent thing. Or use it for the bills. Whatever. It's not fair that you pay for everything.'

I don't know what to say at first. This is what I've been hinting at for months and he's finally got the message. It probably doesn't cover everything I've spent on him in regards to food and bills – but it's better than nothing. We've also got here without a big argument. I wonder if this is what it's like with other couples. Sometimes we feel more like housemates.

'I know we've never talked about it,' he says, as if reading my mind, 'but I think I should contribute. The sales to Sweden went through and I paid off your mum's friends with plenty to spare.'

He smooths down the notes and then passes them over. I don't know what to do with them, so end up holding them. I'm not sure I've ever had this much cash in one go.

'What about the Slovakia thing?' I ask.

'That fell through.'

'Oh…'

He bats a hand as if it doesn't matter, even though I know he was keen a short time ago.

'You go and sit,' he says. 'I'll cook something for you to eat and then we can watch something on catch-up.'

I start to protest but not in any meaningful way. Instead, I go and change into my pyjamas and then decamp to the sofa. I fiddle with my phone, check Facebook and generally don't do very much.

After a while, David comes over with a bowl full of a risotto he's put together. If I'm honest, it's not very good. He's cooked it for too long and the rice has dried out, while the only discernible flavour is garlic. I tell him it's nice anyway because I'm not a complete lunatic.

He sits at my side and scrolls through the list of recorded programmes to put on last weekend's *Strictly*.

'What did you get up to today?' I ask.

'Checked a few websites and followed up a tip about an auction that's happening in Marlborough on Tuesday. I headed out there to ask a few questions and then tried to persuade the owner to sell privately to me. I'm waiting on a callback. I met a couple of interesting locals out there, actually. Some bloke who does house clearances who took a card and another guy who was going on about how he can get fake IDs and passports. I took his card just to be polite. Probably a nutter.' He pauses and then adds: 'What about you?'

'I got my first personal training clients today.'

'Congratulations! I knew you could do it.'

I try not to be too smug – even though I'm definitely pleased with myself.

'I'm hoping I'll be able to do a bit more during the day and have more evenings off,' I say.

'That'll be nice.' He rests an arm around my shoulder. 'I'm *so* proud of you. You've done this all by yourself. So many people lack the ambition to do the type of thing you've done.'

I put my bowl to one side and press my head into his shoulder. I needed to hear this. It's what makes us more than housemates.

'Thank you for believing in me,' I say.

'Of course I believe in you. Who wouldn't?'

'Nobody else did,' I reply. 'Only you.'

TWENTY

Three years, two months ago

The traffic light changes to red with such perfect precision that it might as well follow it up with a flashing middle finger. I could gun the engine and pile on through the junction – but I'm not a taxi driver, so I ease onto the brakes and sit.

There must be some sort of in-built sensors in traffic lights that can pick up on when a person is in a hurry. Got hours to spare? Hey, here's a green light. Running late? Too bad: it's red for you.

It's probably no longer than a minute, but it feels like an age until the light switches back. I hit the accelerator on the 'g' of green and fly across the junction, taking the series of familiar turns until I pull up outside Nick's house. The garage door is open and he's already there in his running gear, waiting for me.

'I am *so* sorry,' I say as I head along his drive. 'I was having problems with the car and then I got caught behind a tractor.'

He waves me away and doesn't question the story, even though it's only cover for that fact that David and I spent twenty minutes arguing over how he never does anything around the apartment. He's not swept up since he moved in and the fridge was empty again today. He never shops for more, as if nipping into Asda is beneath him.

'It's fine,' Nick says. 'I've not been home that long either. It gave me a chance to warm up.'

As my first personal training client, I'm slightly protective over continuing to work with Nick, even though I'm not convinced his heart's in it. He says he wants to train for a marathon, but I don't believe he's sticking to the plan I've drawn up for him. His garage is a makeshift, converted gym – but he's the type with all the gear and little idea. He's packed a weights bench and an exercise bike into the space; plus there's a top-of-the-range road bike hanging from a hook off to the side. It looks like it's never been ridden.

I take him through a short series of warm-ups and then we head off along the pavement for a run. He's out of breath by the time we hit the corner, like a lifelong smoker doing CrossFit. I ease off, slowing until I am, essentially, doing a fast walk. Nick stays at my shoulder as we continue along the pavement. I check the heartbeat on my sports watch and it's steady.

'How are your kids?' I ask.

He gasps slightly for breath, but we're going slowly enough that we should be able to have a conversation.

'Alexa's enjoying school,' he replies. 'She must get it from her mother because I was never a fan.'

'It's basically just painting at her age, though, isn't it?'

'True.'

We take the corner and I tell him that we're going to sprint to the next turn. It is with obvious reluctance that he agrees – and then we bolt to the corner. I have to jog on the spot for a few seconds, waiting for Nick to catch me and, when he does, we drop our pace once more.

In all, we do a little over two miles in a lap until we arrive back at his house. I jog on the spot again, but the lack of breath and stooped stance makes it clear he doesn't have another lap in him.

It's only as I'm watching him that I spot a flicker of movement from across the road. I figure it's the wind at first – but then I see the shape of a person ducking out from behind a bush and then quickly slipping backwards again. I continue to watch as Nick hunches onto his knees.

'Do you want to go inside for some water?' I say. 'I'll wait here.'

'Right.'

He disappears through the back door of the garage into the house – and I dread to think of telling him that he's going to have to do this plus another twenty-four miles if he wants to run a marathon. We've been training for five weeks and there's no improvement.

There's another flicker from over the road – but, this time, I dash across to the hedge. I round the corner just as David pokes his head around to check on me. I wish it was a surprise, though I'm not convinced this is the first time he's followed me to Nick's house. He's wearing a green top I've not seen before, as if he planned this all along and is deliberately trying to blend in with the foliage.

'What are you doing?' I ask harshly.

David backs away until he's deeper into the bush.

'Did you follow me?' I add.

He stumbles over a reply, though there's not really a satisfactory one he can offer. If he didn't follow me, then he went through my diary and used Nick's address to get here.

'Go home,' I say.

David finally pushes himself out of the bush and straightens his clothes. 'I, um…'

'*Go home,*' I repeat. 'We'll talk then. I'm working.'

'It's just, um—'

I turn back to the garage, where Nick is re-emerging from the house with a water bottle. He looks both ways along the pavement, unsure where I've gone.

'We'll talk later,' I hiss, before turning and hurrying back across the road.

The rest of my session with Nick is spent with half an eye on the corner, wondering if David will either return or didn't leave in the first place. Nick doesn't seem to notice, although I realise I'm probably harder on him that I might normally be.

We take breaks in between the exercises, talking about what he's been eating and drinking since I last saw him. Wine definitely seems to be the bigger of the problems, seeing as he puts away 'four or five' bottles a week, which probably means six or seven. It's not like I can stop him, so I simply explain how many calories are in a glass and then leave it up to him.

He's aching by the end, so I tell him about ice baths, which is something he doesn't like the sound of. He pays in cash and then I say that I'll see him next week.

It's only as I'm driving home that the anger starts to build. The sky is darkening, which matches my mood. Leaves drift across the road as a slow drizzle starts and I have to turn on the windscreen wipers. I'm driving too quickly and taking the corners recklessly as I boil.

When I pull onto the patch of land at the side of the building, I spot David sitting on the doorstep to my flat. To *our* flat, I suppose. He's still in the green top, although it makes him stand out against the cream door.

I cross the tarmac and stand in front of him, towering tall.

'I'll leave if you want,' he says, unprompted.

'What?'

'I'll move out and find somewhere else.'

'Why would you jump to that conclusion?'

David shrugs and scuffs one of his boots against the ground. He is refusing to look anywhere other than the ground. It's still raining, although it's more of a mist. The air is damp and clings to my skin as if I've just got out of the shower.

'Did you follow me?' I ask.

'No.'

'Did you look in my diary?'

'Yes.'

'Why?'

David sniffs and, as his shoulders start to rock, I realise that he's crying. I have half an urge to sit on the step next to him for consolation, although the anger is still bubbling away. I'm caught between the two moods, unsure how I feel about it all. Unsure how I feel about him. The argument from earlier about his lack of contribution has been coming. Every time we get close, he does something like give me money, or cook me food. It always placates me – but not today.

'I had a panic attack,' he says. 'I couldn't breathe. I thought you were going to kick me out.'

'It was only an argument. Couples fall out all the time.'

'I know, it's just… I'm not very good at this.'

'At what?'

'Relationships. You and me. I'm not used to living with someone.'

I can feel myself starting to soften. I want to be hard and uncaring, but the betrayal is passing and I'm going to let him off again. It's like all the other times where he takes, takes, takes and never gives. Every time I'm close to ending it, I can hear Mum telling me that men like David don't come along very often. He's so good at making first impressions, which is all she's ever really had of him.

'I've never felt like this before,' he says. 'I'm not used to being… in love.'

He looks up and shows me his big, brown eyes. There are spots of rain running around his nose, reflecting the street lights and making it look like he's glowing. He's not said that to me before and I'm unsure how to react. Do I love him back? Is he saying it to stop being angry?

David stands abruptly and is suddenly directly in front of me. We're almost nose to nose and I know it'll be me who blinks first, metaphorically, if not literally.

'You can't follow me around,' I say. 'I'm working. It doesn't matter if I'm at someone else's house.'

'I know…'

'An argument doesn't mean it's all over. It just means there are issues we need to work on.'

'I know that, too.'

He squeezes my hand and pulls me closer until we're pressed into one another, the rain washing over both our heads.

'I love you,' he whispers.

I gulp as I feel the water running across my eyelids and seeping into my mouth.

'I love you, too,' I reply.

TWENTY-ONE

THE NOW

Veronica is putting a box of documents into the back of her Mini as I hurry along the path away from Mum's bungalow. The light is starting to go, but she peers through the gloom and offers a weak, tired-looking smile.

'Was everything all right?' she asks.

'I'm not sure.'

That gets a frown as Veronica closes her boot and comes across to stand at my side.

'Do the CCTV cameras above the gates actually work?' I ask.

She turns and looks towards the front of the complex. 'I assume so.'

'Do you know where the footage is kept?'

'It's an off-site security firm. I've got the details somewhere.'

'Do you think I can get hold of the footage for anyone who came and went yesterday?'

Veronica takes a moment and a plume of breath spirals from her mouth up into the air. It's going to be another cold one tonight.

'Is there something I should be worried about?' she asks.

It's probably the fact that I can't come up with a good enough lie, but, for whatever reason, I decide to tell the truth. Or *my* version of it.

'That photo on my phone was of my ex-husband,' I say. 'He disappeared two years ago. I think he might have visited Mum yesterday, but I'm not sure.'

Veronica reels her head back in surprise: 'Oh…'

'You know what she's like,' I say. 'She confuses what happened yesterday with what happened years ago. It's probably nothing, but I figure it's worth looking. Do you think you'll be able to get me the footage?'

'I can definitely ask. Do I have your details?'

I'm certain she does, but I give her my phone number and email address anyway – and then she turns to go.

'There was one other thing,' I say before she can get too far. 'There was a framed ticket next to the TV. I've not seen it around. Do you know where it came from?'

Veronica shakes her head. 'I don't think I've ever seen it. I was dusting around there the other week and don't remember anything.'

I thank Veronica for her help and then watch as she reverses out of her spot and heads towards the gate. She eases through and then they close slowly behind her, leaving only the faint whiff of petrol.

I lean on the hood of Andy's car, peering up towards the CCTV cameras. There are two: one pointing at the pedestrian gate; the other at the road. It would be easy enough to sneak around if someone could be bothered – although it would involve a hike along the cliffs, which isn't as easy as it sounds on the type of icy days we've had recently.

I am torn between the car and the bungalow, not sure what to do. It doesn't feel as if Mum is in danger and yet I don't know if I want to leave her alone. That should make the option obvious, except that I know for certain there's no way we can tolerate one another for an entire night. I ration my time with her because I'd rather have quality over quantity. The more months pass, the more that seems an impossibility.

I wanted to tell her to hit the panic button if anyone other than myself or Veronica turns up – but there's a chance she'd get confused and have a full-on meltdown at the postman.

It felt as if the autographed ticket had been left almost like a calling card. An act that was simultaneously thoughtfully kind and overwhelmingly chilling. Mum did tell David – and more or less anyone she's met in the past fifty years – about her regret at not talking to John Lennon on the occasion she saw him. I've never been certain that it was actually Lennon she saw – although I've never voiced that. She probably wouldn't talk to me for a month.

I make up my mind to leave – and it's a chilly, solitary drive back to the studio to take my evening classes. I half expect Yasmine to walk in, although there's no sign of her tonight. Regardless of that, my head is still not in it. I make even more mistakes and it feels as if my world is crumbling.

I say my goodbyes after the class and then lock up the studio before the drive home. I'm nervous to let myself into the flat, even though the locks have changed. Once inside, I turn on every light and poke my head into all the rooms, wardrobes and cupboards before feeling reassured that I'm alone.

It's only when Andy's text arrives that I remember I'm supposed to be meeting him.

Any idea what time you'll be done? X

I send him a quick reply to say I'll be about forty-five minutes and then have a shower before changing into something more appropriate than gym gear.

Before I leave the house, I'm careful to leave a succession of tells in case someone was to enter while I'm out. I set the oven door ajar by a few centimetres, leave open the door to the main bedroom and put the TV remote on the kitchen counter. All small, insignificant instances – but all things I wouldn't normally do.

The roads are already a mottled white as I drive along the country lanes that link Gradingham to Kingbridge. It won't be long before the entire area is a glorified ice rink.

The Kingfisher is a sprawling pub that is, essentially, in the middle of nowhere. It attracts people from both Gradingham and Kingbridge because of the quality of the food. In the summer, the beer garden stretches as far as people want to go. There are B&B rooms upstairs and, regardless of season, it always seems to be bustling.

By the time I arrive, Andy's van is already parked underneath the old stables at the front of the car park. I slot in next to him and then head inside, where I find him sitting in front of a fireplace in one of the side rooms towards the back. His shirt sleeves are rolled up and he's scanning the menu with his glasses on. He removes them when he spots me and stands, before moving quickly. He scuffs my chair out from under the table and waits for me to sit.

'You don't have to do that,' I say, although I don't actually mind. Sometimes, the gallantry is welcome… although David had similar moments, too.

'My pleasure.'

I allow him to shuffle me in and then he takes a seat opposite. The fire is crackling away, spitting sparks into the air as a steady glow warms my fingers.

Andy asks how my day was, but I don't particularly want to talk about it – and I'm only going to tie myself in knots if I go too deep anyway. Instead, I let him speak. He tells me how his youth football team has a big game on Sunday and it seems like he's probably more excited than his players.

Even though we're moving in together, we've not had the full 'children' talk yet. I suspect Andy wants kids at some point and I can easily imagine him being a terrific father. He'd be the type who'd ferry them around to whatever they want, whenever they want. If it's football they're into, then great; if it's music, then he'll buy him or her a violin and drive them off for lessons with whoever's supposed to be good for that sort of thing. After what happened with David, I'm not sure if children will ever be for me. It was kids that led to it all, not that I can tell Andy the truth about that.

We eat and we chat. Time passes and, for a while, I almost forget about everything else. This is when we're at our best. This is when I'm happiest. Ever since David, I've had to ask myself what I actually want from life and a relationship – and I figured it's this. It's companionship.

When we've finished eating, we head through the pub towards the games room at the front. There are a pair of pool tables, a darts board, plus a rack of board games crammed into a shelf at the back. Andy and I have often played pool here and I'm never sure whether he sometimes lets me win, or if I *actually* win. He is exceptional on occasion, as if he spent his teenage years hustling old-timers in a grubby snooker club. Other times, it's like he's a left-hander trying to play with his right. I'm never sure which Andy is going to show up.

I'm busy waiting for Andy to line up a striped ball when a man comes across to the second, unused, table and crosses his arms. At first, I think he's eyeing the table, wondering when our pound coins are going to run out. It takes me a moment to realise he's actually staring at me.

He's probably nineteen or twenty, wearing a tight olive jacket, with a baseball cap that sports a logo I don't recognise. His hands are in his pockets but his upper body is arched forward, as if he's an overly aggressive strutting flamingo.

I look back to him and then he turns and strides back towards the entrance. I figure that's the end of it, but then, less than a minute later, he returns. This time, he doesn't bother standing at the second table, he strides directly towards us. His hands are out of his pockets and he's jabbing a finger towards me.

'You've got some nerve,' he says with a snarl.

I stare at him, wondering if he's someone I know, although my mind is blank. I have no idea who he is.

'Sorry…?' I reply.

'My dad's in hospital because of you. You should be in prison.'

He spits the final word, with flecks of saliva spinning from his teeth and landing on his pockmarked acne-splashed chin. He wipes it away, before pointing his finger at me again.

'Left him for dead.'

It suddenly dawns on me that this must be the son of the person who was hit by my car. Trevor-someone. I have no idea how he knows who I am.

'I'm sorry, I—'

'Don't give me that. You nearly murdered a bloke and now you're here playing pool? Pah!'

He turns to look around the room. There are only a dozen or so people in the games room, though everyone is now turning to watch.

'Sorry?' he continues. 'You're *sorry*? How about you go tell the police what you did?'

'It wasn't me,' I manage. 'I didn't—' I'm stammering and spluttering but the words aren't coming easily.

Andy's far from the combative type, but, before I know it, he has stepped between me and the man. His arms are wide and welcoming; his tone calming.

'Her car was stolen,' Andy says firmly.

The man begins to fire back, though some of the confidence has left him: 'Yeah, sure it was. How'd they get the keys?'

I start to reply, but Andy speaks over me: 'I think you should probably go, mate. This isn't doing any good, is it? It's not helping the police. Not helping your dad…?'

'Don't talk about him.'

Andy takes a step closer to the man, who takes three or four steps towards the door. 'OK, I won't,' Andy says. He angles towards me, although he never takes his eyes from the man. 'We'll leave, all right? We don't want any trouble.'

The man is nodding, though it's clear from the way his eyes are darting to the onlookers that he's suddenly unsure. 'We're going anyway,' he says.

It's only then that I notice a woman hovering by the door. She's half hiding behind the frame, not wanting to be here. Without another word, the man turns and hurries away. As soon as he gets to the door, the woman turns and follows. A moment later and they're gone.

There are a few seconds in which it feels as if everyone has frozen. It takes a moment and then the group by the window playing a board game swiftly turn their attentions back to what they were doing. A dart thuds into the board and, even though I know everyone is still half-watching me, at least it's not their full attention.

Andy turns and threads an arm around my shoulders.

'Are you all right?' he asks.

'I think so. I want to go.'

'Let's give it a minute.'

We wait awkwardly at the edge of the pool table. The balls are still scattered across the baize; a match that will never be finished. Andy returns the cues to the rack and then we leave hand-in-hand. There's a momentary pause when we get outside as Andy scans the car park. A tingle tickles along my spine; a sense of being watched. I'm not sure if Andy feels it, though he grips my fingers tighter and leads the way across to the stable where his car and van are parked.

'Do you want to follow me back?' he asks.

I know the way, of course, but that's not what he's asking.

'Sure.'

There's a crack from somewhere off towards the bushes and we both turn at the same time. There are no lights around the edge of the car park and the slick mud of the autumn months has turned into a thick, solid blend of muck and ice.

I continue staring, remembering the flash from the bushes I saw years before, though there's nothing there.

'Are you OK?' Andy asks – and it's only when I turn to him that I realise this is the second time he's asked. It's as if I blanked out for a moment.

'Yes...'

He goes to take my hand, but it doesn't feel as if there's enough strength in my fingers.

'I know that look,' Andy says.

I'm still watching the bushes, although I'm not sure whether anything has moved since we heard the crack.

'What look?' I ask.

'You're thinking of him...' Andy tails off but the twinge in his voice is hard to ignore.

'Who?' I reply, although of course I know.

'David.'

I bite my tongue to stop my first reply from emerging. It's always hard to hear Andy say David's name; as if he's too pure for it. Like a toddler using the F-word.

'Yes,' I say.

'I don't mind.' Andy takes a breath and then grips my hand.

'Can I stay at yours?' I ask.

'Of course.'

He pulls me gently away from the bushes and then puts both arms around me, pulling me into him. I press into his shoulder, wishing he wasn't so damned understanding all the time.

TWENTY-TWO

THE WHY

Three years, one month ago

David's alarm goes off at half-past-five. There's little more annoying than a morning person – and David does his best to prove that as he springs out of the bed as if he's on a trampoline. It's an ungodly hour, but he turns on the bedroom lights, leaving me hiding under my pillow.

'Best time of the day!' he says.

'Will you turn the light off?'

'I'm finding the right outfit.'

'You could've done that last night.'

'Bit late now.'

David bangs around the bedroom like a cow on a stairwell and, by the time he's dressed, I'm wide awake, too. I sit up in the bed, squinting vampirically into the light. I'm not entirely sure how we got to this point. Perhaps I valued my own space more than I thought? The longer we've been together, the less we seem to have in common.

'Big day,' David says, giddy like a kid on Christmas morning.

'So you said.'

'I'll see you later.'

'Good luck.'

Since we've been living together I've realised David can't close a door quietly. It's never simply clicked into place, it's always banged shut, as if he's an airport worker hurling suitcases marked 'fragile' onto a conveyor belt.

David has a meeting with someone in Newcastle that could mean 'big money'. That's more or less all I know, because he said he doesn't want to jinx the deal by talking about it. I hear his car start and then he's off and away into the November darkness.

Despite the hour, there seems little point in trying to go back to sleep. It's like a day trip to Bolton. No one wants to end up in that situation, but, once there, a person might as well make the best of it.

I get up and make coffee, then potter around the flat, waiting for the sun to come up. It's barely an hour until I'm bored out of my mind. Morning television 'personalities' have similar appeal and charisma as an aggressive STI and there's only so long I can spend looking through other people's Facebook updates until it dawns that nobody I know ever seems to do anything worthwhile. That includes myself.

I have no classes this morning, so spend a bit of time organising my receipts. It is, perhaps, the most boring thing I have to do. The most boring thing *anyone* has to do. Shows like *Dragon's Den* always promote entrepreneurial skills and ideas. That's all well and good, but what they *don't* show is a self-employed person hunched over a desk, trying to hunt down the scrap of paper related to a sports bra that was bought on sale six months previously.

It takes a text message from David to make me realise that it's already past midday.

Just got in. Roads not too bad. Fingers crossed. X

He has attached a photo of what I assume is the Tyne Bridge. There is a curved semicircle of metal, like an upside-down school protractor.

I send him a quick message back to say good luck and then remember I'm supposed to be meeting Jane.

Time travel exists – it involves a load of a receipts and a spreadsheet to make six hours pass in a click of the fingers.

It's a rush to get out the door and into the centre of Gradingham and I'm only five minutes' late by the time I arrive at the new juice bar. Jane has commandeered a pair of stools near the counter and is scrolling away on her phone. Aside from the two of us and the man behind the counter, the place is empty. The walls and floor are bright white and the menu is on the wall behind the counter, written in neat, minimalist black type, as if Apple have launched iJuice.

The man serving is wearing an outfit that's half national service, half trying to seem young enough to get into an indie club. It suits him, though, and he smiles somewhat sheepishly at me as I stop at Jane's table.

'Have you ordered?' I ask.

'I was waiting for you,' she replies.

'Do you know what you want?'

She scans the menu briefly and then shrugs, before calling across 'What's good?' to the man behind the counter.

'Everything's good!'

'That's not helpful,' I reply with a smile.

'I like the acai bowl,' he offers.

'I have no idea what that is.'

'Kind of like a yoghurt trifle.'

I turn to Jane, who raises an eyebrow.

'You had me at the word "trifle",' I say. 'We'll have two.'

As he gets on with making our 'yoghurt trifles', I perch myself on the stool next to Jane. 'How's Ben?' I ask. Jane and I haven't been seeing each other anywhere near as often since David moved in with me.

'I think he's getting promoted at the bank. He had a second interview yesterday and his manager said it's all but his. We're waiting for confirmation.'

'That's great!'

'It means I'll be able to take the career gap I've been thinking about.'

'Is Ben on board with that?'

'He will be.'

She says it with full confidence, although I'm less sure. I've known Jane long enough to realise that 'career gap' means giving up her job for good. There's an irony in that she's been onto me for years about getting into a proper career, while she's seemingly been waiting for Ben to earn enough that she can be kept.

I don't say that, obviously, and then the server brings across a pair of bowls filled with yoghurt, banana, strawberry, some seeds and granola on the top.

We each dig in and there is certainly something trifling about it. I wasn't exactly being honest when I said I had no idea what an acai bowl was. Every diet book or women's magazine has spent the past few years banging on about how it's the solution to everything from weight loss to curing cancer.

'How is it?' the server asks.

'Good,' I tell him – although I was never going to say anything else. He's literally made it in front of us and only a maniac would tell him it was horrible. 'I guess this is what all the fuss is about,' I add.

'What do you mean?'

'Some of my clients told me about this place opening.'

He rocks back on his heels slightly, which is no mean feat considering the tightness of his jeans. 'What do you do?' he asks.

'I'm a personal trainer and run a few different exercise classes.'

'Oh. Hang on a minute.'

He disappears behind the counter into a back room and then reappears moments later with a pile of what looks like business cards.

'Take these,' he says, passing them over. 'They're all for ten per cent off. Give them to whoever you want.' He nods to Jane. 'In return, you and your friend can have a discount whenever you're in.'

'That's really good of you,' I say.

He offers his hand and we shake.

'I'm Andy,' he says. 'I've not long moved down to the area. Hopefully see you around.'

There's a slight moment of awkwardness before he returns behind the counter and starts to scrub at what is probably a non-existent spot of dust.

I lean in towards Jane and lower my voice. 'I think he might have a thing for you,' I say.

She snorts: 'He's got a bit of a yummy mummy following. You should see what they're saying on the secret village Facebook group.'

'What *are* they saying?'

'Put it this way: his skinny jeans are on the brink of getting their own fan page. Anyway, I don't think it's *me* that he has a thing for.'

I turn and glance in Andy's direction and it's as if he's been caught doing something he shouldn't as he quickly spins back to whatever he's supposedly working on.

Almost as if to emphasise Jane's point, the door goes and a pair of women with prams enter. I'm distracted enough by them that I almost miss the significance of what Jane says next.

'I saw David's car this morning…'

When I turn back to her, she is absent-mindedly tucking into the bowl.

'Were you up early?' I ask.

'Not particularly.'

'Where did you see him?'

'At the services just outside Kingbridge. The one where you can cheekily join the motorway if the gate's not down. Next to the Burger King.'

One of the women behind is giggling as she orders a cleansing juice and it's hard to blank her out as I try to piece together what Jane's said.

'When?' I ask.

'About an hour ago. Maybe an hour and a quarter.'

'Are you sure it was his car?'

'It had that weird bobblehead thing in the back. I've never liked that thing.' She pauses for a mouthful of yoghurt and then adds: 'How's he getting on with his, um, job and all?'

She might as well put 'job' into quotations, because it's clear what she thinks of it. Even though I've had those doubts myself, I suddenly feel defensive.

'Don't say it like that,' I snip back. 'It's not an "um" job. It's a job.'

When we were teenagers, we would argue about things like this all the time.

That's a nice, um, top.

Those are nice, um, shoes.

Sometimes I would let it go, other times I'd pick a fight. Jane would rarely, if ever, admit the clear malice she intended. I always took things in the wrong way.

'I didn't mean it like that,' Jane says – although we both know that she did. She can be an, *um*, nice person. I can be, too.

'His job's going great,' I say. 'Everything's going *great*.'

I finish with an audible full-stop that puts something of an end to the conversation.

We continue eating in a silence that's broken only by the girlish giggling of the flirty mothers. Moments later and Jane drops her spoon into the now empty bowl.

'I have to get back to the office,' she says. 'Was great catching up.'

We have a brief hug, although there's little feeling in it, and then she waves a cheerio to Andy and heads out. I wait until she's out of sight and then say a brief goodbye to Andy before hurrying to my own car. I might have been dismissive with Jane – but it's hard to ignore what she said.

I drive through Gradingham and out the other side, then follow the lanes until I reach the unmarked turn into the motorway services. There's a big 'no entry' sign, although everyone ignores it. It is this entrance that staff use to get to work, while, for everyone else, it's a cheeky – and probably illegal – entrance to the motorway.

I drive down the ramp and head towards the main services building, which is when I spot David's car. There are a few trucks on the furthest side of the car park and a coach slotted in across four spaces. Other than that, there are barely any vehicles. I hate that Jane's right, but there's no question she is.

I get out of my car and walk around David's. There's the scuff on the back bumper and the familiar football bobblehead in the back. I agree with Jane that it's weird. I've never liked it, either.

I check the text message with the photo and now know that, if I were to Google 'Tyne Bridge', this would appear somewhere deep in the results. It's probably come from Instagram, or something like that.

After another lap of his car, I stop at the bonnet and turn in a circle. There must be an explanation for all this. He got up at half past five to travel to Newcastle for work. Perhaps he caught a bus from here…? Or he's carpooling with a friend…? He never mentioned either of those things, but there must be some reason for why his car is here.

I head towards the main building and make my way up the grimy steps. I don't need to go any further. I don't even need to go inside. The Burger King is on the corner, a giant splash of red, blue and yellow set against the grimness of this concrete monstrosity. The glass is slightly tinted, but it's easy enough to make out the figure sitting at the table closest to the window. He has his phone in hand, an open box in front of him, with a half-eaten burger spilling onto the table.

David's definitely not in Newcastle.

TWENTY-THREE

Three years, one month ago

How's Newcastle?

I watch as David picks up his phone and reads the message. He licks the fingers of his other hand, wipes them on his top, and then taps something back. Moments later, my phone buzzes with the reply.

Just going into a meeting. The sun's out.

I'm not sure why, but I look up to the darkening sky that matches my mood.

I head into the building and cross to the coffee shop opposite the Burger King. I don't order anything but find a chair in the corner that gives me a perfect view of David. He continues to eat his burger, although it is small bites at a time. I suspect he wants to drag it out, like a teenager trying to make a milkshake last all evening.

Fifteen minutes pass and David does nothing other than use his phone – which is plugged into a socket on a pillar. I wonder how long he's been in the same spot.

He eventually finishes his food and then dumps the rubbish in the bin before heading out the door, into the main services building. I half expect him to see me, though he's not really looking. Instead, he mooches into the arcade, hands in pockets. I almost follow but he's simply trying to waste time. Five minutes later and he's back where he started.

He eventually heads to an empty table that's in the central concourse. He pulls out the uncomfortable-looking metal chair and sits, before taking a book from his bag. There's an unquestionable sadness about a lonely middle-aged man hiding in a service station. I'm not sure whether to be angry or consoling. I want to put my arms around him and say it's going to be all right; but I also don't want to see him again. Like a weighing scale: one side balancing the other. I'm not sure which will ultimately win.

I leave the coffee shop and cross the hall, before scraping back the second chair at David's table and sitting. He looks up, first in surprise and then with eye-popping alarm when he realises it's me.

'You're a liar,' I say.

He opens his mouth and babbles something I'm not even sure are proper words. Then he bows his head and mutters a simple: 'Yes.'

'Is it all a lie?' I ask.

David folds his book closed and sighs. 'Is what a lie?'

'Everything. The job. The travel.'

He shakes his head: 'No. I do buy and sell things. I have *made* money, it's just...'

He tails off and then returns his book to his bag, before pressing back into his chair. He stares past me towards the arcade and it feels like the clouds from outside have descended within.

'It was what my dad did,' he says. 'I thought I could carry it on, but it's not been as easy these past few months. Times are changing and I don't know how much of what I do has a place any longer.'

I follow his gaze to the arcade and it's there, too. There are a pair of kids probably bunking off school. When I was young, they'd be on primitive, clunky dance-step machines. Those have now been replaced by high-definition, motion-sensor games with cameras that put the youths onto the screen itself. Everything is changing. It always has and it always will.

I turn back to him: 'Did you really go to Bath last month?' I ask.

'Yes. I didn't buy anything, though. It was a waste of time.'

'What about Cardiff?'

'This is the first time I've ever told you I'm going somewhere and then I haven't.'

I examine his face, looking for any sort of tell. I can't tell if it's the truth. If this is the first time he's faked a trip, then he's extremely unlucky to have been caught.

'I know you don't like me sitting around the flat all day,' he says. 'I didn't want to look like a loser to you. Didn't want to let you down.' He gulps and then adds: 'Didn't want to lose you…'

I turn away because it's hard to look at him like this. I can't figure out where those scales are balanced; whether I'm sorry for him or annoyed with him.

'I know Jane and Ben aren't fans of me,' he says.

'That's not true… it's just they don't know you so much now.'

He scratches his chin and fiddles with the cuffs of his shirt. Anything that means he doesn't have to look at me directly. He can probably sense the unease, too. The feeling that our lives will change here and now. He doesn't know which way it will go but neither do I.

'I've been jealous,' he says. 'Your career is taking off. I knew you'd be able to do it – and it's happening. I suppose I wish it was happening for me, too. I want to be able to provide for you.'

I snort and think of Jane with her 'career gap': 'It's not the 1950s. I don't need or want to be a good little housewife.'

'I know. I'm pathetic.'

'Don't say that.'

'I don't deserve you.'

'Don't say that, either.'

He finally meets my gaze. 'I love you so much.'

'I love you, too.'

It's like a reflex. I love you-I love you, too. One sentence follows the other like night after day. I've said the words without thinking about them and then, before I know what's happening, our lives *are* changing. In the middle of the service station forecourt, David drops to one knee and pulls my hand towards him.

'Will you marry me?'

TWENTY-FOUR

THE NOW

Wednesday

It takes me a few moments to figure out where I am. The mattress is too hard and the covers are too warm; like sleeping on a pavement next to a bonfire. I fight against the quilt, freeing myself from the temporary straitjacket and then roll over to see Andy's eyelids fluttering. He's breathing deeply, lost in a dream, and I watch him for a couple of minutes. He always looks older in the mornings, before he shaves. Shearing the stubble from his face each morning skims a few years from his age.

Sometimes when we're like this, I see David in him. They don't look alike and they couldn't be more different in terms of personality, but, when they're sleeping, they share the fact that they are completely out of it.

I roll off the bed and pad around the bare-wood floor until I'm in the hallway. Andy doesn't have a cleaner and yet his place is always immaculate, as if there are pixie maids who visit in the night. Sometimes, I feel as if I'm making the house dirty simply by being around.

The bedroom next to the main one has been cleared, ready for me to move in. Andy has put three identical wardrobes side by side into an alcove; and there is a pair of shoe racks under the window.

This space is mine to do with as I please… although it will never feel like *our* house. It's his space and always will be.

Back into the main bedroom and Andy is still breathing deeply. He's not snoring, because it's not the type of thing I can imagine him doing. He has far too much control over his life for that. I'm not sure I've ever seen him sneeze, either. David was all about chaos and lethargy; Andy is calm and meticulous planning. His clothes for today are laid out neatly on a chair at the end of the bed, with a chosen pair of shoes underneath.

I watch him and it's easy to see the circle continuing. I married David because I didn't want to grow old and be lonely. Here I am, three years on, moving in with someone else for the same reason.

I close the door to the bedroom and head downstairs into the kitchen. There's so much white, just like Andy's juice bar. Everything clean and in its place. A bowl is on the counter, filled with a precise measure of bran flakes that Andy will top up with an exact amount of almond milk when he gets downstairs. The espresso machine is already loaded with a levelled, double shot of coffee; the mugs are lined up perfectly on the side, ready to go.

I wonder if living together will work. Whether Andy will end up trying to organise me in the way he organises everything else in his life. Even if he does, I don't know if it will necessarily be a bad thing. Perhaps that's what I need?

The inside of his fridge is like a spread across the pages of a health food magazine. There are juices, obviously; plus fruit, vegetables, almond milk, soy milk, and five different types of yoghurt. One day soon, this will all be mine.

Or *jointly* mine.

I put a small handful of raspberries into a bowl and head for the sofa. There's a photo of Andy and me on the coffee table that I don't remember being there before. It was taken when Andy did a charity race up Snowden last summer. I helped the support team at the top and he raised almost £13,000 for the scouts to buy a new minibus. Our faces are smushed together and, though he's slightly red-faced, I'm the one who's a sweaty mess, as if I did all the running. It was taken on Andy's phone by one of the other volunteers and I have no idea when Andy printed it out, or found a frame. It's certainly not very flattering to me, although it was a fun couple of days away. We drank beer in the sunshine and I ate the best roast meal of my life the afternoon after the run. It was then that I decided Andy and I might just make it; that I wasn't destined to become a bitter, divorced middle-aged spinster.

There's a power cable that leads to the shelf underneath the coffee table. I follow it to Andy's laptop, which is sitting with the lid half-open, as if he put it away in a hurry. The screen is glowing a bluey-white onto the keyboard as I lift the lid and pull it out. The main screen shows the desktop but Word and Chrome are minimised into the corner.

I know I should close the lid and leave it – but it's not what people do, is it? Not what I do. I click to open the web browser, which reveals the BBC Sport home page. The next tab along is the *Guardian* – of course it is – and then there's the home page for Andy's scout troop. The three pages are him in a nutshell; all it's missing is a fourth from *Men's Health*.

I'm about to snap the lid closed when I'm drawn to the 'History' button. I almost want Pornhub to be top of the list – it would prove he wasn't quite the saint he always seems to be.

That isn't what he was looking for before he drove out to the pub last night, though. Instead, there are a series of Google searches: 'Morgan Persephone', 'Morgan Noble', 'Morgan Persephone award', 'Morgan Persephone talk'.

It's like a tree where I'm the trunk. He'll search for something relating to me and then the branches take him off in varying directions. Andy looked at the awards page to which Steven directed me that contains the photos of the night. He spent five minutes clicking around the home page for my studio. He did an image search.

And then, below all that is the two-word search term that leaves me feeling as if I can't breathe.

'David Persephone'.

TWENTY-FIVE

THE WHY

Three years ago

Jane waves me across to an alcove underneath the trophy cabinet. It's the first time I've visited the rugby club since I was a teenager and this was one of the few places that would serve underage. It also helped that it was largely frequented by beefy men. It's probably the only time in my life that I've ever remotely noticed men's thighs. Sometimes it feels like I was a completely different person then. As if I woke up one day and the person I used to be had gone to be replaced by whoever I am now.

With a bottle of wine in one hand and an empty glass in the other, Jane is already a large part of the way towards sleeping while slumped over a toilet seat tonight. We've both been there before. She takes a swig from the bottle and then fills the glass and has a mouthful from that, too, before nodding across to where my mum is sitting at David's side. They're close to the bar, but it feels like he has eyes only for her tonight.

'Your mum loves him,' Jane says.

'More than me.'

Jane looks between us but doesn't deny it. The great love of my mother's life was my dad. When he went there was nobody else. I was a square peg who had no chance of getting through the round hole. A part of her died with him.

Jane has another mouthful of wine, though I know her well enough to realise that this is to stop her from having to reply. She doesn't understand why I said 'yes' to David's proposal. She's been with Ben for such a long time that she's never had that fear of growing old alone.

David waves across to someone behind the bar and the waiter scuttles across with a small glass of sherry for Mum. If there's no one around to hold her up, she'll be down like a pensioner on a winter's day within the hour.

What Jane doesn't understand is that a marriage proposal is a line in the sand. A 'no' is the end. It's not as if the couple carry on as they did before, waiting for the subject to come up again at a later date. A no is a no is a no.

I love that David believed in me.

He was the only one. Not Jane and definitely not Mum.

Since we met, my life has got better. It's like his faith in me forced things to happen. I got personal training clients; I was offered more classes. I had my first chance to talk in front of an audience, when the local college wanted me to address a group of young women. My career was going nowhere and now, ten months after meeting David, it's finally heading in the direction I want.

A no is a no is a no – and so I said yes.

Across the room, Mum has her sip of her sherry and, almost as if it's some sort of potion that has transformed her, she starts to giggle. It's often hard enough to get anything from her other than a frown – but then this is, perhaps, where David's true talents lie. It's not in the buying and selling; it's in the way he makes people feel about themselves.

'Don't take this the wrong way,' Jane says with a nervousness to her tone, 'but it's only been ten months…'

'I know.'

'I'm not saying you're wrong, or anything like that. It's just…'

I could make her squirm, but the truth is that I know what she's saying.

'I know it's quick,' I say, 'but if he'd asked me in a year, I'd have said yes then. All it's doing is bringing things forward.'

A no is a no is a no.

'I'm thirty years old,' I add.

'That's still young.'

I can't help but glance across to the group of young women who are hanging around near the rugby players on the other side of the bar. The room is split in two, with this side for our engagement party and the other for a regular night in the rugby club. The women are either late-teens or early twenties; all slim and wearing short dresses and too-high heels. Their backs will hurt in the morning, or maybe they won't because they're young. Youth is everything.

I want to say that I don't think any other men will get down on one knee for me. It took me this long to find someone who will.

A no is a no is a no.

David insisted on having an engagement party, saying that he wanted to show me off. I put down the deposit on my credit card because they don't take cash. It's strange, largely because there's almost nobody he knows here. It's mainly my friends from school. He didn't invite Yasmine, even though I said he should. There are a handful of people that went to university with Ben, Jane and David – but he's not speaking to any of them anyway. He's giving all his time to my mother. Over the past ten months, I've often wondered how many friends he really has – but the same is true of me. There's Jane, possibly Ben, and then… I'm not sure.

Mum rests a hand on David's knee and then rocks back laughing. The last time I saw her cackling like this was at the repeat of the Morecambe and Wise Christmas special. She insisted it was new, even though one of them had been dead for a good thirty years at the time.

'I better go and help him out,' I say.

Jane raises her glass and says she's not planning on going anywhere soon. 'Ben's busy with his football mates from uni,' she adds.

As I cross the floor, I glance across to Ben, who is in the middle of a circle of sporty-looking thirty-somethings. They each have pints of lager and I can imagine them reminiscing about the glory days of when they spent semesters playing football and getting pissed.

When I get to David, I stand over him and touch his shoulder. It's hard not to notice that my mother's features instantly sour.

'Why don't you go and spend some time with your friends…' I say, not making it a question.

He takes the hint and stands, squeezing my hand almost imperceptibly. I expect him to head off to be with Ben and his old football mates, but, instead, he crosses to the other corner of the room and disappears behind a group of people.

I take the seat he was in next to my mother, although she is seemingly now interested in an unremarkable patch of wall.

'Thanks for coming,' I say.

'What else was I going to do?'

'I don't know – but it's nice you're here.'

She clears her throat and I'm not sure if it's genuine, or if she's annoyed about something.

'What music is this?' she asks.

I stop to listen: 'I'm not sure,' I reply.

'It's terrible. Music was so much better in my day.'

'I think everyone believes the same thing.'

'Yes, but I'm right.'

She finishes her sherry and passes me the empty glass.

'Do you want more?' I ask.

Nobody rolls their eyes quite like my mother. It's always been able to make me feel a couple of inches high. As if not reading her mind is some sort of crime. 'What do you think?' she replies.

'I don't know – that's why I'm asking.'

She stretches for the glass: 'I'll get it myself if it's too much trouble.'

I stand abruptly, saying that I'll go and then crossing quickly to the bar. There's nobody else after a drink, so I get another sherry for Mum, as well as a glass of red for myself. It's only when the barman returns that I ask for a double whisky and neck it when nobody's watching. I'm going to need it to get through the evening.

After that, I load a paper plate with food from the buffet and then head back to Mum, who is still sitting by herself. She takes her drink and then points at the food.

'What's that?' she says, her top lip curled.

'That's a samosa,' I say, pointing to one side of the plate, before motioning to the other, 'and that's a yam roll.'

Mum wafts a hand across the plate. 'I don't know what's wrong with a plain ham sandwich. Never killed anyone, did it?'

'Not everyone eats meat, Mum.'

'Pfft. People weren't so fussy in my day.'

I open my mouth to reply, but then close it. Nothing is going to be worth turning this into a full-on argument. I should have left her with David. He's more or less the only person around whom she turns into a pleasant person. If he was anywhere in sight, I'd nod David across and hand over the reins once more – but he seems to have disappeared.

'I've got to mingle,' I say, wanting a way out.

'Oh, don't worry about me,' Mum replies. It's hard to tell whether she's being sarcastic, or if she actually wants to be left alone.

'I'll see you later,' I say, although she's back to staring at the wall. I can imagine her saying that nobody needed phones in her day because they had perfectly good walls to stare at.

There's still no sign of David and I assume he's gone to the toilet, so I head back to Jane, who is still in her alcove. There's a slim hint of a smile on her face that makes it clear she knows exactly what's happened between my mother and me. She's known us too long.

She's also tipsier – and holds up the half-empty wine bottle. 'This is my last one,' she says.

'It's a long night,' I reply, though she shakes her head.

'Not only tonight: for a long while. Ben and me are going to start trying for children. This is my last weekend of drinking.'

It takes me a couple of seconds and then I reply with the only thing I can: 'You'll be a great Mum,' I say – although I'm looking at my own mother as I say it. Maybe I believe it; maybe I don't.

David is back in the room. He walks gingerly across the floor, like an old man who's forgotten his stick, and then turns in a circle, seemingly not knowing where to plant himself. He said he pulled a muscle when he decided to go running on a whim. I was taking a spin session at the time. I've never known him do that before, but I suppose that's why he pulled a muscle.

Jane is watching him, too and I can feel the tension from her. 'I should've told you this a long time ago,' she says, somewhat abruptly.

'Told me what?'

'Ben and David were never really friends at university. We didn't really know him. After my birthday party, we spent a good hour trying to figure out why he came and who invited him.'

I turn to her, wondering if this is some sort of joke. Her face is serious as she switches her attention from David back to me.

'I should've said something ages ago,' she repeats.

'I don't know what you mean. Weren't Ben and David on the same football team?'

'Ben says they were in the same *squad*. Ben was in the first team and David would come along to training sessions. That was about it. He couldn't get in the team.'

I watch David float around the room and, now I'm looking for it, it's suddenly obvious that he's studiously avoiding the corner where Ben and the rest of the university football team are congregating. It wasn't David's idea to invite the members of the football team still living in the area; it was mine. I insisted on it. He even tried to talk me out of it, but I said there had to be some people he knew at the party. I know Jane's telling the truth and yet I can't quite take it in.

'I don't get what you're telling me,' I say.

'Maybe I'm talking out of turn,' Jane says, 'but that's what happened. If he'd been a proper member of the football team, I'd know him. I hung around with all the players because I was seeing Ben. I honestly don't think I'd ever met him until you introduced us. When he and Ben were arguing outside your flat on the day he moved in, it was because Ben was asking him why he'd turned up to my birthday party.'

'Why had he?'

'We're still not sure. We think he'd seen the invite via a friend of a friend on Facebook, something like that, and tagged along. We didn't know if we should say something… You seemed so into one another and I didn't want to spoil things…'

Neither of us speak for a while. David takes out his phone and rests on a table at the furthest end of the room. He's by himself, making no attempt to mix with anyone.

'Haven't you noticed how all his stories make him out to be either a hero, or wronged in some way…?' There's a wobble in Jane's voice. The wine taking hold, though there's truth in what she has said.

I had noticed before and put it to one side. Most people are like that, aren't they? We're all the heroes of our own stories. Except that so many of David's tales *do* end up with him being wronged. Whether it's by his sister or unscrupulous buyers or sellers, he's almost always the victim.

'That's untrue,' I say, not wanting it to be the case. It's not just about him – it's about being wrong in front of Jane.

'I just want you to be sure. Marriage is so… final.'

Jane is trying to help and I know it's partly the booze talking. It's partly her, too. The jealousy that I'll be getting married first. I could probably get pregnant first if I tried. When she talks of a 'career gap', what she really means is to stay home, spread her legs, and pop out a series of babies. She wants to be a stay-at-home mother. I think she always has.

David may not be a hero, he may not be popular or even always truthful, but he wants to marry me and who said marriages were ever perfect. They take work and effort, and at least I'm going in with my eyes wide open. We both know what we're getting into and we both know the alternative.

'David supported me,' I say. 'You didn't. You said I should get a job at a bank. He pushed me into visiting gyms and leisure centres a bit further out. That got me more serious jobs closer to home.'

Jane shrugs and finishes her glass. 'I'm not saying—'

'What *are* you saying?'

She sighs and glances away. 'I don't know.'

'It's not my fault your boyfriend is stuck for life shuffling papers around a bank and won't marry you. Talk about living the dream.'

I can feel her staring sideways at me, her mouth open. I'm watching Ben, who's busy laughing with his old football friends. For so long, I've thought that Jane and Ben were the perfect couple. I've wanted to live up to everything they are – and, now that David and I are close, I see how jealous Jane can be.

'I think I'm going to go,' Jane says – and, as she pushes herself up, I know that I'm never going to say sorry for this.

TWENTY-SIX

Two years, seven months ago

The sun is beaming through the back windows of the Rolls-Royce and I can feel the sweat starting to pool in the space where the zip sits at the back of my dress. Mum is sitting indignantly with her knees crossed, facing me as if we're in the back of a black cab. Meanwhile, Jane is at my side. It's only her presence that's stopped my mum criticising what I'm wearing.

'Are you nervous?' Jane asks.

'I wasn't until you asked,' I say.

'Sorry.'

I smile at her and try to laugh, although it comes out as more of a cough. 'I'm joking,' I reply.

She smiles weakly and I think she's probably more anxious than I am. The argument between us has been forgotten in the sense that we've not spoken about it since. It's as if the night in the rugby club never happened. But none of what she said – or what I did – has gone away. It's like a blister that's bubbling and ready to pop at an indeterminate point in the future.

Not today, though.

Jane is my only bridesmaid, largely by default. It was only that decision – if it can be called that – which made me realise how much of life itself is 'by default'. Everyone goes through the motions and things happen to us, rather than the other way around.

The driver sets off from Mum's bungalow and edges slowly through the gates, before accelerating onto the country roads. The three of us are largely silent in the back. In my case, it's because I'm worried about what might come out if I allow myself much time to think about today. It feels like we're on the way to a funeral, rather than a wedding.

We're a little out of Gradingham when Mum waves me closer. I lean in, unsure what to expect, and her voice is barely audible over the hum of the engine.

'Don't mess it up today,' she whispers.

I press back and bite my lip before letting it out anyway. 'Don't, Mum.'

'Don't what?'

'It's my wedding day. Can you please be happy for me? For once? We're doing it at the same register officer where you and Dad married.'

Of all the things to say, I accidentally hit the right one. A smile slips onto her face and she grips the armrest hard as she looks between Jane and me.

'It was such a lovely day,' she says. 'Your father looked spiffing in his suit – and then we all went off to the Legion for tea and cake. We had to get special permission because they didn't usually let in women after five, except for on a Sunday.'

Jane and I exchange a glance and it's hard to believe that this was only a little outside our lifetimes. The world has changed so much.

'Course, couples stayed together then,' she adds, her features darkening. 'Not like now where people break up after one little argument.'

'How many people were there?' I ask, wanting to hear about my parents' wedding; not my mother's opinions on life today.

'Where?' she snaps.

'Your wedding.'

It's as if a cloud is floating overhead. Mum's face brightens and darkens depending on its position. It shifts again and the light returns.

'Everyone we knew,' she says. 'We couldn't fit everyone inside. They were standing in the doorway, clinging to the windows. Everyone loved your father.'

'You, too,' I say, although she doesn't react. I'm not sure if she's listening.

'He was like the Pied Piper afterwards,' she adds. 'Leading everyone back down the High Street to the Legion.'

The cloud above her shifts again and the hardness returns to her jaw. 'Your David's just like him. I honestly don't know what he sees in you.'

It feels like the air has been sucked from the back of the car. My dress was tight to begin with, but now it feels as if it's shrinking, pushing the breath out from my lungs.

Jane squeezes my shoulder momentarily and then pulls away. I can't dare face her.

I can't bring myself to say anything during the rest of the trip. Mum starts humming to herself as we reach the edge of Kingbridge – and she doesn't stop until we pull in outside the register office. The driver is all action, opening doors and offering arms. Going anywhere in a wedding dress is like trying to cross an ice rink while wearing bowling shoes. It takes planning and a large amount of luck to get around without falling over.

The registrar is waiting for us: a prim woman who, I suspect, can judge the potential success of a marriage within two minutes of meeting a couple. I wonder what she thinks of David and me.

She looks me up and down and beams 'You look lovely,' though I can't believe she ever tells a bride anything else. It would be quite some career gambit to turn to a bride and say, 'You look quite the state.' I feel it, with sweat pooling down my back and Mum's words bouncing around my head.

Jane guides Mum off towards the main room, while I go with the registrar into a side office. She keeps it light, talking about the weather and the journey, but it's easy to see that she's trying to smooth away any nerves. She says she has to go and prepare – and that she'll see me in a few minutes – and then I'm alone.

The room is lined with books and a plush red carpet, like someone's private library. I can imagine other brides sitting or standing in here, looking around and wondering what life will bring after the day. This is the line in the sand that's been in the back of my mind ever since I saw David in that service station. I suppose it isn't even a line; it's a junction. Left or right. Yes or no. Marry or don't.

The Rolls-Royce is parked outside the window and the driver is polishing an already spotless part of the wing. It was David's idea for me to arrive in the fancy car. He insisted and so I went with it. If nothing else, I thought Mum might enjoy it. In the old days, she'd take me to the seaside for the annual parade of fancy cars. I can't remember why it happened, or what it was actually called, but there were sparkling sports cars alongside classic vehicles. Mum would always point out the Rolls-Royces, possibly because it was the only make of car she knew. When I told her we'd be travelling to the register office in one of the cars she'd long admired, she shrugged and said there had never been such a parade.

As I watch the driver move around to the front of car, I think about knocking on the window and telling him to start the engine. I could duck through the side door, rush along the corridor and be out front before anyone knew. I'm sure he'd drop me off at my flat – or anywhere else I wanted.

What then?

I've heard stories of women who walk out on their husbands-to-be – but there never seems to be a follow-up to say what happens after that. David and I have only known each other for fifteen months and, suddenly, it feels like it. This is the problem with living somewhere small. Cities give anonymity, home towns give notoriety.

The door clicks and then Jane appears. I turn away from the window and she must see what I do. She stands with her body angled towards the second door. The way out. I wonder if she knows.

'You ready?' she asks. I take a breath and then she adds: 'Everyone's here.'

There's a moment, just a second, perhaps two, in which is feels like she might ask me again whether I'm sure. Last time, it caused an argument; this time I might tell the truth.

And then the moment passes. Jane offers her arm and says: 'Shall we go?'

I link my arm into hers and she leads me through the door, along a short corridor, to the entrance of the wedding chamber. It doesn't feel as if there's any turning back now. A no is a no is a no.

When we came to plan the day, I realised there are so few men in my life. It isn't by design, it just sort of… happened. There's no one to walk me down the aisle and, though Ben volunteered, it didn't feel right. I said I'd do it by myself and so Jane gives my shoulder one final squeeze and then waits off to the side.

The Wedding March begins with a boom and the doors open, leaving me nowhere to go. Light beams from the windows at the furthest end of the chamber but the room still feels dark… or perhaps it isn't the room at all. Perhaps it is me?

My legs feel unsteady, a dog in booties for the first time, though I somehow remain upright. Each step is a tiny bit easier than the previous, though that isn't saying much. Jane slots in behind me and I can feel her presence close, almost as if she's blocking me in. Mum is on the front row, though she continues staring towards the windows at the front, not turning to watch. Other than that, it is mainly acquaintances. Some of the gym managers I know, a few old school friends, a couple of neighbours. It's not much to show for thirty-one years on the planet.

David is there, of course. He looks good in his hired suit. I know he hasn't – but it makes it look like he's shed half a stone. Yasmine is at his side and this will be only the third time I've met her. We've only spoken once – that first time in the gym. The second, David was giving her a lift somewhere and they stopped outside my flat. He said he saw her on the side of the road, though he never talks about her. She'll be my sister-in-law and yet I know nothing about her. She's not quite wearing white, but she might as well be. It's a shoulderless silky cream dress that I should probably be more annoyed about than I am.

Like my mother, Yasmine is refusing to turn and watch – but the one person whose eyes are fixed on me is David. It's true that he adores me. It's complete. I wonder if that's what's in my eyes when I look at him.

How many other people will ever show that devotion to me?

I reach the front and my legs are jelly; my mouth a desert. The registrar goes through the things that everyone's seen a hundred times before. When she gets to the part about anyone objecting, I half turn to take in the room. This is the final moment; the last chance. Jane doesn't move and neither does Ben. Mum continues staring at the floor; Yasmine is picking her fingernails. Nobody speaks.

There are vows and rings: I do, he does, we all do. And then it's over. There's a kiss, claps and cheers. Job done. We're married. Happy ever after and all that. The thing all young girls dream of.

So why does it feel as if I've made a terrible mistake…?

TWENTY-SEVEN

THE NOW

I wish it had been porn on Andy's laptop. I could shrug it off if he was interested in various questionable acts he's never mentioned wanting to try. People's internet browsing histories are a murky business at best. I would imagine most would rather do a naked lap of Trafalgar Square than have to unveil their list of visited websites. No one wants the truth to come out that they clicked onto the *Daily Mail*'s site.

After seeing the name 'David Persephone' in Andy's history, I continue scrolling through the rest of the things he looked for.

I Googled Andy before our first meal out together. I stalked his social media and looked through his juice bar's webpage. I found out everything I could about him because, like it or not, that's how things work nowadays. It's easier than asking questions. To find the answer, put the question into Google, and there it is.

Andy's history from the past few days includes visits to the websites of various wholesalers and suppliers. He did an Ocado shop and browsed The *Guardian*. He likes the BBC website and spent time on Twitter. Much of it is normal… except there is a huge gap in the history from Sunday evening. I have no idea where Andy was but, at the time I was getting my award, he wasn't using his laptop. There is no activity from 4 p.m. through to Monday morning.

It proves nothing, of course – except that the final thing he looked for on Sunday was 'David Persephone'. Hours after that, I was seeing the ghost of my dead husband.

I glance away from the laptop towards the door and the stairs beyond. There's no sign of Andy getting up. I could go and ask him why he was searching for David, but it's another of those lines in the sand. I'd have to tell him about going through his browser history and where would that leave us?

While I was travelling to the venue on Sunday, Andy read almost two-dozen articles about David's disappearance. He spent almost two hours in total looking through details. I'm there too, of course. The devastated wife with all the questions about where my precious husband had gone. I always found it a surprise how quickly things went away. One minute, the police and the media had a sustained interest in David vanishing; forty-eight hours later and it felt like nobody cared. A week on and the only people who remembered were those who knew him.

Andy and I have talked about David in the past and it's natural that he'd be curious. My concern isn't so much that he is looking at these articles, it's that he's looking *now*. What's changed?

There is a creak from the stairs, so I snap closed the lid of Andy's laptop and push it back underneath the coffee table. I'm leaning back on the sofa, casual and carefree, when Andy appears in the doorway. He stretches high and fights a yawn.

'How did you sleep?' he asks.

'Good. You?'

'Perfectly.'

I don't know why couples talk about sleep. We take the most boring of subjects and somehow drag it out to be a daily conversation piece. I'm not convinced anyone cares anyway.

I watch Andy go through his routine. He pours almond milk onto his cereal and sets it to soak while he sets the espresso machine to heat. With that bubbling, he checks the news headlines on his phone and then, when the green light appears, he turns the dial to set the coffee pouring. As that's filling a cup, he pours a glass of juice that would've been prepared the night before. He's done that just in time for the espresso cup to fill, so he turns off that machine and quickly disposes of the grinds into the bin. After washing the filter, he then carries everything to the table. Finally, he fetches the laptop and takes that to the table, ready to browse the news properly.

He does all this with little emotion or even thought, I suppose. Like a robot fulfilling its programming.

It's not to think of David and all that happened. All *I* did. There's a part of me that unquestionably liked the unpredictability. With Andy, it's all stability and certainty.

'…want anything?'

I blink back to the sofa, realising that Andy's talking to me.

'Pardon?' I say.

'Do you want anything?' he asks.

I clamber off the sofa and try to remember where I put the BMW keys. 'I've got to go,' I say. 'I have classes later. I'll text you.'

'Do you need help packing for the weekend?'

'I don't think so.'

He gets up from the table, probably wondering why I'm suddenly rushing. I'm not sure I can explain it. I should ask him why he was searching for David but know that I won't.

My phone buzzes and I glance down to see the text from Jane:

I need to see you. Urgent.

Hyperbole is unlike her, so I quickly thumb back a message while Andy watches:

Your place? Mine? What's up?

'Everything all right?' Andy asks, nodding towards my phone.

'I'm going to stop by Jane's on the way home.'

He nods acceptance and then pulls me close. His fingers clutch my back, but I start patting his almost straight away, wanting to be released.

'If you see that guy from last night, call the police,' he says.

It takes me a second to remember the son of the guy hit by my car.

'I will.'

My phone buzzes once more and it's almost as if I can feel the urgency of what's come back. I resist the urge to check.

'I'm looking forward to moving in,' I say.

'It will be a new start for both of us.'

I'm not completely sure how it's a new start for Andy – but I would love it to be true. I should have let my flat after what happened with David. Life changed – except that it didn't.

Andy kisses me on the forehead, though that's as passionate as it gets. 'See you at Jane's later,' he says. 'It should be good.'

I'd forgotten that she'd invited us over. I'm not sure if I can agree that it'll be good – but I nod along anyway.

I head for the stairs to grab the rest of my things, which is when I check the message from Jane.

It's such a shock that I stumble over the bottom step and clatter my knee into the one above. I have to pull myself up and act like it never happened. A clumsy child with out-of-control limbs. I read the message a second time, but it hasn't changed, and it's just as heart-stopping as it was the first time:

I think I saw David.

TWENTY-EIGHT

THE WHY

Two years, five months ago

A squirrel stops momentarily on the path ahead, stopping to look towards David and me. I go for my phone, but the animal quickly decides he or she has better things to do than pose for pictures. The squirrels skips away into the undergrowth with a rustle.

'You'll have to be quicker next time,' David says.

I don't reply as we continue along the dusty trail, deeper into Little Bush Woods. It's not rained for weeks and the green along the edges is starting to turn a yellowy-brown.

This isn't an official country park, but locals from Gradingham use it as such. It's busy at the weekends, with dog-walkers and parents using the trails as free entertainment for their children.

'You got in late last night,' I say.

'I know – you were out like a light.'

'How was Estonia?'

'Wet – but I found a Hank Mobley LP that should be worth a fortune.'

'I have no idea who that is.'

'There was an Agincourt, too – and some Led Zep. I brought it back in my hand luggage. Didn't want to risk them losing it in the hold.'

He stretches and takes my hand. Apart from a groggy coffee this morning, it's the first time we've seen each other in ten days. This has been the pattern since we got married. Instead of being the start of something, that wedding day has increasingly been feeling like the end. I'm not sure if that's my fault, or his.

We continue along the path, my hand in his.

'How much can you get for them?' I ask.

'Maybe a couple of thousand for the Mobley if I can find a buyer.'

'Wow.'

'What about you?'

'I dropped a class this week because I signed up two more PT clients. I'm up to 400 followers on Twitter, too.'

He squeezes me hand. 'That's great. I'm so proud of you. It's good that the name change didn't create a problem.'

'No…'

We had discussed keeping my name as Morgan Noble, figuring that it would be easier to pitch as someone running their own business. David wasn't keen and so I went with him. He was insistent that we should be linked through our names. There are battles to pick and this didn't feel like one of them. Morgan Persephone, which rhymes with 'knee' and not 'phone', is quite the mouthful. It doesn't feel like me and perhaps it never will.

David lets go of my hand and we continue along the path slowly as a pair of boys race past us, heading in the other direction. Another couple is walking towards us and we swap a series of smiles and hellos until we've gone our separate ways.

The sun is dappling through the leaves, throwing a speckled quilt of rays across the track. I find myself sticking to the shadows, stepping over the patches of light without trying to make it obvious. Like avoiding the cracks in a pavement.

It's as we're walking that I realise how nice it is to have David at my side. The doubts have never really gone away, ever since that afternoon in the service station, but it's true what they say about absence making the heart grow fonder.

That's not stopped me wondering if his ten days in Eastern Europe has really been ten days in cheap motels. He's been forwarding me emails of his itinerary under the guise of me being able to check whether his flights and trains are on time. We both know that wasn't the only reason he was sending on those things.

'How long are you home for?' I ask.

'I'm not sure. There's a fair out Bristol way in a couple of weeks – but that should be down and back in a day. You can come if you want…?'

He knows I won't, but that isn't the point.

'I'll see what I have on,' I reply, which is a not very subtle code for 'no'.

We continue along the path, which is gradually starting to fill with more and more walkers. There are some in flip-flops and shorts; others with hiking poles, backpacks and enormous water bottles, as if they're on their way up Everest. The route takes us in a full loop until we arrive back at the car park. It's just off a country lane, half a mile down the road from the rugby club. There's a barrier that was installed after an outcry in the local paper because of apparent doggers during the summer nights – though it never seems to be down.

The day is getting warmer and it doesn't feel as if either of us is ready to head back to the flat yet. It's taken us a while to find this groove, but perhaps morning walks on a sunny summer's day is what married life is supposed to be.

Without needing to discuss it, we stroll along one of the other paths that quickly leads to a bridge that crosses the lake. There are signs warning of 'deep water' and I remember kids at school saying there was a shark in here. That was before we knew how ridiculous it sounded. I think *Jaws* had recently been on TV, which got everyone's imaginations racing.

There are waterlilies dotted around the edge of the lake, though many are massed on the soil verge. The water is low and there are footprints around the slope down from the bridge, where kids have gone wading. A family of two-point-four children are crossing the other way, with the father holding onto the youngest son's shirt to stop him charging ahead. There are more nods and smiles. The countryside code, I suppose.

It's after they've passed that David stops and half turns, resting his forearms on the rail of the bridge and peering down to the water below. I swing around until I'm at his side, elbow to elbow.

'Yasmine's pregnant,' David says.

It's the first time I've heard her name since the wedding two months ago.

He pauses and then adds: 'I was wondering…'

David doesn't finish the sentence because there's no point. In everything that's happened between us, we've never properly had this conversation. We each said that we'd like kids one day – but it was vague and undefined. There was never a timetable; never a plan.

'We're both self-employed,' I say. 'I'd have to put my career on hold. I don't think we can afford that.'

It's a practical reply to a question from the heart.

'I think I might be running out of time…'

I fix on a point on the furthest side of the lake, where a deer has appeared from the trees. It stoops and laps at the water and there's a beautiful serenity to the moment.

Sometimes I forget that David's a decade older than me. I wonder if I can do this for us.

For him.

'You'd have time afterwards,' he says.

'Time for what?'

'To still have a career.'

I don't reply, though he's probably right. I'm young enough to get my body back after a birth and then, with the free time he has, perhaps he can take on the role of day-to-day carer? Perhaps that's what he wants? Perhaps it's what I want?

'Maybe…' I say. 'But what about money?'

'What do you mean?'

'Your work is so unpredictable.'

Since marrying, we have a joint account, into which we both pay a certain amount each month. We still have our separate accounts, though I have no idea how much David has squirrelled away – if it's anything at all. He's never asked about my accounts, either – although I want the flat to remain in my name. I want it to be *mine*.

'We can figure it out,' he says. 'I think we're ready to be parents.'

'We'd need something bigger than my flat.'

'That's the other thing – perhaps we can look for a house…? Something with three bedrooms – or four?'

I don't know what to say. Five minutes ago, there was none of this in my mind – and now we're talking about houses and children.

'Where's the money going to come from?' I ask again.

'It will work out.'

I move my weight from one foot to the other and the wooden bridge creaks ominously. The deer looks up, perhaps startled by the noise. Its ears are pricked high and then it turns and darts off into the trees. Perhaps that's the omen? That should give me my answer.

'What do you say?' David asks.

'I don't know.'

TWENTY-NINE

Two years, two months ago

I bluster through the door as the bell jangles above. Outside, the wind is howling as the hail blasts the pavement. If it was anyone other than Mother Nature, it would be common assault.

My inside-out umbrella has long since been abandoned to the bin, while my coat is so wet, that it's more liquid than solid. I drip my way across the floor, apologising the entire way until I get to the counter. The glass cabinets are filled with various necklaces, rings and jewels; none of which are marked with prices. The man at the counter looks on somewhat disapprovingly as I continue to drip on his carpet.

'I brought my watch in a few days ago,' I say. 'It had stopped working…'

He gulps and looks sideways to an empty space, as if hoping someone will come and save him.

'I'm afraid there was a problem, Mrs Persephone,' he says.

'What sort of problem?'

'It's a bit of an, um, *delicate* matter…'

The television is playing in the background as I sit and stew on the sofa. I've not really been watching it, but the shows have scrolled around on a loop until the news came on. The lead story is about a one-punch murderer who's been given a life sentence. It's hard not to think of all the lives that have been destroyed. Not only the victim and his family – but the attacker, too. One stupid, momentary decision, if it can even be called a decision.

The door bangs behind me and David blusters his way in, followed by a few litres of rain. He slams the door behind him and then puts his soaking coat onto the rail next to mine. He offers a quick 'need a wee' and then dashes for the toilet, leaving a trail of water behind.

The news story has moved onto the mother of the victim. She's devastated and struggling for words as she says that the attacker should never be released from prison.

I wait and I fume until David returns. He's taken off his shoes and socks and has a towel around his neck. He heads towards the kitchen and then he stops still, turning to peer over his shoulder like a wronged cowboy in a Western.

I've never quite understood how emotions can bleed out into the surrounding atmosphere. As if feelings themselves can be so intense, so strong, that they can become something physical.

'What's wrong?' David asks.

'When we were at my mum's last year, you gave me a watch for my birthday,' I say.

'I know…'

'Where did you get it?'

He takes a small step backwards, but the counter is behind him and there's nowhere to go. 'I, um… don't remember.'

'It's worth three grand. How can you not remember?'

I watch as his eyes flick to my wrist, surely noticing the empty space where it used to be. I hold my wrist up higher so that he can see clearly.

'It's gone,' I say. 'Why do you think that is?'

He slides around the counter, putting it between us as I stand and move towards him.

'Where did you get it?' I repeat.

David's doing a goldfish impression; the first time I've seen it since we were in the service station a little under a year ago.

'It had stopped working, so I took it to the jewellers,' I continue. 'I went back to pick it up, but he said the serial number was on file. It had been reported stolen eighteen months ago.'

David is like a dog stuck in a cat flap.

'I've been walking around with stolen goods on my wrist for more than a year.'

He holds his hands up, still backing away – this time into the fridge: 'I didn't know,' he says. 'I bought it from a pawn shop. I buy all sorts of things from places like that. It's my job...'

'I don't believe you.'

I shake my head. If that really is his job, then he should be able to tell the difference between something stolen and something that isn't.

'It's the truth.'

'Even if it is, that's the point, isn't it? It's *not* a job. It never has been. It can't be a job if you're buying stolen goods.'

'I wanted to buy you a new one, but—'

'I didn't *need* a £3,000 watch. I never did. You must know that's not who I am...?'

David stumbles over the words, but it's not that he can say much anyway.

It's not even the watch. Not entirely.

'I can't work out when you're lying to me,' I say.

'I'm not lying.'

'You have before. You kept quiet about Yasmine. You lied about knowing Ben. You lied about going to conferences. You lied about your stolen goods.'

He doesn't say anything, so I keep going.

'I could've been arrested. I think the jeweller felt sorry for me, which is why he said he'd deal with it indirectly. I still don't know what that means.'

'I didn't steal it.'

David speaks through gritted teeth and everything about him screams that he wants to be somewhere else.

'I love you,' he says.

'Don't.'

'Don't what?'

'You can't give me something stolen and then make it all right by saying you love me. It doesn't work like that. Tell me the truth.'

He opens the fridge door and then closes it, then takes two paces to the other side of the kitchen, before taking a couple of steps back. His breathing quickens and then, finally, after everything: 'I knew it was stolen.'

Deep down, I think I always knew. David never had that much money, let alone that much *for a watch*. The rugby club spent three months phoning me, wanting final payment for the engagement party – and, even though David said they didn't take cash, the secretary specifically told me they did. I suppose it was another reason for me to pay and not him. This is how it's been ever since he moved in. The 'rent' is sporadic. Everything is. I pay for most things under a fantasy premise that he'll one day pay me back – and I've largely stopped asking because he's bought me off with other people's property.

'Where did you get it?' I ask.

'Someone I know.'

'A thief?'

He shakes his head. 'Just someone who sells things…'

'Someone who sells stolen goods?'

He turns away and it feels like something is broken – or, perhaps, it was never whole in the first place.

'I can get the money I owe you,' he says, even though I've not asked about it.

'I don't care about money, David. It's the lies. Maybe you *have* been in Estonia all week – but the fact I even question it is what matters.'

'I'll make it up to you…'

It's me who turns away this time, backing towards the sofa. The anger is gone and now there's only resignation.

'I don't think you can,' I reply. At first, I don't know what to add, but then, from nowhere, I do: 'I need a break.'

David stands staring at me. His shoulders have slumped and his bottom lip is wobbling.

'What does that mean?' David's voice cracks, like a teenage boy's. 'Are we breaking up?'

'No, just a break. Tonight. I want time to think and I can't be here.'

'Where are you going?'

'Somewhere.'

I move into the bedroom and grab a bag from the bottom of the wardrobe. There's nothing methodical about my packing as I pull a handful of clothes from my drawers and stuff them inside. When I turn, I expect David to be in the doorway. I'm surprised that it's empty as I fumble with my mobile and then call Jane. We've barely spoken since the wedding and yet she answers so quickly, and says my name with such conviction, that it's as if she's expected this all along.

'Are you safe?' she asks.

The question stops me momentarily.

'Can I come to yours?' I reply.

'I'm away in Nottingham for a hen do this weekend. I'm not drinking, but…' The thought ebbs away and then she adds: 'I'll send Ben.'

'OK.'

'He's not hurt you, has he…?'

It takes me a second to realise that she means David. I've never felt in danger around him, but then I've missed so many things – some of them wilfully.

'No,' I say.

Something rustles in the background and then it's Jane's voice again: 'I'm going to hang up and call Ben now,' she says. 'You can have the spare room. Stay as long as you want. I'll be back in the morning and we can talk then.'

She's efficient and in control, which at least makes one of us. It's hard to admit that other people were right all along about getting married so soon. Perhaps even specifically about David.

I hang up and sit on the bed, bag at my feet, waiting. The wind is still raging outside, rattling the windows as if it's trying to get in. I think back to being on the stairs of Jane and Ben's house, wondering if I would have ended up with anyone who sat next to me and said nice things. I was looking for anyone who'd encourage and offer comfort, assuming love would come. I'm not sure it ever has. There was a big part of me that wanted to win, as well. To be married first. To prove I was happy.

The bedside clock changes time agonisingly slowly. Minutes pass and then David's shadow appears in the doorway, blocking most of the light as he leans into the frame.

'Please stay,' he says.

'I need a night to think.'

'We can keep trying for a baby if you stay.'

This is how it's been with David and me. I think I've made up my mind to do one thing and then, from nowhere, I find myself doing another. I made a decision on the bridge that day, the same way that I made a choice in the service station. David might have suggested it, but I went along. I decided that having a baby was what *I* wanted.

Except that it isn't happening.

I didn't want it – and now that I do, I can't have it.

It's been three months, which I know isn't long enough to know for certain – except that, somehow, I *do* know. I can feel my body rejecting our attempts at making a baby. It's telling me something that, perhaps, I knew all along.

'I love you,' David says.

'I know.'

He crosses to the bed and sits at my side, stroking my hair. 'I'd never let anyone hurt you.'

'Stop.'

'I'd kill for you. Do you know that?'

It's a strange, mixed-up, almost clichéd thing to say. It's supposed to convey a degree of romanticism, as if anyone would want that. But who would? It's an incomprehensibly manic idea to love a person so much that killing someone else is somehow acceptable.

'Why would you say that?' I ask.

'Because it's true.'

For perhaps the first time in our relationship, I genuinely believe him.

The doorbell sounds three times in rapid succession and I jump to my feet, spurred on by the urgency.

'Don't go,' David says.

He trails me all the way to the door and, when I open it, Ben is standing there.

'How's it going, Morgs?' he asks.

'It's been worse.'

He glances past me towards David and then pushes the door wider. 'Shall we go?'

I take a breath and then step outside, where the rain continues to lash: 'Yes.'

THIRTY

THE NOW

Toddlers are much like brides-to-be on a hen do at the end of the night. They stagger around in circles, babble nonsense, crave attention, and then fall over and burst into tears. They also sometimes vomit on themselves.

Jane's daughter, Norah, is at the stage where she can generally walk around by herself, although she's like a mini human bumper car. She bumbles around my living room bouncing off the sofa arms and coffee table, before setting herself right again.

Jane is on the sofa, nursing a cup of tea.

'You saw David?' I say.

'Norah likes walking,' she points to her daughter, who is seemingly trying to prove the point as she does a wobbly lap of the living room. 'Well, sometimes. Other times, I'll strap her into her buggy and she'll refuse to get out for hours. She won't sit on a chair, she'll have to be wheeled into the living room in her buggy. Anyway, we were at Elizabeth Park and there was a bloke sitting at the edge of the pond by himself. I'd glanced away for one second – and then Norah was bumbling towards the pond.'

She gives the *what can you do?* sigh that only mothers can manage. I think there's an acceptance that deep water is for jumping into; fire is for touching; anything with a danger sign can be ignored. Kids are like lemmings and it's only parental reflexes that prevent the inevitable.

'I had to rush to catch her and, when I got there, I looked up and the man on the bench was watching us.' She gulps and then ends: 'I could have sworn it was David.'

A week ago, I'd have known she was imagining it. Now, I'm not so certain.

'How close were you?'

'One side of the pond to the other. Not far. I started to go around there, but Norah was wriggling and, by the time I got halfway there, he'd gone.'

It's hard to know what to say. On its own, I'd say it was probably someone else who looked like David. Combined with the hotel photo, the possible break-in and my missing car key, it doesn't sound so crazy.

'Have you heard from him…?' Jane asks.

Sometimes I forget that everyone else thinks David is missing. When people say things like 'Have you heard from him?', I have to remind myself that it's not a ridiculous question. Of course I haven't heard from a person who's dead. After the last few days, it definitely doesn't feel like a ridiculous question.

'No,' I reply.

Jane chews her bottom lip and, for a few seconds, all we do is watch Norah toddle around the table. She bumps into the corner and then plops onto her backside. It could go either way – laugh or cry – but she breaks into a grin and starts giggling to herself.

'I'm not saying it *was* him,' Jane says, 'just that it *looked* like him. I thought you should know.'

My phone is almost always on vibrate, because otherwise there would be a constant *ding-ding-ding* as I walk around. Like a dog with a bell. If spam emails were actually printed on paper, there'd be no trees left on the planet. Perhaps it's because of that, I jump when my phone actually rings. There's a part of me that expects to see David's name on the screen – but it reads Veronica instead.

I tell Jane I have to take the call and skirt off to my bedroom and close the door before pressing to answer.

I think I've been bracing myself for this type of call ever since Mum moved into the bungalows. A message to say that she's had a fall and not got up, or that she hasn't been answering her door. I think everyone does when their parents get to a certain time of their lives. There must be a crossover point from where parents dread the middle-of-the-night call about their children to where the children fear the unexpected call for their parents.

'This is Morgan,' I say.

I can tell from Veronica's first intonation that my mother is fine. 'Hi,' she says. 'I just wanted to say that I talked to the security company about the camera footage from the gates.'

In all that's gone on, I'd almost forgotten about the autograph that appeared next to Mum's TV.

'What did they say?' I ask.

'That they can only release the footage if there's some sort of criminal investigation. Something to do with their contract and data protection. To be honest, I think it's because they don't want to. They want the police to contact them, so what should I do?'

'Leave it,' I say. 'It's nothing anyway. I'm really sorry for wasting your time.'

There's little else I can do considering the last thing I want is go to the police with possible sightings of the husband I killed.

Veronica sounds unsure, like she knows it's more than I'm letting on. 'I can keep onto them if you want. If it's something important…?'

'No…'

There's a gap and then: 'If you're sure.'

I tell her that I am and then hang up. It takes me a short while to feel ready to face Jane again. There was a moment when my phone rang that I felt certain it would be to say that the worst had happened. Anticipating something and being ready for it are two different things.

Back in the living room, Jane looks up expectantly. There's a rudeness about asking who was on the phone, even though we all want to know.

'Nothing important,' I say.

I can feel her watching me as I sit, as if she's trying to read my mind.

'Are you sure you're OK?' she asks.

'Yes… just busy.'

'You can tell me anything…'

This is the moment where I can either let it out, or I'm going to have to hold onto it. Even with that, there is truth within truth. If I tell her that I think David was in the back of her photo from the hotel, then do I leave it at that? Do I say that David's dead? That I killed him? It's the problem with lying. It's like chocolate digestives with a cup of tea: one is never enough.

'It's nothing,' I say.

Jane continues to watch me and there's a moment in which we both know it's a lie. She's asking if I want help and I'm telling her no, even though the answer is yes.

'I have to get going,' she says. 'I wasn't meaning to stir things up, or anything like that. I just thought you should know what I saw.'

She calls for Norah, who spins at the sound of her name and fumbles her way around the living room. Jane straps her into a buggy and then I hold the front door.

'Are you and Andy still all right for later?' she asks.

I want to say 'no', but it feels too late.

'Sure,' I reply.

'Fab. I'll see you tonight.'

She's reached the pavement when she stops and turns, offering me a final chance to tell her what's wrong. I don't take it and she offers a knowing, slim smile before she turns and disappears out of sight.

I close the door and know I should start packing. It's only a few more days and I'll be moving out to put this chapter of my life behind me. My keys are on the otherwise bare kitchen counter and I wonder if the Tigger pot will show up while I'm packing. If I could find it, it would almost make everything else that's happened seem explainable.

Andy sorted me out with a pile of packed-down boxes, that are now in the corner of the bedroom. I fold the first one out and place it on the bed. I am about to start filling it with summer clothes that I definitely won't need this week, when the doorbell sounds. My first thought is that Jane has forgotten something and returned to retrieve it. That is instantly forgotten as I get into the living room and spot the police car through the window. I consider finding somewhere to hide and pretending I'm not in. There is no good that can come from answering the door, although I know I have no choice.

It's the same two officers as from the other day: one a head shorter than the other. I can see in the eyes of the taller one that he recognises me, but I suppose he has to say it anyway.

'Mrs Persephone…?'

'You got my name right that time,' I reply.

He doesn't smile and instead angles himself towards the police car. He doesn't need to say it because I know.

Something bad has happened.

THIRTY-ONE

THE WHY

Two years, one month ago

Keeping a secret is like being constipated. It's a pain in the arse and then, sooner or later, it all comes out anyway.

I've somehow lost two hours through watching mindless television, skimming around the internet, browsing videos of cute dogs, scrolling through Facebook and finding out what type of cheese I am via a Buzzfeed test. I am a cheddar because, apparently, people know where they stand with me. I can only imagine that being a stilton involves crumbling at the first sign of resistance and stinking like old socks.

David yawns his way into the living room at a few minutes past six in the evening and heads to the kitchen. 'I needed that nap,' he says, partly to himself. He rests on the counter, waiting for the kettle to boil as he fiddles with his phone. 'I thought you had classes?'

'I had to cancel them.'

'You're still not feeling well…?'

'Not really.'

He takes a couple of slices of bread and starts to smear margarine across the surface. 'Do you think you need to go to the doctor? You might have the flu. I think it's going around.'

'It's not the flu,' I say.

He drops the mucky knife into the sink and returns the margarine tub to the fridge, before removing a block of cheese. He picks up a sharp chopping blade from the block and stands poised.

'What do you think it is?' he asks.

'I'm pregnant.'

It's what we talked about; what we wanted – and yet, now it's here, everything is wrong. There's a sinking sensation in my stomach that isn't down to the pregnancy. It feels like I've woken up on an airbed with a leak and that I'm being swallowed into the centre.

The cheese hits the floor as David stares open-mouthed across the room, knife still in his hand.

'*Pregnant?*'

'Yes.'

'But we haven't…'

'That night before you went away a month ago.'

He nods, but he's dazed, like he's staring into the sun. It's not like he could have forgotten that night.

'Are you sure?' he asks.

'About when it happened?'

'About whether you're pregnant.'

I wasn't sure how David would respond – but this is probably the one question I didn't expect.

'There are pregnancy test kits in the bin under the sink if you want to check. I've peed on them, though.'

He takes a breath, steps backwards, steps forward, scratches his arm, then pulls up his trousers. All the while, he never stops staring – and he doesn't put down the knife.

I get to my feet and cross to the counter. It's all that separates us.

'I thought this was what you wanted,' I say.

David shakes his head slowly and it's now that I notice the tears that ring his eyes: 'It's not mine, is it?'

'Why would you say that?'

His tone is firm and unerringly knowing. 'Tell me.'

'Tell you what?'

'Whose is it?'

'It's yours.'

The knife wavers in his hand, but then he grips it tighter. I can see the veins bulging in his arm as he squeezes the handle.

'I had a vasectomy,' he says, looking up to catch my eye and hang onto it.

'What?' I say, stumbling. 'When?'

'Before the engagement party.'

I remember him limping around the room at the rugby club because of what he said was a running injury. It didn't sound right at the time – but so much of what David says doesn't sound right. I figured it was another white lie to disguise something unimportant – now it couldn't be more important.

'I've never wanted children,' he adds flatly. His stare is stone cold, a different person from the man who gazed longingly at me along the wedding aisle.

'It was *your* idea to try for a child!' I say. 'When we were on the bridge, *you* brought it up.'

It's as if a switch has been flicked as, suddenly, I get it. It's like minor politicians promising policies they'll never have to implement because they have zero chance of winning an election. It was easy for David to suggest us having a baby because he knew it wouldn't work. As long as we were trying, we would be together. It gave a foundation to our marriage. Without that, perhaps there was no purpose for us as a couple. He knew I had doubts all along and this was his way of keeping me.

I've finally seen the truth – and he knows it.

'How much of this is a lie?' I ask.

'You tell me.'

'*Me*? This whole *have-a-baby-thing* was a trick to keep me with you. Like everything. The fake trips, the fact you and Ben were never good uni friends. I'm asking you how much of the last two years have been a lie?'

David doesn't flinch and it feels like any warmth I ever saw in him was a mirage. Perhaps I did that to him?

'You first,' he says, with steady and terrifying calmness.

'What do you mean?'

'You're pregnant, but it can't be mine – so who were you with?'

It feels like the truth doesn't matter any longer. Things are broken anyway.

'You,' I say. 'Only you.'

'Whose is it?'

He repeats the line three times, with each time sounding more and more like a growl. I simply stare at him, not sure what to stay. I can see his forearms starting to tremble as his upper body tenses. I've never seen him like this before. This is a different person and, perhaps for the first time since we met, I realise how helpless I could be up against him.

'Tell me.' His lips move but his teeth are clenched.

'David—'

'You've destroyed us,' he says. He should be shouting but his tone is steady, almost calm – which makes it feel so much more dangerous. 'You're ruined everything. I'd have done anything for you – but you're just like all the others.'

'I—'

I don't have a finish to the sentence and it's only now that I remember the knife. The overhead light catches the blade as it sags in David's hand. He notices it too and suddenly grasps it tighter.

It's strange how things that happen the quickest can feel as if they're occurring in slow motion. At regular pace, it's easy to miss the details. Two people side by side can spot completely different things in the same scene.

Even though everything happens in an instant, I see it all with absolute clarity. David lunges towards the side of the counter, the knife clenched in his hand; the tip angled in my direction. His teeth are bared, like a cornered animal; his arm muscles tensed. In a blink, he slashes the knife towards me. The glint of the kitchen lights flash off the blade as it arcs through the air towards my cheek. My back is pressed hard into the counter and I feel the swish of the air as it passes millimetres away from my skin when I angle away.

I'm acting on instinct as I grab the Tigger head pot from the counter at my side. David's attempt to cut me has left him slightly off-balance and, as he straightens to come at me again, I throw the pot towards him. Anything to gain myself a second or two so that I can dash towards the door.

I've always had some degree of fitness and athletic ability – but I never tried javelin or discus when I was young. I didn't play cricket or rounders and threw 'like a girl' according to the boys I was at school with.

Not today.

The throw couldn't be more perfect, or devastating. David glances to his own hand, as if surprised he is still holding the knife and, in that millisecond, the pot thunders into his temple. His eyes roll into his head as he slumps to the side, thwacking his other temple on the corner of the counter. His head snaps back and then he drops limply to the floor, surrounded by broken ceramics, unmovingly still.

There's a sudden second of silence and I'm gasping for breath as I take a couple of steps towards the door. Flight not fight… except that David hasn't moved.

There's something else…

When I glance down, there is a drizzle of red across the centre of my top. I'm not sure how I missed it – but there is a throbbing sting as I touch the base of my neck and then remove my blood-soaked fingers.

David's knife didn't miss me.

THIRTY-TWO

THE NOW

Good solicitors have the ability to make grown adults feel like uninformed children. They're like parents who can explain why the sky is blue with the assurance that the world is in safe hands as long as they're in charge.

The room at the back of the police station is small and cramped, with barely space for two seats and a table. Some sort of fan is buzzing overhead, as if there's one giant bee trapped within the walls.

None of this fazes Mr Patrick, because I can't believe anything would. He's one of those distinguished middle-aged men for whom first names don't seem appropriate. I can imagine his wife and kids calling him 'Mister'.

'It appears that the man struck by your car has taken a turn for the worse,' he says, as he peers at me over his glasses.

'He's not going to die, is he?'

'I don't know.'

'I ran into his son in the pub last night,' I say.

'How do you mean "ran into"?'

'My boyfriend and I were playing pool out at the Kingfisher. I had no idea who he was – but he came over and called me a murderer.'

This brings the merest of frowns and, perhaps worse, Mr Patrick rubs the bridge of his nose. 'You should have called me,' he says.

'I didn't think. It was all a bit of a shock.'

'What happened?'

'Not a lot. He shouted and then my boyfriend talked him down. He left and then we left.'

Mr Patrick notes something on a pad in writing that might as well be hieroglyphics given the state of it.

'I can mention it to ensure it's on file,' he says.

'I don't want any trouble.'

He taps his pen on the pad and nods along. When he looks up, it's obvious we've moved on. 'So, we're clear about what happens when we go back in?'

'I am… but I don't get it. I haven't done anything. My car was stolen. What's wrong with saying that?'

Mr Patrick removes his glasses and uses the handkerchief from his pocket to wipe them clean. 'Perhaps in an ideal world,' he says. 'Let's remember that it's innocent until proven guilty. You don't have to prove you were in bed: they have to prove you were driving. The more you talk, the greater the risk of accidentally saying the wrong thing.'

'Like what? I know what happened.'

'Perhaps you say you left the hotel at 2.30 – except they have camera footage of you leaving at 2.25 because you weren't paying perfect attention. Then you say you were home at five – but they've got footage from a motorway camera of you being nearby fifteen minutes earlier than you thought. Say you gave one time when you last spoke to them, but, today, it's slightly different.' There's an edge of annoyance to this, like being scolded by a teacher. Disappointment, not anger. 'You've not lied,' he adds. 'It's just that humans are imperfect. We round up and down. We don't pay complete attention. Everyone does it – except that, in cases such as this, timings matter. The more you talk, the more chance there is of getting the small things mixed up. Put together a few things like that and it suddenly looks like you're trying to hide something. They're after inconsistencies – even unintentional ones.'

'I always thought guilty people said nothing…'

It's the same interview room as the last time I was here. Constable Robinson is back – the one who barely said anything – but, this time, he's alongside someone called Inspector Bainbridge. I wonder if it's a bad sign that a sergeant has been swapped for an inspector. Whether this means it's more serious. Bainbridge is of the same mould as my solicitor – a similar age, build and level of charismatic distinguishment. I suspect they've each been doing their respective jobs long enough that they could swap places and argue equally as passionately for the opposite side.

The room still feels brown and encompassing. In a kidnap movie, the victim would be chained to a wall in here.

Bainbridge sets the interview up by introducing everyone and then he gets to business: 'Where were you at five-oh-five hours on Monday morning, Mrs Persephone?'

I want to answer, to make it clear I was in bed, but Mr Patrick steps in and speaks for me: 'My client has already made it clear where she was at that time, Inspector. If you want the answer, I suggest you check the transcript from the last time you spoke to her.'

I expect Bainbridge to be annoyed, but his lack of reaction makes it seem like he expected something along these lines. The interview – if it can be called that – goes on in much the same fashion.

'*My client left the hotel in search of a more comfortable sleep.*'

'*My client is a* victim *here, Inspector.*'

'*You already have the answer to this.*'

It reminds me of the few times I've caught Parliamentary footage on the news channel. Someone will ask a question and the MP will say: 'I refer the honourable gentlemen to the reply I gave some moments ago.'

It's clearly a giant middle finger, although we all continue as if it's perfectly fine. Bainbridge asks me a question, I say nothing; and my solicitor – in not so many words – tells him to do one.

Everything he says on my behalf is correct, but it still feels wrong in his mouth.

It feels like frustration is finally starting to kick in as Constable Robinson sets up something that looks like an iPad on the desk. There's a video that must have come from the hotel's reception area that shows me entering through the main doors with Jane.

'Is this you, Mrs Persephone?' he asks.

'Yes.'

My reply gets a raised eyebrow from Mr Patrick, which is the equivalent of a monumental telling-off.

The video shows me walking through from reception into the main suite where the awards dinner took place. I say hello to a couple of people I know and then, in a moment that is so cringey, I find myself covering my eyes, I start to dance.

'Would you like to describe what's happening here?' Bainbridge says.

I know I'm supposed to stay quiet, but it's so bad that I can't shut my mouth: 'A pretty bad attempt at the cha-cha slide by the look of it,' I say.

'Do you perform the, ahem, cha-cha slide often?'

It sounds so ridiculous in his fatherly voice that I can't stop my lips from twitching upwards. Like a dad claiming he's into hop-hip. The smile passes as quickly as it arrived and then Mr Patrick answers for me.

'Come now, Inspector. If this is all you have to ask about, I think we'll be going.'

He motions to stand, but Bainbridge fires back with another question: 'How much did you drink, Mrs Persephone?'

I suppose he's suggesting I was already drunk *before* the awards, meaning I might have been drunker later on when I drove back.

'I believe my client passed a breathalyser test,' Mr Patrick says. 'Hours after the crash.'

'Was there any indication in those results that she drove drunk?'

There's no reply, which is an answer in itself.

The video finishes with Jane and I walking away from the awards room, back towards reception, ready to check in. I'm not sure what came over me in that moment.

'When did you last see your husband?'

Mr Patrick acts far quicker than me. I'm wondering whether he knows something he can't possibly.

'Sorry, Inspector. Are we talking about a stolen car, or my client's husband?'

'One thing could be linked to the other, considering there was no apparent break-in to take the car keys…'

It's the flaw in my story that can't easily be righted. I can't explain how someone got those spare keys because I have no idea.

'Have you changed your locks?' Bainbridge asks.

I figure there's no reason to avoid this question: 'I have now.'

'Have you seen your husband in the two years since he disappeared?'

The pause is momentary before Mr Patrick steps in: 'I don't see how this is relevant.'

I think of the photo Jane took with the man in the blue suit in the background. David or not David.

'No,' I say.

THIRTY-THREE

THE WHY

Two years, one month ago

Blood is starting to pool, creating a soggy, crimson halo around David's head. I keep expecting him to blink and climb groggily to his feet. Seconds pass; maybe a minute, maybe more – but he doesn't move. The knife has clanged free from his hand and is poking out from the small gap under the cooker.

There's my blood, too. When I look at myself in the mirror, there's a narrow slit that arcs across the top of my collarbone, near the base of my neck. David was aiming for my face and it was only my last-second flinch to the side that made him miss. It's not deep – nothing for which I'd have to go to the hospital – although there's plenty of blood.

As I look at my reflection, I tell myself I did the only thing I could. Not only that, the outcome was an accident.

If I tried another hundred times, I doubt I could muster the accuracy I had when the clay pot hit David's head.

Then there's the voice at the back of my mind that says he was simply moving around the counter. He was holding the knife because he was making a sandwich and, in all the drama, he forgot he was holding it.

'David?'

I crouch, avoiding the blood, and gently pinch his fingers.

'Come on, David. Time to get up.'

The shattered pieces of the clay pot are spread around the kitchen. There are four or five large shards and then a couple of dozen smaller pieces. I push some of the bigger ones towards the side, out of my way, as I move around David's body and then gently slap his face.

'David?'

I hold his wrist, trying to check his pulse, but my fingers and trembling and I can't control my grip. I try his neck, but there's nothing. I even press a hand to his chest, looking for even the merest of inflations.

Nothing.

I start pumping his chest – one-two-three-four-five – aah-aah-aah-aah-staying alive – but then I stop. What happens if he does come around? An assault charge? Attempted murder? How can I explain it all?

And then…

I remember the news from a few weeks ago. David and I argued about the stolen watch he'd given me, but, before that, I was watching the story of the one-punch man. One stupid action and two families lost everything. David is already dead and it isn't like he's close to his sister. He doesn't have anyone else, except me. Should I lose everything because of one action that wasn't even deliberate?

It suddenly feels as if I'm out of my body. Like someone, or something, else has taken over – and I'm now watching myself. It's either rationality or the complete lack of it.

I clamp a square of kitchen towel to my neck and then head into the bathroom, where I grab a bandage from the cabinet. It looks ridiculous as I wind the material around my neck and secure it with a plaster – but it does the job in stopping the bleeding.

After that, I move into the bedroom and strip the bed. The sheets were one of the few things on which I spent decent amounts of money when I first moved in. I couldn't afford much in the way of luxury but figured anything that contributed to a good night's sleep would be worth it. The value is worthless now as I carry the sheets into the kitchen and cover David's body. I start to wrap him, like he's some sort of Egyptian Mummy, folding the corners until he is fully entombed. Blood is seeping through the top part, so I wrap a second sheet around his head, which, for the moment, seems to stop the worst of the flow.

With David entombed, it's not that difficult to drag him across the laminate floor until he's by the front door. I return to the kitchen, pushing the larger parts of the clay pot into the corner and wiping away the worst of David's blood. I squirt some Mr Muscle onto the floor, leaving it to soak in.

The reddened cloths all go into a bin bag and I'm about to dump the pieces of Tigger's head in with them when I stop. There are very few tiny shards and I wonder if it could be glued back together. It would be like keeping the gun or knife after a murder and yet, for the first time, I realise why someone might do that. There's something close to a mystical quality about an object that's done so much damage. A fascination that cannot be matched.

Instead of dumping the broken pieces of ceramic, I brush the rest of them into the corner and then get back to work.

It's not a deep clean – there's time for that in future – but I finish clearing away anything obvious, until I have a pair of black bags full of cloths and paper towels.

I've never been a fan of the end of a year, when it feels like the sun never comes up. Darkness has a grip on the day, which it seems so reluctant to relinquish. It's a blessing now, though.

My car is backed onto the patch of land by my door. I've often thought about installing some sort of motion-detecting security light overhead because the nearest street lamp is diagonally across the road and offers little light in this direction. Now, I'm grateful for the gloom.

It takes me a short while to find my car keys. They were in the pot when I threw it and, for a moment, it's like they've fallen through a wormhole. David is here, the broken pot is in the corner, my house keys are next to the knife, which I realise is stained with my blood – but there are no car keys. Five minutes pass before I finally discover them in the sink, next to the buttery knife David left. It's as if they've broken the laws of physics by somehow travelling in the opposite direction to everything else.

I open my car boot and then drag David out of my door and heft him into the back. I add the two bin bags and then return into the flat to grab the ball of string from under the sink. I can't ever remember using it, nor why I bought it – but it will be useful now. I get the scissors from the kitchen drawer and then take a pair of the bricks from the wall next to my car that always looks like it's on the brink of collapsing.

I wipe away a few final smears of blood from the floor inside and then lock the flat, while leaving the lights on. My dad used to be obsessed with things like this back in the day. He was convinced anyone passing was secretly planning to break in and, every time we left the house, he'd leave the lights on. As crime prevention methods go, it's relatively basic – although we were never burgled, so perhaps he was onto something. Either way, I figure any neighbour who casually glances across the road will see the lights and assume I'm in.

The car feels sluggish from the back, although I take it slowly as I head out of Gradingham and head for the road out towards Little Bush Woods.

I'm only a couple of minutes past the village sign, when I hear the clunk from the back. I ease off the accelerator, wondering if I've bumped over some roadkill, when it comes again. My mind races: David's still alive – and he's banging on the side of the car, wondering what's going on.

I slow and ease the car onto a verge at the side of the road. High hedges surround both sides and it's colder in the countryside. My breath ekes into the air as I open the driver's door and edge around to the back of the car. I rest a hand on the clasp at the back, wondering what to do. It will be impossible to dress this up as some sort of misunderstanding. It's not like I'm taking David to the hospital…

The boot creaks as I pull up on the handle. I half expect it fly open as David springs free… except, when I peer inside, he's still there, mummified and covered. I have to use the light from my phone and it doesn't look as if any more blood has leaked through the sheets. The two black bags are still wedged into the corners and I can't see anything different. There's no escaping the fact that David is dead – and that I killed him.

I close the boot and look back along the road, wondering if it was roadkill, after all. Or even my imagination?

I get back into the driver's seat and continue along the road. My neck is throbbing from the cut but I try to ignore it as I continue on.

It's hard not to have the twinge of remembrance as I pass the rugby club. David had a vasectomy in the days before our party and spent the evening limping around, saying it was a running injury. Then he said he wanted to have children. I have to blink it away, because, for now, I can't personalise what's happened. I need to act first.

The gate to the car park at Little Bush Woods is up and it's apparently too cold for any potential doggers to hang around at this time of year. There's a big sign saying that the park closes at five during the winter – but it's not as if there's anyone to enforce it. The car park is deserted.

I'm glad for the semi-regular weight training as I heave David out of the boot. His body feels heavier than it did when it went in. I suppose that 'dead weight' is a literal thing, not simply a vague saying.

I end up dropping David's body on the floor, largely by accident because of his bulk. I grab the end of the sheet and drag him across the car park. There's a charity clothes bin that I've never noticed before, though the lid has been levered apart and is hanging open. Random pieces of clothing are strewn across the weed-ridden tarmac.

It's far easier to drag David than it is to carry him. I pull the sheets along the trail, stopping every few minutes to catch my breath. Half an hour on a treadmill cannot prepare a person for this.

It isn't long until I get to the bridge. The moon is engulfed by clouds and yet the light is still managing to cast a bluey glow across the water.

Raindrops start to ripple across the lake as I drag David's body onto the bridge. It's gentle at first, the merest of pitter-patters, and then, as quickly as it started, it's a deluge. My hair is plastered to my face as the water soaks my clothes to my skin. It's only now that I realise I'm not wearing a coat. Not that it matters – everything I'm wearing will be burnt within a day or so.

I continue heaving David across the bridge until we're in the middle. It was only a few months ago that we were here. I can picture David and myself, leaning on the rail, as he said he thought we should try for children. It feels like another lifetime.

David's body is left on the sodden wood as I rush back to the car, from which I retrieve the string, scissors and bricks. The bin bag can go in a builders' skip somewhere, or one of those bins outside a supermarket. It's not as if anyone's going to go hunting through it.

When I get back to the bridge, the signs warning of deep water are being battered by a thunderous blast of rain. David's cocoon is still in the centre, but I cut away the sheets and toss them to the side, until it's only me and him. I look at his waxy face and there's a part of me that still expects him to sit up. When I roll him onto his side, there's a second in which I wonder if his leg twitched. I stop and watch, waiting for it to happen again. I have to convince myself that my mind is playing tricks.

My fingers are trembling as I thread the string through the holes in the brick and then loop it around David's legs. I wrap it around over and over, passing it through the brick each time until the ball of string is half gone. I've never been great with knots, so I tie it like a double-knotted shoelace – except that I keep tying it until there's no string left. I repeat this with the second brick, attaching it to his midriff.

His skin is clammy and wet and I constantly have to stop because, every time I touch him, I'm convinced he's still alive. He doesn't move, no matter how many times I pause. In the end, he's left with a pair of bricks knotted to his body.

'David?'

The lashing rain almost hides the words and he doesn't respond.

'David?'

There is no comeback, so I prod him with my foot, before rolling him onto his back. His eyes are closed and I can't bring myself to open them to check whether there's anything there. I know there's not – and yet that niggle of doubt won't leave me. The blood is being washed away by the rain to the degree that I can see the slash close to David's ear from where the pot hit him. It's not as large as I thought it could be. I had a bigger cut last year when we went hiking in the Peak District and I snagged my bare leg on a thread of barbed wire. I suppose I have a bigger gash on my neck now – although it isn't as deep. I thought it would look far worse than it does.

'David?'

I stand and take a breath, peering out across the rippling lake. The raindrops make it look as if the water is alive, as if something is going to breach the surface with a monstrous roar.

All it takes is a nudge with my foot.

That's it.

David rolls off the bridge, momentarily snagging on one of the posts before I push harder. He slides under the water almost instantly. There might be a flurry of bubbles, but I can't know for sure because it's obliterated almost instantly by the raindrops.

I watch for a few seconds, still expecting him to burst back up, like the shark in *Jaws*, or the one we once thought lived in this lake. The rain is so hard that it's painful to stand in the open; like being smashed over the head repeatedly. The irony of that is not lost as I turn, scoop up the bloodied sheets and then run back to the car.

THIRTY-FOUR

THE NOW

I've often wondered where the clarity came from on the evening that I got rid of David's body. Whether, somewhere deep down, I had been thinking about it for a while.

His lies were big and small – some that mattered, many that didn't – and I think there was a part of me that always knew he had a loose relationship with the truth. If he ever had a storage unit full of collectibles, then I never found any information about it within his possessions. The police have never mentioned it, either. There was almost no money in his bank accounts and it was far eclipsed by the amount he owed on credit cards. He came into the world with nothing and he left it in more or less the same fashion.

I wait in the car park of Little Bush Woods, wondering if I should have come here direct from the police station. I have no reason to think they're following me, though if they are, I've led them directly to where I dumped David. I could be out for a walk, of course.

There is still an hour or so until the park closes, although I suspect the barrier will remain raised. I wait in the car for five minutes, wondering if someone will follow me in. A marked police car would probably be excessive – but there are no other cars anyway.

Unlike the last time I was here two years ago with David's body, there is a smattering of vehicles across the car park. The surface of weeds poking through the tarmac is almost identical to how I remember it.

As I wait, a man emerges from the path to the lake. He has his hands in his pockets, his hood up, and barely looks in my direction before hurrying across to a battered Ford. A few seconds later and he's gone.

I'm as convinced as can be that I wasn't followed, so get out of the car and set off towards the lake. Almost instantly, I pass a woman with a dog. I'm not sure of the breed, but it's one of the big, fluffy ones who would probably try to make friends with Godzilla if it came stomping down the High Street. The dog sniffs at my ankles and I stop to ruffle its collar as the owner and I share a quick 'hello'. They head back to the car park, so I continue onto the bridge.

When I get to the deep water sign, I stop and lean on the bridge rail, turning and waiting in case a police officer does appear. Mr Patrick said they had no reason to hold me as there's nothing to indicate I was driving the car. That is, of course, because I wasn't. My DNA will be all over it – but that's because I drove it not long before it was stolen. It proves nothing. He seemed to think the police were on a fishing expedition because they have no clue who was driving. There isn't a lot of crime around Gradingham and, perhaps because of that, very few resources to look into anything that does happen.

Minutes pass and nobody emerges. A breeze is fizzing across the water, sending a gentle flurry of waves across the surface. The bridge is coated with a delicate layer of frost that's dented by intersecting, scuffed footprints.

I used to visit the woods most weekends, either for a walk with David, or some sort of training run around the trails. I found the soft soil easier on my joints than the harsh concrete of the pavements around Gradingham. Anything's better than the monotony of a treadmill. It's only now that it occurs to me that not coming here for two years is far more suspicious than continuing what used to be predictable. If anyone was watching my day-to-day routine, they would surely conclude that something happened here. I was consumed by those news reports or TV shows, in which experts say that criminals always return to the scene of the crime. I live in the scene of mine – but this place means something, too. I always thought David's body would be found sooner or later. That didn't mean it would be linked to me, but I've expected a knock on the door ever since I kicked him into the water. It's not happened.

As I stand in the centre of the lake, I picture David's body below me, still weighed down by the bricks. In the aftermath of that night, I thought the string might erode and David's body would float to the surface, to be found by an unfortunate dog-walker. That hasn't happened, either.

Sometimes the thought flitted through my mind that the reason I've heard nothing for two years is because David was somehow alive. That the bang from the rear of the car was him and not roadkill or a pothole. That, after I turned my back and headed back across the bridge, David hauled himself out of the water. The thought always evaporated as quickly as it arrived – until I saw him in the back of the photo at the hotel.

I'm not sure what I expected by returning here. All I have is an eerie sense of déjà vu. I keep thinking it might rain, even though it feels more like it might snow. I'll always picture this bridge with splattering raindrops and the noise of water crashing into water. I eye the surface of the lake as the ripples continue to ebb towards the bridge, spurred on by the bristling wind. I can hardly jump in and dive down to see if there's a body there.

'You OK?'

I spin to see a woman standing behind me with a forlorn-looking dog. I'm not sure how she managed to get so close without me hearing anything. The animal doesn't seem too keen to be out in the cold and is straining in the direction of the car park.

'I, um…'

'Are you looking for something?' she asks.

'No,' I say.

She looks past me towards the water and then shrugs a *suit yourself* dismissal. 'Have a good walk,' she says.

'You, too,' I reply.

She turns and heads along the bridge. The dog continues to watch me, as if it somehow knows the reason I'm here.

'David,' I say – as with the last time I was here, there is no answer.

THIRTY-FIVE

The evening's Zumba class is enough to take my mind off the police investigation, even if it is temporarily. I'm supposed to be on an evening off, but my body is itching to do something that doesn't involve moping around. I end up taking a space at the back of a class that's being hosted by one of the trainers who rent a space at my studio. We all have something of an agreement that any of us can tag onto anyone else's sessions if there is room.

I can tell that the trainer is nervous as she goes through the routine. She tells everyone to move left while simultaneously heading right, and then misses the beat on a couple of the track changes. It's still plenty enough to help me work off the restless energy I've felt since being at the police station.

I shower, change and check my phone after the class – though there are no further messages from the 'Miss me?' number. There's nothing from the police or my solicitor, either. All I have is a text from Andy asking if I'm going to meet him at Jane's, or if we're going to go together. I'd almost blocked it out, though there's no getting out of it now.

I take the alternative route to Kingbridge, avoiding the country road that would have taken me past the rugby club and Little Bush Woods.

Andy's work van is already parked on the road outside Jane and Ben's when I arrive. I parallel park behind him, all the while cursing him for not pulling further forward.

It's only when Jane answers the door and beckons me in that I glance towards the stairs and remember when David and I met. So much can happen in three years. At the time, this house felt like glorified student digs, as if Jane and I had never quite grown up properly. Now, there is a child gate at the bottom of the stairs and another at the top. When we get into the living room, Ben has a framed diploma on the wall. There's a child monitor on the side, with a blinking green light. The kitchen counter has a soft polystyrene sphere covering what would have been a sharp edge. We act as if everything is the same as it's always been, but I suppose that's life. We spend large parts of it telling everyone else we're perfectly fine, even when the opposite is true.

I've been interviewed twice by the police because they think I drunk-drove and hit an innocent pedestrian in the early hours of a morning – and yet I'm acting as if it's nothing. I've seen my dead husband in a photo – and then gone to bed and got up the next day. Everything is an illusion.

Jane doesn't mention being at my flat earlier, or the fact that she says she might have seen David. She's put on a dress for the occasion, for which I don't blame her. It's been a long time since I've seen her in anything other than loose clothes that are cheap enough to cope with being vomited on. She's pushed the sofa to the side and set up the dining table in the living room. Andy and Ben are sitting next to one another, although, when I enter, they are silent like kids outside a headmaster's office.

Andy stands and we share a misplaced fumble in which neither of us seems sure whether we're trying to hug or kiss.

'You got here,' he says.

'What gave it away?'

It doesn't feel very funny and neither of us laugh as Jane enters with a plate of breads. As soon as we're all sitting, she and Andy are chatting as if they're the couple. She starts off by talking about a typical sort of day with Norah and that evolves into a conversation about his scout group and the football team he coaches. Before long, they're on to schools, catchment areas, various school governors he knows, a nursery she's been looking at – and so on.

I catch Ben's eye and we share a brief smile that leaves me cold, before we each turn away.

Jane brings in the main course – some sort of fishy rice thing – but we've barely had a mouthful when the baby monitor sputters and Norah starts to cry. Ben and Jane swap a quick glance, but she's already up and on her way before a word is swapped. It's at that moment that Andy gets to his feet and disappears off towards the toilet.

Ben and I are opposite each other. Aside from brief, passing hellos, we haven't seen each other in a long while.

I nibble at the rice dish, but my hunger has gone. It was a bad idea to come; I should have said I couldn't make it. Excuses are easy to come up with – I have to pack; I'm not feeling well – whatever.

'How are you doing?' Ben asks.

'Not bad. You?'

'I'm fine, too.'

He mushes his fork into the rice, mixing it all around in a circle. He sighs and won't look up, although he isn't eating, either.

'I didn't *ask* for this,' I say.

His fork pauses mid-stir and then he glances up to me. His voice is a hissed whisper: 'You're the one who keeps calling her and texting. You're the one who meets her for lunch and coffees.'

'We've been friends our whole lives. I knew her long before you. What do you want me to say to her?'

There's a bump from the hallway and we both wait, although nobody appears. 'We've got a daughter together,' Ben mutters. 'It's not like it used to be.'

'Again – what do you expect me to do? Even if I wanted to stop being friends, it's not going to happen just like that. We only live a short distance apart. We've seen each other at least once a week for as long as I can remember.'

Ben clinks his fork into the side of his plate in annoyance. Where once I saw big, blue buttons for eyes, now I see an inferno. He opens his mouth to say something but never gets the words out because Andy breezes back into the room, utterly oblivious.

He sits, eats some of the rice, and then turns to Ben: 'How's life at the bank?' he asks.

Ben eats some of the food himself, although, such is his anger, he ends up spilling some of it on the table. 'I've got a conference starting tomorrow,' he says. 'I'm going to be away for four days.'

'Where's that?' Andy asks.

'London. They're putting me up at a place near Euston.'

'Nice.'

'I'd rather be here.'

Ben glances towards me, but I quickly turn away, focusing on my own food. He's made his point.

'How's your juice bar?' Ben asks, although he doesn't sound overly interested.

'I'm looking to expand,' Andy replies. 'I've been talking to my own bank about possibly getting a loan to open a second bar. We've been going over possible properties.'

'Exciting times.'

Ben couldn't have sounded less enthused, although I'm not sure that Andy realises. It matters little anyway because there is a series of thumps from the stairs and then Jane re-emerges.

'Norah went almost straight back to sleep,' she says, before re-taking her seat. 'Sometimes she only needs her hair stroking and that's enough.'

We get through the rest of the meal with relative normality. Jane and Andy still make much of the conversation, while Ben and I routinely blank out everything that's going on around us while umming and aahing at the appropriate times.

There's always an awkward moment after people have finished eating in which nobody's quite sure what happens next. Everyone really wants to head either home or somewhere far more comfortable than a dining table – though nobody wants to be the first person to bring it up.

It is Ben who finally breaks the impasse. He mentions his collection of football programmes, perhaps accidentally – and then he and Andy disappear into the garage to look through them. Jane waits until they've left and then pours herself another glass of wine.

'That is such a blokey thing to do,' she says. 'Can you imagine me dragging you upstairs to go through old Cosmos?' She swallows a mouthful of wine and then adds: 'At least they're getting on…'

I'm not sure how to respond because I would far rather they *weren't* getting on. My hushed altercation across the table with Ben has brought that closely enough into focus.

'How's the car?' Jane asks.

'They've impounded it for some sort of inspection. My solicitor said I might not hear back about it for another week.'

'I meant Andy's BMW.'

'Oh… His indicator stick is on the other side of the steering wheel, so I keep setting the wipers going when I'm trying to go around a corner – but it's fine other than that.'

She holds the glass in front of her face, lowers it and then lifts it again. It feels like she's mulling over whether to say something. In the end she places the glass on the table.

'Are you still OK for tomorrow?'

I stare at her blankly, trying to figure out what she means.

She must see it because she quickly adds: 'You're taking Norah in the afternoon…'

'Oh, of course. I thought you meant something else.'

I'm not fooling anyone. I'd completely forgotten I am supposed to be keeping an eye on Jane's daughter while she gets a mole removed.

'Take her to the park,' Jane says. 'The forecast says it'll be dry and she loves going there. She'll want to stroke all the dogs and, before you know it, ninety minutes will have gone past.'

'You're dropping her off at…?'

'One o'clock. Do you want me to bring her to the studio or your flat?'

'The flat. I've got packing to do in the morning anyway.'

Jane nods along, though my gaze is momentarily drawn towards the baby monitor, panicked that Norah might start crying again and I'll be asked to go and sort it out as some sort of indoctrination. It wasn't that long ago that I was telling David I was pregnant – and now it seems incomprehensible that I ever felt ready for that.

'Are you looking forward to the move?' Jane asks.

I hesitate, wondering if, perhaps, Andy has returned and is now standing behind me. Under the guise of stooping to scratch my ankle, I check there's nobody there and then sit up straighter again.

'Of course,' I say.

'I think it's great that you're finally moving on,' she replies.

'From David…?'

'Who else? I've been thinking about what I saw in the park earlier and perhaps I was wrong. I was trying to keep an eye on Norah and there was a bit of mist around. I don't know…'

I'm not surprised that she might try to backtrack on what she said she saw. It's natural. We see something we can't explain and then, in the hours afterwards, we convince ourselves it wasn't really like that. My problem is that I have a photo to confirm what was there.

'Are you sure you're fine to look after Norah?' Jane asks.

It's not as if I could say 'no' when she first asked, let alone now.

'Of course,' I say.

She obviously sees it within me. 'But…?'

'I'm on bail,' I say.

'It's not like you did anything, though, is it?'

'No.'

THIRTY-SIX

THE WHY

Two years, one month ago

It's four days since I pushed David's body into the lake – and it's only now that a pair of officers are visiting to find out the circumstances around his 'disappearance'.

I think it would genuinely concern most people to know how long the police take to respond to cases of missing people. It's probably cuts and diminishing resources – but there's also a distinct sense that there isn't a lot they can do when an adult disappears.

I've been wearing turtle-necks ever since, which is enough to cover my own wound. Aside from that, it had got to the point where I think I'd over-cleaned in the aftermath of what happened. I had swabbed the floors between the kitchen and the front door to the degree that they looked overly sparkling in comparison to the rest of the flat. It smelled too clinical as well, so, after all that cleaning, I had to dirty up the apartment a bit. I trampled in a few footprints and emptied a little dust from the vacuum into the corners around the kitchen appliances. I even left a small Marmite stain on the counter, close to the glued-together Tigger pot. My keys are sitting inside, as they always have.

I have no idea how I'm supposed to be behaving – whether I should be crying my eyes out, or answering their questions with a blank-eyed, glassy stare. Perhaps I should be full of hope that this is all a misunderstanding and that I'm confident David will return quickly enough? In the end, I figure I'm better offering a bit of everything.

The officers are on the sofa, both wearing uniforms, one of whom is carrying a notebook. I'm in the chair facing them, my legs curled underneath me.

'The last I heard, he was off on a work trip,' I say. 'He takes them often. He buys and sells collectibles and goes to trade fairs all over Europe. He was in Sweden recently – and Estonia.'

'Have you looked for his passport?' one of the officers ask.

'It's gone. It was in the drawer next to our bed, but there's no sign of it. His phone is gone, too. He said he'd be back in a day – but that was two days ago. I've not heard from him since.'

The officer motions towards the window. 'Did you say that's his car outside?'

'It is. He said he was getting a taxi to the airport because of the parking fees. I'd gone to work at my studio and, when I got back, he wasn't here. I assumed he was already on his way.'

'Where was your husband headed?'

'He said Denmark. I assumed Copenhagen – but I'm not sure if he ever specifically said that. I can't remember.'

I speak as confidently as I can – but it took me a while to decide upon Denmark as the place where David was apparently going. I was thinking about a place in the UK but then figured it might mean that various British police forces join together. I found a list of collector fairs around Europe and there is one happening in Copenhagen at the moment. I hope they'll check and put two and two together to make five.

'Was there a reason he was going to Denmark specifically?'

'I assume some sort of fair, or that he was buying or selling from someone specifically. We didn't talk that much about those sorts of things – he was always going somewhere.'

That gets a nod and another note on the pad. The officer counts on his fingers and then says: 'So the last time you saw him was on Monday morning…?'

'Correct.'

'When did you last hear from him?'

'That morning. He usually texts when he gets to the airport – but not always. I assumed I'd get something when he landed in Denmark but nothing came. I'll show you my phone.'

I figure they'd be able to check through the phone company if they really wanted – but I pass him my phone, where it highlights the messages I sent to David after I'd already killed him.

Hey. Not heard from you. How are you? How was the flight?

Are you OK? Hoping you get this. I had a good day. Hoping yours was all right.

Can you text or call me? Getting worried.

On it goes. Message after message sent to a phone I'd already smashed to pieces and dumped in a bin outside the Tesco Express in Kingbridge, along with the remains of David's burnt passport.

The officer skims along the screen before handing it back.

'Do you know where he might have stayed in Copenhagen?'

'No idea.'

'What about the taxi company he used to get to the airport?'

'I don't know that either. I think he kept the details on his phone – but I don't know where that is.'

I can feel my hand starting to shake with the pressure of the lies building up. It's a lot of front to maintain. I stand abruptly and ask if they'd like some tea. They each say yes, so I cross to the kitchen and find myself standing on the precise spot where David died. It only occurred to me this morning that I don't know how deep the water is at the lake in Little Bush Woods. There's a 'deep water' sign – but that doesn't necessarily mean much. I keep thinking his body will appear, despite the bricks.

There are a few moments of respite as I make three teas and, by the time I get back to the living room area, my nerves have settled.

The officer asks questions about the length of time we've been together and how long we've been married. I play up a little ditziness by counting on my fingers and glancing upwards, as if counting the months is an enormous challenge.

The next question is the one I expected. I've been practising the answer in my head, knowing it's what will matter when it comes to it.

'Has he ever done this before?' the officer asks.

I pause for a moment and then: 'No, well…' I stare wistfully off towards the window and sigh loudly enough that it can't be missed. 'I suppose I caught him out once,' I say.

'What do you mean?'

'He told me he was going to an event in Newcastle, but my friend, Jane, saw his car at the service station just outside Kingbridge. I went there and he was sitting in the Burger King by himself.'

The story gets the confusion I hoped for. The officer with the pen stops writing as the other glances sideways.

'Why?' the officer asks.

'He said it was because his business wasn't going well at the time. He didn't want to sit around all day and make it obvious, so he invented the trip. He said he was afraid of losing me…'

I can see in their faces that they're hooked. It isn't simply a missing person now; it's a person shamed by a failing business who has probably jumped off a cliff somewhere.

'What was your relationship like?' he asks.

I leave another gap and throw in a smaller sigh. 'We only got married six months ago.' I point him towards the photo at the side of the TV which was taken on the day. All these types of pictures end up looking the same: blokes in suits and brides in white smiling for the camera. Wedding photos can reveal a lot about the bride – simply look to see what the bridesmaids are wearing. If it's a sensible colour and style, she's probably sane. Something garishly bright, or hideously poufy, and she's a divorce waiting to happen. Jane is in something slimming and turquoise that was chosen entirely by her.

'How was the marriage?' he asks.

'It had been good. We were trying for a baby.'

The officer with the pen tilts his head ever so slightly and I know I have them. It's sympathy for the wronged woman whose husband disappears on mysterious trips all the time. He'll be having an affair, or living a second life. Maybe he'll show up in five years married to another woman, who knows nothing about me. Cogs are turning. They know something isn't right – except it's something not right with David.

'I was happy,' I say. 'He was a bit moody sometimes, but I suppose everyone is.'

'Did he drink?'

'Socially. He liked the odd whisky and lager. Sometimes he'd come home with a bottle of wine he'd bought wherever he'd been.'

'Drugs?'

'No. That wasn't him.'

'Could he be with any friends or family?'

'He's never really had that many friends that I know of.' I let that settle and then add: 'As for family, there's only his sister. She's called Yasmine and lives in Kingbridge. I've only met her a couple of times. I don't think they're in contact that often – but I guess she'll know better than me. I don't have her number, so I haven't called. I don't know why he'd be at hers, though. The last I heard, she was pregnant.'

They check the full details of her name and then ask if there's anything else I can think of. There isn't – but I give them his laptop, even though I don't know the password. I also give them his car key and an envelope of documents, including a few innocuous letters from his bank.

I lead them to the door and they wait on the precipice.

'What happens next?' I ask.

'We'll do what we can,' the officer says. 'We'll check his bank records and see if there are any reports of him getting onto a flight out of the UK.'

'How long will that take?'

Her features soften, seeing me as a concerned wife – even though I'm more curious about how long this will drag on.

'I wish I could give you a precise answer,' she says, 'but I don't know. If anything happens, you'll be the first to know.'

I watch them head to their car and then pull away. Unless David's body floats to the surface of the lake, I'm not expecting to hear anything soon. A thought niggles away that I'm not as smart as I think. That a detail will have escaped me somewhere along the line.

But there's the fact that I am, apparently, good at this sort of thing. Everyone has their talents. I'm not sure what it says about me, but perhaps mine lie with deception. I suppose the truth of that will be shown by what happens over the next few months. If I get a year or two along the line and things have gone quiet, then that will be that.

'Goodbye,' I say – and then I turn and walk back into the flat.

THIRTY-SEVEN

THE NOW

Thursday

The world swims into focus as I roll onto my back and stare at the ceiling. Whoever decided that people should sleep together – literally sleep – was an idiot. There's so much more space and freedom when a person has a bed to themselves. I starfish my arms and legs wide and close my eyes again, breathing in the morning. I'm in *my* bed, in *my* apartment. The idea that I decided to share this with David seems so outlandish that I sometimes have to remind myself that it happened.

And now I am giving it up again… this time for Andy. Except that this is different. I know what I'm letting myself in for this time – and Andy isn't David.

It's a few minutes after nine, so I yawn myself into a sitting position, before padding into the kitchen to put on a pot of coffee. I check the front door, though it's still on the latch. There have been no more mysterious texts, or possible sightings of David. If Mr Patrick is correct about the police, then they can't be far away from concluding that there's no proof I was driving my car, which means that should be finished with.

Is this it?

Thirty-six hours of mystery, suspicious police, and now everything goes back to normal? Perhaps the past can finally go back to being the past.

I return to bed for half an hour and sip the coffee while skimming through the emails on my phone. I answer a call from Jess at the studio, who's querying something about the rota, and then get on with the job of packing.

David's things are long gone. I went for a long drive and left his clothes with a charity shop. I could have taken them to one more locally, but it would have been too strange to see someone local wandering around in something David owned. It also might have aroused suspicion if I was seen dropping off his things when he was supposedly only missing.

Everything else was either taken to the tip, or sold – including his car. The police returned me the keys and it sat outside the flat for almost a year until I was sick of the sight of it.

I find myself flicking through old fitness magazines, wondering why I ever kept them. I think part of it was being with David and somehow believing that one person's junk was another's treasure. It doesn't matter now, because I end up putting more of my things into bin bags than I do the boxes that I will be taking to Andy's. Some people are apparently addicted to the endorphins that come from buying things, but I think there's something equally intoxicating about heading to the tip with a carful of junk, while wondering why it was ever bought in the first place.

It's less than half an hour until I've packed enough rubbish bags to fill my car. I head outside and only then remember that I have Andy's BMW. I dump everything into the back and then go for a drive out to the tip.

When I get there, some burly bloke offers to help and everything is dispatched with maximum prejudice. Apart from the magazines that will go off to be recycled, the man reckons everything else will be in landfill by the weekend. How easy it is to shed an old life.

Back at the flat, I struggle to reverse-park Andy's BMW into the space. The car is needlessly big and the mirrors seem to move themselves. I'm never convinced that I'm in control. It takes me three attempts and then I figure it's close enough.

I spot the package straight away.

It's sitting on my step, neatly wrapped in brown paper and thirty or forty centimetres square. When I reach it, I see the rectangle of white paper that's been taped to the front. 'Morgan' is printed in capital letters and sans serif font, with no last name. I pick up the box and it's surprisingly light. There's no rattle from inside.

I turn and take in the street. The box has been hand-delivered in the half-hour I was out, so it's either a coincidence, or someone was watching and waiting for the moment. I walk to the pavement and look both ways, then follow the street until it gets to the turn that leads to the alley that runs around the back of my flat. There is no one hanging around; no mysterious out-of-place cars. It's the type of street where an unknown vehicle outside someone's house will get a series of angry curtain-twitches at least and a letter on the windscreen if someone's really annoyed.

A sniper's dot is prickling the back of my neck. I'd swear I'm being watched, except there is no one in sight. I hurry back to my flat and open the door, before waiting in the frame; one foot in, one out.

'Hello?'

There's no answer and, when I poke my head inside, no obvious sign of anyone being there. I tell myself that I had the locks changed.

After a final check towards the empty street, I move fully into my flat and lock the door behind me. There's warmth and safety here. The worst thing I ever did happened steps from where I am – but I'm still here.

I put the box on the counter and then get the scissors from the kitchen drawer. The corners of the brown paper have all been meticulously taped down, so I'm left snipping away at the package until there is enough room to slip my fingers inside. I pull the paper apart to reveal a plain brown box. It gives me a vision of boxes within boxes all the way down to some sort of thimble in the centre.

It's not that. As soon as I unfold the flaps at the top, the contents of the box are clear.

Baby clothes.

THIRTY-EIGHT

There is a pale blue onesie with 'Daddy's little boy' printed on the front, plus a pink one that reads 'Daddy's little girl'. As well as those, the box contains matching hats for the outfits, plus small white socks and tiny booties that look like they would be too big for a doll.

Everything smells fresh and new. The labels read Marks & Spencer and I can imagine this being the type of thing a grandmother-to-be might buy in anticipation of a birth.

Other than me, only two people knew about my pregnancy: David and Jane. It was literally the last thing David and I talked about, or, I suppose *argued* about. It's impossible to resist the pull to look down at the spot in the kitchen where he hit his head. Sometimes I think I can still see the pool of blood, even though it was cleared years ago.

It's not as if the package was left by accident, or that it could be someone else's. My name was on the front. It was meant for me. It's not exactly upsetting, more of a jolt to times gone by.

Daddy's little boy.

Daddy's little girl.

I find myself rubbing the scar at the base of my neck again. In the days after David slashed me with the kitchen knife, I feared the mark would end up being far darker than it ever became. The narrow line is only a little muddier than my actual skintone and, unless a person is standing close to me – and actually looking – I doubt anyone would notice.

I spend much of the morning doing little other than pacing my flat, looking for answers where there are none. I find the clothes online. They're part of Marks & Spencer's current season, so would be available at any of their stores. Whoever bought the clothes did so recently.

It has always felt like a cliché that someone can jump when they're surprised. It's a figure of speech – and yet, when my doorbell sounds, I yelp like a dog whose tail has been stepped on. I leap high enough that I have to cling onto the counter to stop myself from tumbling. I quickly sweep the baby clothes into the drawer in which I usually keep tea towels and then crush the empty box into the bin under the sink.

The doorbell sounds a second time, though I'm ready for it now. When I answer, I'm not sure why I was surprised at all. It's two minutes to one and Jane is there with Norah strapped into a buggy.

She blusters into my flat buggy-first and then places a couple of bags onto the counter.

'Norah's slept on and off all morning,' Jane says, by way of a greeting. 'She'll probably be awake most of the afternoon.'

'No worries,' I reply, while thinking, *thanks for that*.

Jane seems flustered as she checks her coat pockets and then reaches under the pram to check on something.

She speaks quickly: 'If you do take her to the park, then she likes being strapped into the buggy most of the time. But it might tire her out enough for her to sleep if you take her out, so that could be the best idea.'

There is little subtlety there – and I guess this means I'm definitely taking Norah to the park.

Jane indicates to the space under the buggy: 'There are two changes of clothes just in case, plus blankets, her monkey and a bottle of milk for the fridge.'

Presumably because she's about to have it removed and it's on her mind, Jane starts to scratch the mole next to her bra strap.

There are a rapid couple of scritches, but she stops when she realises what she's doing.

'Are you worried about it?' I ask, nodding to her shoulder.

'They say it doesn't hurt, but who knows?'

The mole is the type of thing I wouldn't have noticed until Jane pointed it out a year or so ago. The doctors said it wasn't tumorous, but she wanted it removed anyway.

'You look terrified,' Jane says, looking from me to the buggy.

Norah is awake, though happily sitting and staring. I'm not sure if all infants do the same, but she will sometimes stare at something seemingly innocuous like a lamp as if it's a wonder of the world. I suppose there's a part of everyone that wishes the world could still be viewed in such a way. Norah seems to be interested in the skirt I have drying over the radiator.

'I think I can handle a sixteen-month-old,' I reply, although not particularly confidently.

'I have to get going,' Jane says, checking her phone. 'I'll let you know when I'm on my way back.'

She crouches and says goodbye to Norah and then heads out to her car.

I stare at Norah, who stares back at me. I undo the straps to release her from the buggy, but she doesn't move.

'Do you want to come out?' I ask.

She points at the radiator: 'Tree.'

'It's not a tree,' I say.

'Tree.'

I actually look, though the radiator is still a radiator.

'Tree,' she insists.

I've looked after Norah before – but only in small doses. There was once for an hour at Jane's house because she had some sort of meeting, then a few times where it's been minutes at a time because Jane's had to go to the toilet or something like that. An entire afternoon is a new one.

When Norah was first born, Jane would say things like, 'It'll be you again soon', seemingly oblivious that my husband was gone. She was thinking of herself while trying to be comforting – but I suppose we're both guilty of that. Either way, it quickly tailed off. We never talk about me having children now. I suppose I wondered myself if seeing someone else with a young daughter would somehow get me broody, but, if anything, the opposite is true. Parenting always seems like so much work.

'Tree,' Norah says again.

I crouch so that we're at the same level. I've never told Jane this, but she and her daughter look nothing alike. Norah has the same big, blue eyes of her father, along with Ben's light hair. Jane has been dyeing hers for so long that I forget she isn't a natural blonde.

'Do you want to go and see the trees in the park?' I ask.

She puts her fingers into her mouth and starts to chew on them. 'Tree,' she says.

'I'm going to take that as a "yes".'

It's still cold, but there's none of the biting fury from previous days. It's back to feeling more like a winter's day in Britain, as opposed to somewhere in the Arctic Circle. Norah is already wrapped up in a coat, scarf and gloves – and I find a folded blanket on top of the other things Jane has left below the buggy.

'Do you want to walk?' I ask her.

Norah stares at me and gurgles something that I'm almost certain is not a word. I finger walk across my palm, wondering if this might be a better way of communicating. When she doesn't respond, or make any attempt to get out from the buggy, I strap her in, grab my phone and keys and then set off.

Walking with a child in a buggy is something close to having an internal monologue that is no longer internal. I find myself asking Norah if she can see the cars, the trees, the clouds – and more or less everything else directly in front of us. She makes almost no indication that she can hear me, let alone understand what I'm waffling about. It is a little bit like having a conversation with a wall.

Elizabeth Park is a short distance from the centre of Gradingham. Whoever named it had such a level of inventiveness that he or she must have looked at the monarch and said, 'That'll do.'

There's a path that loops around the park, so I start to push Norah along. She is happily pointing at various things and saying 'tree'. I'd give her a fifty per cent hit rate of actually identifying a tree. The sky, the grass, the toilet block and a bloke with a bottle of cider are all accused of being trees. I stop a couple of times, wondering if Norah might want to hold my hand and walk for a little bit. Each time I attempt to undo the straps holding her in, she starts to scowl, seemingly moments from tears, so I secure her back into the buggy and she smiles once more. I don't blame her – I wouldn't object to someone wheeling me around a park all day.

We get to the pond and Norah shouts something that I hope is 'duck'. If not, she's been overhearing some words that are definitely not child-friendly. After the third such declaration, a woman on her way past with a pair of shopping bags stops to turn and look.

'She likes the ducks,' I call across to clarify, although I'm not sure the woman hears.

It's a mild day, although there are the usual park weirdoes with their hoods up, who have congregated in the bushes to drink cider. A little away from them, some lads who should probably be in school have created a goal with their bags and are playing football.

I try again to see if Norah wants to get out of the buggy, though she's happily identifying crows as ducks. Occasionally, she'll point at an actual duck – although her hit rate for this is a lot lower than when she was identifying trees.

I look across to the other side of the pond and the empty bench, wondering if it really was David who Jane saw here. It's a smaller distance than I thought, definitely close enough that someone should be identifiable. Jane knew David for long enough that she should be able to distinguish between him and someone else… except that she won't have seen him in two years. My memory of his face has faded in that time – and hers will have done as well.

Norah seems happy enough, so I crouch by her and we watch the birds for a while. She points a lot, along with opening and closing her mouth vicariously. She's one of those children who constantly seem on the brink of letting out full, eloquent sentences, though she isn't quite there yet. I've known grown adults who are much the same.

I find myself drifting back to the package of clothes, wondering who sent it and what it means. Someone is playing with me. Someone who knows me.

As we set off for a second lap of the park, I'm beginning to think that this parenting lark isn't that tough, after all. A grandmothery type stops us partway round and starts making goo-goo noises towards Norah, while saying how she's got my eyes. I don't correct her, although, when Norah points at the woman and shouts 'cow', the moment is somewhat soured.

Clouds are starting to mass and it's the time of year in which it never quite gets light anyway. Aside from the footballing boys, there are only a handful of people in the park, almost all of whom are wearing heavy, thick coats. It's only as I pass the toilet block that I realise I really need to go. In some parks, it would be a strict no – but these were renovated a couple of years ago and, as public toilets go, they're more or less acceptable for human use.

I wheel Norah around the zigzag doorway and then leave her next to the sinks. I'm not sure whether to face her towards the graffiti that accuses someone named 'Claire' of a rather graphic act or the open stalls.

I'm also not certain of the etiquette for going to the toilet while looking after a young child. It doesn't feel right to leave her, while, at the same time, I don't think I can take her into the stall with me.

Do mothers walk around all day holding their bladders? It's not the sort of question I can believe anyone has ever asked out loud.

In the end, I wheel Norah into a spot close to the hand dryers, where she's facing the opposite wall.

'I'll be one minute,' I tell her, without a response.

I head into the cubicle and lock the door, trying to will my body to get on with it. I've only been sitting for a few seconds when my phone rings. It's a scramble to get it from my bag and, though I think about ignoring it, the word 'solicitor' appears on the screen.

Mr Patrick announces my name as if he's summoning me: 'Morgan...?' he says.

'It's me.'

'I'm calling to let you know that the police are not pushing further charges over the collision involving your car.'

I'm staring at the scratched markings on the back of the door, where someone has taken to it with a knife. It takes me a couple of seconds to take in what he's said.

'That's it?' I reply.

'That's it. Someone should be in contact to sort out what's happening with your car and I'm sure you'll need a conversation with your insurance company. Other than that, your bail conditions have been lifted.'

'Why?'

It's so out of the blue that I'm sure I sound guilty. 'Usually,' he says, 'this sort of speed would indicate that new evidence has come to light.'

'New evidence...'

I've become a parrot.

'I can't say for certain,' he replies, humouring me. 'I wasn't able to get a proper answer from anyone at the station and, frankly, I'm not sure it matters at the moment. The upshot is that you no longer have anything to worry about.'

'Thank you...'

'Not a worry. I'll be in touch if there's anything more.'

He hangs up and I'm left staring at the scratches in the door, wondering what's happened. Has someone else been arrested? Is there a new witness?

Everything has taken me by such a surprise that I only now realise I've forgotten to do the one thing I came in here for.

'Hang on a moment, Norah,' I call, although there is no reply.

A minute or so later and I'm out of the cubicle. I head for the sinks and set the water flowing. It's only then that I glance across to the buggy, which still sits next to the hand dryers.

The *empty* buggy.

THIRTY-NINE

THE WHY

Two years, one month ago

The doorbell and loud knocking combine to create a tsunami of noise through which no normal person could ever sleep. I roll one way in the bed, then the other, squinting through the gloom to the clock that reads 06:53.

Ugh.

I'm trying to get the sleep out of my eyes as I realise that I've slept on David's side of the bed. I'm almost certain I started where I would usually sleep, but, in the absence of my husband, I've unknowingly spread myself across onto his.

The doorbell continues to ring over and over as thumps also bounce through the flat. I pull myself out of bed and stumble into the main area, before peeping through the window to see who's at the door.

I suppose I should have expected this.

When I open the door, Yasmine shoves her way in with such force that she almost stumbles into the counter. It would almost be funny, if it wasn't for the fact that she is one of the most pregnant people I've ever seen. Some women can disguise a pregnancy almost up to birth, whether through flattering clothes or some sort of wizardry. Yasmine is definitely not one of those women. She is so huge, it's as if she's smuggling a small hippo under her top.

'You can't just come in here,' I say.

'What happened?' she fires back.

'What do you mean?'

'I had the police around. They say David's missing.'

'I know. Who do you think reported it?'

'So, where is he?'

I have to fight away a yawn, which only seems to make her angrier. It's only now that I realise I've never given her my address. She must have got it from David.

'If I knew where he was,' I say, 'I wouldn't have reported him missing.'

Yasmine stands up a little straighter and smooths her top across her stomach. Her belly button has popped and looks like the cherry on top of a bakewell. Her eyes scan my roll-neck neck top and it's as if she knows.

'What did you do to him?' she asks.

Until now, I thought I'd have no problem dealing with her, but it's as if the force of the accusation is too much as I find myself taking half a step backwards.

'What are you on about?'

'He wouldn't just disappear.'

I'm not sure why I react in the way I do. I should sympathise and perhaps try to force out a tear. We could be sisters in arms. Instead – and I suspect because I simply don't like her – I fire right back.

'He disappeared all the time,' I say. 'He'd claim to be off in one place – and then I'd find him sitting in a service station by himself.'

Yasmine's arm remains half raised. 'What do you mean?'

'What do you think I mean? It's not a metaphor, it's a fact. There's plenty he didn't tell me – including who you were, until you showed up in my class.' A pause. 'And why *did* you turn up?'

Things have swapped and now Yasmine folds her arms defensively across herself. 'Because he's my brother,' she says. 'He'd never had a proper girlfriend before and I wanted a look at you.'

'Why not tell me that at the time, instead of running away?'

She slumps a little, unfolding her arms and gripping the counter. There's a moment in which I wonder if she's about to go into labour. I'll have to bundle her into the car and get her to hospital.

'I'm not sure,' she says, quieter this time. 'David's a complicated person. He's been hurt by girlfriends before – or at least that's what he's said. Sometimes I wondered if he was the problem. I was going to ask if you knew what you were getting yourself into… but then I thought you were playing games in pretending not to know me.'

'I *didn't* know you.'

'Well, I know that now…'

It's now that I know I should stop – except this is when I twist the knife. It's one thing to tell lies to cover; another entirely to tell them to cause someone else pain.

'Do *you* know where he might have gone?' I ask.

I picture the lake and the bridge.

There was no need for that – and yet I feel like she started it by announcing herself after my class and then storming away. What goes around, and all that.

'I did tell the police,' Yasmine says. Her tone has changed from angry and accusatory to soft acceptance.

'Tell them what?'

'Dad's old house is out in a place called Greatstone on the Kent coast. We've not known what to do with it since Dad died. It's too run-down for anyone to live in and neither of us have the money to restore it. Developers have been interested – but only to knock it down. David would never agree to that, so it's still sitting empty.'

'He never told me…'

Yasmine shrugs and there's a moment in which it feels as if we could – and maybe should – be closer. It wasn't only me from whom David kept things.

'Dad was a hoarder,' she says. 'He wouldn't get rid of anything. I can't even bare to look at the place. David and me have been arguing about it for years.' She stops and then adds: 'I guess he didn't tell you that either…?'

'No.'

She glances towards the doorway and, I suspect, is starting to wish she hadn't come. 'David always was one to keep things to himself.'

'I've come to realise that.' I point towards her belly, while thinking of my own. Yasmine's child will be a cousin to mine… at least in everyone else's mind, even if it's not the truth. 'Do you know if it's a boy or a girl?'

'Girl. She's due in ten weeks, but nobody seems to think I'm going to last that long.'

She turns towards the door and it feels like we're done – not just now but for good. I suspect that, unless we run into one another in someplace like a supermarket, we'll never see each other again.

'I should go,' Yasmine says. 'I, er… hope I didn't wake you.'

I wave it away as if it's all fine – of *course* she woke me.

She starts to head for the door, before spinning somewhat abruptly. She picks up the pen on the counter and scribbles something onto the pad next to the Tigger pot.

'That's my address,' she says, 'just in case you need it.'

'OK.'

We don't swap numbers and I wait until I hear the sound of an engine disappearing before checking what she's written. It's a place in Kingbridge that I will likely never visit.

I figure I might as well go back to bed, but, when I turn, it's as if someone has jabbed knitting needles into my midriff. I double over, struggling for breath and wheezing like an asthmatic. I have to hold onto the back of the sofa to steady myself as I stumble across the room before eventually reaching the toilet. I've barely managed to get myself into a sitting position when I realise the true horror of what's happening.

There's blood.

Lots of it.

FORTY

THE NOW

There's not a strong enough word to convey the absolute raw terror I feel as I stare across to the empty buggy. It's such a shock, it's like I've been punched in the stomach. It feels as if the ceiling is falling; that the sky itself is collapsing. I felt like this once before – and I lost a child that day, too.

I rush to the buggy and check the straps, almost to make sure it's not some sort of illusion. The straps hang unfastened and limp, with no sign that they were ever being used to secure a child. There's only one stall with the door closed, although I know there's no way a sixteen-month-old could release themselves from the straps and open it. I look anyway. The hinges are wonky and noisy, and, when I shove it open, there is no little girl inside. The toilet block is far too small for someone to hide.

'Norah?'

I'd love to hear her confident voice calling 'tree' or 'duck', but there's silence. I don't know what else to do, so wheel the buggy outside. I half expect someone to be there with Norah – *ha ha, look who I found trying to run away* – but there's not much of anything. The sky is grey; the grass is tinted with white – and, aside from the boys playing football at the furthest end of the park, I can't see anyone.

There is a separate disabled toilet, the door already partly open. The nappy-changing table is down and the bin is overflowing, though there's no sign of a person.

I move to the other side of the block and the men's toilets. There is a similar zigzag entrance as there is for the women's and I edge along slowly.

'Hello? Anyone in there?'

There's no answer, so I move quicker. It's darker and smellier than the women's toilet. The floor is wet – but it still doesn't take me long to figure that there's no one here.

Back outside and the empty space in the buggy is gaping. There's a rushing sensation in my stomach as if I'm going to be sick – but it's not a physical thing. I thought that what happened with David was the worst thing I'd ever do – but this is worse.

'Norah...?'

My voice barely carries, as if the atmosphere is so shamed by what I've done that it can't be bothered to transfer my voice. I keep turning to the buggy as if expecting Norah to materialise with a dramatic 'ta-da!' She doesn't. Of course she doesn't.

I wheel the buggy around the entire toilet block with increasing speed. There's nobody here. I was only on the phone for a minute or two. Where could she have gone? There is a moment of clarity as I stop in front of the ladies' and look around the grass for footprint trails. I'm so convinced that this will work that it's a shock when I find myself back at a crossroads where the path meets another stretch of tarmac. There are no trails on the grass.

Other than the path and the grass, the closest thing to the toilet block is a large, wiry tuft of hedges. In the summer, it will be an enormous green dome, though it is more a collection of weedy sticks at this time of year. I try to peer towards the centre, though there are bits of crisp packets and plastic bags stuck to the branches. The twigs are tightly packed and tougher than I thought – and I can't believe there are many adults, let alone children, who could batter their way into a hiding place.

The soil is mushy as I edge my way around the bush, though there are no obvious footprints. On the other side, there's a steady slope towards the pond.

I know what's happened. I can feel it, almost as if I actually watched it happening. Norah's drowned. I did the unforgiveable and took my eyes off her and she staggered away to the water. She'll be face-down and that will be that. How could I ever explain this to anyone, let alone my supposed best friend?

Except the pond is empty, too. The ducks and crows have disappeared to the other side of the bank, close to the bench. There's barely a ripple to the water; hardly a breath of wind. The world feels still.

I turn in a full circle, unsure where to go and what to do. I end up heading back up the bank and around the copse until I'm at the empty buggy. I look to the furthest side of the park, but even the boys have given up their football game and gone home. I feel alone.

I take out my phone, unsure who to call first. The police or Jane?

It's the same feeling I had when David's body was in the back of my car and was driving him to the lake at Little Bush Woods. That sense of knowing that life can never quite be the same again. Even if she's found, this is the end of my friendship with Jane. Things can never recover from this. Everyone in the village will know me as the woman who lost someone else's child.

I open the phone app and have already dialled two nines when I hear a soft, babble of a sob. It's such a shock that I almost drop the phone. I start to shake as I spin, trying to figure out if the sound is actually there, or if it's in my imagination.

The second cry almost sets me off. It's a steady wail now and I follow the noise into the disabled toilet. I checked here a few minutes ago – but that was then and this is now. The nappy-changing table is still down, but, this time, Norah is straddled across it, wrapped in a blanket. Her blue eyes are stained by tears and they stare accusingly at me as she quietens to breathy sobs.

I pick her up and, though she fights against me, I hold her close. I have to tell myself not to grasp her too tightly because I can barely believe she's actually real.

'I'm here,' I say. 'I'm so sorry.'

I carry Norah out and place her into her buggy. As soon as I put the straps across her, she's instantly silenced. I kneel, pressing my knee into the hard concrete and lower myself until we're eye to eye.

'Are you OK?' I ask.

Norah doesn't reply, though I gently press my fingers to her face, looking for any incriminating marks. She's still wearing the same outfit; with the only addition being one of the blankets that were underneath the buggy.

It's as I'm standing that my phone buzzes. I'm expecting Jane – but it's a text from the unknown 07 number that messaged me before.

Tonight. 9 p.m. Just You. You know where.

FORTY-ONE

In the end, it is Ben who picks up Norah from my flat. It's been a long time since his car last pulled up outside. It was that time I'd been arguing with David and said I needed a break. It feels like a different lifetime.

He straps Norah into the car seat in the front seat and then collapses the buggy into the boot. It's the type of folding mechanism that looks like it's amputated a thumb or two in its time, but Ben packs it down with the ease of a person who's done it many times before. Even this comes easily to him.

'I thought you were at a conference?' I say.

He closes the boot and turns: 'I was on the way. Jane called to say she was running late, so I ended up coming back here. I'm going to drive down to London later. I'll miss the opening banquet but…' He tails off and shrugs, as if to say that it doesn't matter too much.

'Has something gone wrong?' I ask.

His brow creases with momentary confusion: 'With Jane?'

'Who else?'

'I don't think so. She sounded fine when she called.' He turns to the car and stoops to check on Norah. 'You all right, sweetheart?' he asks.

She turns to him and replies with a clear: 'Daddy!'

The grin that spreads onto his face couldn't be any larger. I'm not sure I've ever seen him smile like this. Perhaps not only him, but anyone. It's joy in its purest form.

'How was she?' Ben asks, although it takes me a moment to realise he's talking to me.

'She liked being strapped into her buggy,' I say, fighting away those feelings of guilt about the *empty* buggy.

He nods and the smile trickles its return. 'It depends on the day of the week. Sometimes she wants to walk everywhere, other times she'll point to her buggy and cry if we don't put her in it. We have to wheel her into the living room to watch her shows, or read her a story.'

The smile fades sadly. It would have disappeared more quickly if I'd told him that I'd lost his daughter for ten minutes.

'I should get off,' Ben says. 'Thank you for having her.'

'See you around,' I reply, not thinking about the words. It's a reflex of a reply. A thank you/you're welcome of an exchange. There was something firm and final in his tone.

He stops and stares: 'No,' he says pointedly. 'You won't.'

I don't bother waiting to see him leave. Instead, I head inside and lock the door. It feels as if the world is imploding.

I text one of the other trainers from the studio, asking if she can take my evening classes because I have a sore throat. The reply pings back almost immediately that she will. 'Something going around,' she adds – which is the explanation for everything. Got a cough? Something's going around. Flu? Headaches? Herpes? Split ends? Everything's always going around.

There is more paperwork to do – there always is – but I can't even look at my laptop. There's the baby clothes that turned up out of nowhere – and then Norah's disappearance almost seems like a dream now. It felt like hours, but I can tell from the time of Mr Patrick's call through to the text message arriving that it was a little under ten minutes. It was nothing and yet it was an age.

You know where.

Of everything from the text message, that's the bit that really gets me – because I *do* know where.

The minutes tick by slower than ever and there are moments in which it feels as if 9 p.m. will never come around. I'm a kid waiting for Christmas morning – except nothing good is going to happen when the time finally arrives.

It's ninety minutes after Ben leaves that I text Jane:

How did the op go?

A reply comes back almost immediately:

Good.

That's it. She doesn't mention any specifics, or Norah. I try typing out a couple of replies, but nothing feels right. I wonder if Norah has moved up from single words to full sentences in the last hour-and-a-half and is busy singing like someone's nephew in a Scorsese movie. I end up leaving it at that. If Jane wants to tell me anything more, then she will.

It's a little after eight when I can wait no longer. I'm going to be early – but that will be better than late.

After a warmer, cloudier day, the night feels like the panicky moments directly before something goes horribly wrong. The hedgerows are painted a speckly white and the car windscreens are already crusted with ice. I can feel the cold in my bones as I sit, waiting for the windows of Andy's BMW to defrost. Warm air blasts from the vents, though the conditions outside the car are apt for whatever's about to happen.

Nobody sensible is braving the roads tonight and, as soon as I get past the boundary of Gradingham, I'm swallowed by the night. The car's headlights barely make an imprint on the countryside's cavernous depths of black. The once familiar lanes that lead towards Kingbridge are now like looking down and seeing someone else's hand.

It's such a surprise to see the sign for the rugby club that I almost swerve towards it, instead of around the bend. The hedge rushes towards me and, when I turn the steering wheel, I half expect the wheels to lock and the car to spin. In the split-second, I'm almost certain I close my eyes, but it's hard to know for sure because, all of a sudden, everything is fine. I'm on the carriageway as I should be.

By the time I pull into the car park at Little Bush Woods, my heart is still pounding. I've not seen a single vehicle since leaving home.

You know where.

Where else could it be? Everything leads back to the place where I rolled David's body into the water.

It's almost ten minutes to nine. There are two cars parked at opposite ends of the parking area, neither of which seem to have anyone in them. I doubt anyone has come here for a late-night walk around the park and yet I can't think of another legitimate reason why they might be here. I suppose the same is true of me.

I wait a couple of minutes to see if anyone will appear. When nobody does, I get out of the car. The cold instantly leaves me gasping, like vines snaking into my lungs. I've forgotten my hat and gloves – and there's nothing for it other than to jam my hands into my coat pockets as I set off for the bridge. The spindly, bare tree branches rustle steadily around me; a fanfare heralding my arrival. There are no secrets here.

You know where.

It is 8.58 when I get to the ramp of the bridge. I almost expect to see the shadow there in the centre, forearms leaning on the rail. David back from the dead. It only now occurs to me that I'm utterly unprepared. I have no idea how he could have survived – but he's hardly going to be happy about everything that happened. It's not like I'm here for a cheery reunion.

The centre of the bridge is deserted, but I set off towards it anyway. The wood underfoot is clammy and sodden, though there's a hint of frost clinging to the rail.

The time on my phone reads precisely 9.00 as I stand in the centre. I wait and then turn in a circle, expecting someone to be there. Expecting *David* to be there. He's not. Nobody is. There are no animals, no people, no anything. The night is still except for the gentle bristling of the tree branches.

When 9.01 arrives, the bridge is still deserted. By 9.02, I'm starting to lose feeling in my fingers. They're at the stage where, if it wasn't for what I can see, it would be hard to know for certain whether they are hot or cold. The glacial air tickles my throat and I have to cover my nose and mouth with my hands in an instantly failed attempt to try to warm myself.

Time continues to move. When 9.05 arrives, I am still alone. By 9.10, I'm wondering if I was wrong. The message said I'd know where to go – but, aside from my flat, I can't think of anywhere other than here.

At 9.15, I start to pace. There's the now familiar sense of being watched, even though I've not seen a soul in hours. By 9.20, my shoes and socks are no longer effective against the chill. It's like my toes are being squeezed in a vice as I try to wriggle some life back into them.

It's 9.25 when I give up. My teeth are chattering and it's so cold that even blinking has started to hurt. As I hurry back to Andy's car, I hear every snap from the woods; every whisper from the undergrowth. I tell myself it's the wind, but even my thoughts are frozen solid.

I fumble with the fob for the car, stumbling not only to hold it but also to press the button to unlock the doors. I can hardly get a grip on the handle and pulling on the door sends scorpion stings shooting through my fingers. I practically throw myself into the driver's seat, before hooking the door closed and then putting the fans onto full heat and power. My skin is so numb that I can't be sure whether the clash of temperatures is a good or bad thing. I hold my fingers in front of the vents, willing them to come back to life.

You know where.

I'm still sure this is where I was supposed to be – and yet I was here alone. Or I *felt* alone. The woods provide enough places for someone to hide. It's not as if this is the only place to park, either. The trails lead out to other roads, some that are on maps, some that aren't.

What I can't figure out is why someone wanted me here.

The answer comes as my phone starts to ring. It's Jane – and I can tell from the quiver as she says my name that something is wrong.

'What is it?' I say.

'It's David,' she replies. 'He's here.'

FORTY-TWO

Nobody answers when I press Jane's doorbell. It took me until I was halfway here to remember that Ben's off at his conference. I wonder why she called me and not him – although it's largely irrelevant if he's now hours away.

I press the bell again, before knocking on the window next to the door. The curtains are open, giving me a clear view of the living room. With the angle, I can see through the door to the hall and the steps on which David and I sat when we first met. It's amazing how much can happen in a short period of time. Three years to change our fortunes for good.

How can he be alive?

How?

I call Jane's phone. There's a brief pause and then I hear a tinny-sounding 'Don't Look Back In Anger' from inside. We were always such big Oasis fans, even though their best stuff was out while we were still in primary school. We were far too middle-class to really understand what Liam was singing about – but that didn't stop us belting out 'Cigarettes & Alcohol' like the rebels we definitely weren't.

I try the bell again and it's only then do I notice the door is slightly open. There is barely a gap between the door and the frame – and a gentle push from the inside would close it. I already have a foot on the doorstep when I stop and realise it's as if it was left open *for me*. I feel like the person in a horror movie who knows something is wrong and yet charges in anyway.

'Hello…?'

My voice echoes into the house and rattles around before curving back without response.

'Jane…?'

Nothing.

I step forward, nudging the door open with my elbow.

'Ben…?'

I've only managed a few steps into the hall when I hear a scuffling from behind. I start to turn but it's already too late. Something slams into my neck, like a snake's fangs. My head starts to spin and it's as if my body is no longer my own. I think I hear a crackling and my last thought is that something's burning. After that, there is only darkness.

The world is swimming as my eyelids flutter open. I can smell something burning as I roll onto to my side and explode in a series of hacking coughs. It takes me a few seconds to realise that I'm on the floor of Jane's living room. The carpet is short and bristles into my cheek as I roll onto my back. I see her sofa, as well as the candles, the abstract prints and books she hasn't read.

I try to gain some sort of momentum to push myself up. My arms ache and my head is whirling, while my neck burns.

It's only as I peer across the room a second time that I notice Jane. She's laid on her side, one arm splayed, the other cocked under her head. Her eyes are closed and she isn't moving.

'Jane?'

She remains still and unresponsive.

'Jane?'

I pull myself up using the sofa and the fog at the edge of my thoughts starts to clear. I stumble across to Jane and crouch next to her, fearing the worst. David wanted me somewhere else because he always planned to be here.

She moans as I gently rock her shoulder and then her eyelids start to flutter. I squeeze her hand as she rolls onto her back and then blinks her eyes open to take me in. She rubs her head with her free hand and squints.

'What happened?' she asks with a croak.

'I don't know. I—'

I stop because Jane's eyes have widened. When I check behind me, there's nobody there.

'What?' I add.

'Your hair...' she says.

I push myself up and drift across to the mirror in the corner, now able to see why Jane was so shocked. My hair has been butchered off.

FORTY-THREE

THE WHY

Two years, one month ago

Andy places the juices on the table between Jane and me. He smiles kindly and says: 'On the house.'

'You don't have to,' I reply, even though I feel Jane tense momentarily at my side. Never look a gift horse in the mouth and all that. It's been three weeks since what happened with David. His body hasn't been found and everyone still believes he's simply disappeared. It's at the stage where all the people I know – and many I don't – are giving me those closed-lip smiles with the *are-you-OK?* head-tilts. I play along, allowing myself to stare longingly out of windows. I also do a lot more sighing than I ever did before. I should probably miss him for real… except that I don't. Other people were right about him and I was wrong. I don't miss his lies and I don't miss second-guessing everything he ever said.

'It's my pleasure,' Andy says. He hovers at our side for a moment before turning and heading back to the counter. Jane waits until he's out of earshot before speaking again.

'Have you heard from the police?' she asks.

'Not really. They said they'll be in contact if anything happens. I think they're keeping an eye on David's bank accounts, that sort of thing.'

I allow myself another sigh, although there is some truth to this exhalation. We're a couple of weeks away from Christmas and Andy's got some sort of festive playlist on the go. On its own, it wouldn't be so bad – but these songs are in every advert break; in every store and on all radio stations. After a while, it makes a person want to rip their own ears off.

Jane slurps at her sympathy juice and then glances towards Andy, before looking back to me: 'What happens next?'

'I don't know. I've been trying to find out how long someone can stay missing before, well…'

I tail off because mentioning that he might be dead doesn't seem like something someone in my situation would want to bring up.

'I don't know what to do with his things,' I add. 'They're still in his drawers and the wardrobe. A windscreen company came out and fixed the glass in his car – but it's still parked outside. Nobody seems to know what I should do with it all. He could be back tomorrow…'

I'm becoming used to following up sentences like this with a lingering stare at a blank patch of wall. This time I settle on the Christmas wreath that Andy has pinned to the wall next to the toilets. There is tinsel around each of the windows and a small fake tree near the door. My mind wanders to wondering whether he put it all up himself.

Jane reaches across and squeezes my shoulder for reassurance. This has gone on for far too long for me to ever tell her I don't like it.

'It's good to see you out,' she says. 'But how are you *actually* doing?'

I'm not sure why but, from nowhere, the truth slips out: 'I miscarried.'

The pressure of keeping everything else to myself has finally become too much, as if my brain only has space for a certain amount of secrets. I'm keeping back so much that this one has to be spoken.

There is silence, though I can feel Jane staring at me. Seconds pass as she searches for the words: 'You were pregnant…?' she asks.

'I wasn't far gone. Maybe a few weeks.'

'Is that why David, um…'

She tails off and it takes me a few seconds to realise she was going to say 'disappeared'.

'I don't know why he left,' I say.

'Did you tell the police?'

I shake my head: 'Only you and him.'

She has another sip of her drink and we watch as a group in Santa hats enter the shop. It's a mix of men and women, probably on a lunchbreak from work. The woman at the front knows Andy by name and sets about ordering as the rest sit near the Christmas tree. I don't know any of them, though one of the women catches my eye and seemingly recognises me. I wonder how long it'll be before people forget who I am.

'It's the not knowing, isn't it?' Jane says. Her voice is a murmur now, hard to hear over the music and voices. 'If David said he was leaving, at least you'd know. If he was, um…' she presses in slightly closer and this time actually whispers '*dead*' with such reverence that it's as if saying the word might make it true. 'I'm not saying he is,' she adds. 'But it would be something final, wouldn't it?'

'I know what you mean…'

'Are you sure there wasn't a trigger for it all?'

'Like what?'

'I don't know. An argument? Was he upset about the pregnancy? Or something else?'

I shake my head.

'How's your mum?' Jane asks.

'She blames me and says I must have done something to make him leave.'

I suppose there's a degree of irony to the fact that, of everyone, my mother is the person who is right.

Jane shuffles back, unsure what to say. She has almost finished her drink, so I slide mine across the table towards her. 'Not in the mood,' I say.

We sit quietly for a moment as the volume increases from the group next to the door. I sense a couple of them sneaking sideways glances towards me, before my phone beeps to distract me. It's an email and, as I skim through it, Jane glances in the other direction in the way people do when they're too polite to ask what's going on.

One thing I never could have expected is that David's apparent disappearance has brought about what can only be called sympathy business. There is a fitness circuit of conferences and health expos that is an industry in itself. People become almost too famous for things like personal training and end up giving talks about the subject, instead of actually doing it. I've never understood how someone could get to that lucrative point – but this email is asking if I'd be interested in hosting a session at an upcoming expo for up to 500 people. It's the third similar offer I've had this week. I'm also swamped with potential clients wanting personal training sessions.

What an irony that, even now, David is finding a way to support my career.

'Word's gone around,' I say to Jane as I put my phone away.

'What do you mean?' she asks.

'People keep offering me work. I've never been so in demand.'

'Wow… at least something good is coming of this, I suppose. Not that it's a good thing, I mean…'

We're interrupted by Andy returning to the table to collect Jane's empty glass.

'Would you like anything else?' he asks, talking to me.

'I think I'm all right,' I reply.

'Just say if I can help.'

He lingers at the table for a couple of seconds too long and then heads back to the counter. I wonder if Jane is going to comment on it because she must have noticed it as well.

'What about you?' I ask, wanting to change the subject.

'What about me?' Jane replies.

'All we do is talk about me…'

She snorts a little: 'Ben's not been himself for the past month or so – but he has busy periods at work, so I suppose it's that.' She pauses for a moment and then adds: 'You should come over one evening soon. Or we'll go out somewhere?'

'We'll figure something out,' I reply, which everyone knows is code for, 'not now'.

Jane finishes my drink and starts shuffling with her bag. 'I have to get going,' she says.

She asks if I need anything and then we do the usual goodbye hug before she heads off.

I continue sitting and it's less than a minute until Andy appears at the table.

'Are you sure you don't want anything else?' he asks.

'I've got to head off,' I reply.

He glances to the door and then focuses on me. Ever since I first started coming here, there's been something of a buzz between us. Always unspoken, but undoubtedly there. Like two magnets at opposite ends of a table that are far enough away not to be pulled together.

'I'm sorry to hear about what happened with your husband,' Andy says.

'Thanks.'

'If there's anything I can do, you know where I am.'

He waits for a few seconds, but I'm not sure what to say. Not yet, anyway. Not properly.

'See you around,' I say.

'I hope so.'

FORTY-FOUR

THE NOW

My hair is jagged and short, like a child who's found a pair of scissors for the first time. There's no style – it's been slashed into sharp angles and, for the first time I can remember, is cropped enough that my ears are on show. I stare at myself in the mirror but it doesn't look like me. I have to touch my face and my hair to know that it's really me and that there isn't some sort of trickery. There is still a sharp pain on the side of my neck close to my scar and, when I half turn, there are two small red dots imprinted into my skin.

'In here,' Jane calls.

I turn from the mirror to see that she's no longer in the living room and then I follow her voice into the kitchen, where my chopped hair is on the floor.

'I don't know what happened,' I say as I stare.

'Is Norah OK?' I ask.

There's a dawning second where Jane's eyes widen and then, without a word, she skips past me and bounds up the stairs. I should follow and yet I'm transfixed by the hair on the floor. It's not even necessarily how ridiculous I now look, it's that this feels like an invasion. I can't quite process what's happened.

There is the sound of more footsteps on the stairs and then Jane reappears. She peers down to the hair and then back to me.

'Norah's fine,' she says. 'She's asleep. I rolled her over to make sure she's unharmed – but she is untouched…'

She scans across me and there's an obvious implication that I'm not. I still feel a little unsteady.

'What happened?' I ask, partly to myself, partly to her.

Jane shifts onto one of the dining chairs: 'I heard noises outside,' she says. 'I went to the window and there was someone at the end of the drive. It looked so much like David that I didn't know what to do at first. We stared at each other and then I went to the front door. By the time I'd opened it, he'd gone.'

'What time?'

'Nine o'clock or so? I texted you not long afterwards.'

'I came straight here.'

It took around twenty minutes to drive along the country roads from Little Bush Woods. If David sent me there for nine, it gave him a good head start here.

'I thought I heard noises at the back,' Jane says. 'I went to the door and the next thing I know, you're here.' She stops and then adds: 'How did you get in?'

'The front door wasn't locked. Not enough that anyone could see from a distance – but enough that it could be pushed open. I came in and then… I don't know. I heard a noise, but then I woke up in your living room. I think someone stabbed something into my neck. I sort of remember shaking, but I'm not sure.'

I touch the spot on my neck without thinking, then I fill a glass with water and drink it down.

'Let's see,' Jane says, and I tilt my head to the side as she peers closely at it like a mother with a child's scabbed knee. 'What do you think it was?' she asks.

'I don't know. Maybe a stun gun? Something like that?'

'Have I got them?' She steps away and tilts her head back so I can see her neck.

There are a pair of similar dimples in the same place on her neck – but they are already fading, with the redness disappearing back to the regular colour of her skin.

'Sort of,' I say.

'Could it be David?'

Jane has finally asked the question specifically. He's dead – and yet I saw him, too. Someone's been texting me. I can hardly tell her that I rolled his body into a lake. She thinks he disappeared.

'Why would he do this?' I say, trying to think of something better.

'I don't know.' She pauses for a second, glances away momentarily and then adds: 'I suppose I was never quite sure why he left. Did you have an argument? Did something happen between you…?'

She reaches inside her top and scratches her shoulder. It's something done so absent-mindedly that I almost miss it. The mole she was supposed to have removed is still there. Jane catches herself scratching, but, by then, it's already too late.

'One of the surgeons was off,' she says. 'Some sort of miscommunication. I've got to go back.'

I'm not sure precisely why, but it's as if a switch has been flicked. It's not even the fact she still has the mole, it's more the way she phrased her questions about David. We've talked about reasons for him leaving before. I've always said I didn't know – because that's all I have. This time, she was pushing the points specifically.

We lock eyes and there, in that moment, I know.

Not only that, she knows that I know.

'Norah,' I say, quietly.

Jane's eyes narrow: 'What about her?'

'When I woke you up, she would have been your first concern. Not my hair, not whether David was around – but Norah.'

Jane is silent for a moment. After everything, it's her own daughter who has caught her out.

'It was you, wasn't it?' I say. 'All of this was you. David. Everything.'

Jane bows her head slightly and bites her lip, before pushing up until she's standing with her arms folded. Her features are fixed and unblinking.

'Well,' she says. 'It took you long enough…'

FORTY-FIVE

Jane is between me and the door, but I'm not sure if she feels like a threat anyway. Then my neck starts to singe with pain and I remember that I've already been knocked out once.

'What was the point?' I say. 'To cut my hair...?'

'It wasn't a bad start,' Jane replies. Her posture has changed from slumped and downtrodden to being rigid and primed. She reaches into the drawer that's closest to her, fumbling underneath some tea towels until she finds what she's looking for and places it on the table at her side. It looks like some sort of plastic gun, like a heavier water pistol.

'Is that a stun gun?' I ask.

'What gave it away?'

I rub my skin once more and look up to see Jane smiling.

'I thought I'd be able to keep this going for months,' she says. 'I was going to see how much I could get away with and slowly drive you mad.'

I look from the Jane to the gun and back again. It's much closer to her, although I have no idea whether these sorts of weapons need to be primed or loaded. Whether they simply work with a point and a click.

'What did you want to achieve?' I ask.

'What do you think?'

'Did you want to... *kill* me?'

Her lips are tight but, from nowhere, Jane snorts with derision. '*Kill you?* I don't think I'd have it in me. I suppose I thought about it some nights – but never seriously. I thought I could mess with you and then watch as you blamed everything on your missing husband. You've got to admit, it's a good alibi?'

It takes everything I have not to laugh. It *would* be a good alibi if it wasn't for the fact that David is dead. I knew that. I *know* that, even though I had a momentary wobble.

Jane thought she could mess with my mind by making me believe David was back – but that's only because she doesn't know the truth.

I killed him.

Her plan would have been perfect if David really had disappeared.

She's so assured that I know I have to ask the question to which I don't particularly want the answer. The question to which I probably already *know* the answer.

'Why?' I say.

It's Jane's turn to look away. She glances upwards towards Norah's room and then focuses back on me. 'All I want is the truth,' she says. 'I think you owe me that.'

FORTY-SIX

THE WHY

Two years, two months ago

'I'd kill for you,' David says. 'Do you know that?'

It's a strange, mixed-up, almost clichéd thing to say. It's supposed to convey a degree of romanticism, as if anyone would want that. But who would? It's an incomprehensibly manic idea to love a person so much that killing someone else is somehow acceptable.

'Why would you say that?' I ask.

'Because it's true.'

For perhaps the first time in our relationship, I genuinely believe him. The doorbell sounds three times in rapid succession and I jump to my feet, spurred on by the urgency.

'Don't go,' David says.

He trails me all the way to the door and, when I open it, Ben is standing there.

'How's it going, Morgs?' he asks.

'It's been worse.'

He glances past me towards David and then pushes the door wider. 'Shall we go?'

I take a breath and then step outside, where the rain continues to lash: 'Yes.'

I quick-step across the pavement to his car and clamber into the passenger side, before clipping my seat belt into place. Ben slides into the driver's seat and starts the engine. I slouch slightly, watching David in the doorway of my flat as we pull away. He stands unmovingly, leaning with one hand above his head, resting on the frame. It's only a few seconds until we are around the corner and out of sight.

'Are you all right?' Ben asks.

'I am now. Thanks for coming.'

We drive in silence for a while, following the road out of Gradingham until we reach the welcome sign. After that, the street lights are behind us and darkness looms.

'Jane's worried,' Ben says.

I turn sideways to take him in, though his eyes are focused on the road.

'What about?'

'About you and David. She thinks he's taking advantage. That he's living with you rent-free and that you pay for everything.'

'It's not like that,' I say.

'Isn't it?'

'He works hard.'

'Are you telling me, or yourself?'

I open my mouth to reply and then realise that I don't know what to say. We both know that Ben's right.

'He was never one of my friends at university,' Ben says.

'Jane told me.'

'I'd wanted to say something for ages. Jane and I talked about it, but the time never felt right. We figured you'd break up sooner or later. After a while, it was too late.'

'Does it matter whether you were friends?'

Ben continues driving, missing a beat, and then says: 'Maybe not. But if he lied about something your friends could easily disprove, then what else would he lie about?'

He leaves it there, though I'm not ready to cave on the point quite yet.

'David's just... misunderstood,' I say. 'He's unorthodox.'

Ben takes a hand off the steering wheel and touches my arm. It only lasts a moment but, in that second, I know we both feel something. Almost as soon as he put his hand there, he removes it again.

'Why did you marry him?' Ben asks.

'Why *haven't* you married Jane?'

He laughs a little, but it feels more like deflection than anything humorous. 'I'm sure we will,' he says.

'You've been together a long time.'

'Maybe I'm not the marrying type...?'

'You're not answering the question.'

'Neither are you.'

Ben reaches forward and adjusts the air conditioning. For a few moments, we sit and listen to the warm air firing through the vents and then I can't take it any longer.

'I didn't want to be alone,' I say. He doesn't reply, so I continue: 'Do you remember when I broke up with Gary? It was at Jane's birthday party at your house. I'd lost my job, too and you told me that everything would come together.'

'I remember.'

'I thought everything was going to fall apart, but then I met David on your stairs and... it didn't. Things got better.'

'But was that because of him – or because of you?'

There's quiet again as I wonder if he has a point.

'Did you know him at all at university?' I ask.

'Do you really want to know?'

'Yes.'

'He was a weirdo. It didn't help that he was older than everyone, but that wasn't a problem in itself. It was more how he was. He'd have all these stories about how he was a great footballer as a teenager – but he was terrible. He tried out for almost every club. He was a great climber – except he couldn't even get a quarter of the way up a wall. He'd been in a choir all his life – but couldn't sing a note. He'd acted in numerous plays but fell out with everyone in the drama club. Most societies had stories about him. I thought he was probably lonely – but nobody's going to make friends by trying to join clubs and acting like they're an expert when they're obviously not.'

I don't reply. It's hard to know whether it matters. Whether it would have made a difference if I'd known this when David and I first met. It probably wouldn't, although, with all I know now, I suppose it's hard to reach any conclusion other than that my husband is a habitual and compulsive liar.

'He told me he was off to Newcastle one time,' I say. 'But then I found him at the service station outside Kingbridge. He was hiding because he was basically unemployed. I don't know if he has a job at all. I'm never sure when he's telling the truth.'

Ben sighs. He takes his hand from the wheel and, for a moment, I think he's going to take my hand. I anticipate it, I *want* it – but then he grips the gearstick and changes down, before returning his hand to the wheel.

'I don't know what to tell you,' he says.

We say little for the rest of the journey. The dark lanes soon become well-lit suburbs and then we're into Kingbridge and the estate on which Ben and Jane live. Ben pulls onto the driveway, takes my night bag from the boot, and then unlocks the house to let me in. I wait in the hall as he locks the door behind us.

'The spare bed is already made up,' he says. 'There's a bit of a new paint smell in there – but it's from weeks ago and shouldn't be too bad. We've been leaving windows open, but it's still taking ages.'

He puts my bag on the bottom step and then turns to the living room.

'Do you want a drink?' he asks. 'There's wine in the fridge, or whatever you want…?'

'Wine sounds good.'

He ushers me into the living room and I wait on the sofa. Moments later, he comes in from the kitchen with a pair of glasses and a bottle. He sits next to me, before emptying a good third of the bottle into my glass. He fills his with the same amount.

'Shall we drink to something?' he asks.

'Old friends…?'

He clinks my glass with his. 'To friends. Old and new.'

We drink and then he presses back onto the sofa. 'Do you want to talk about it?' he asks.

'Not really.'

'Is there something you want to watch on TV? We've got Netflix, plus there's iPlayer and so on.'

I pause for a second. David controls the television in the apartment and it is perhaps only now that I realise how uncomplicated life is for Jane and Ben. No games. No tall stories. A normal life with normal people.

'I'm not in the mood,' I say.

We sit for a short while, each sipping at our wine; each too afraid to say any more. It's Ben who finally crosses the divide. He puts his glass on the table and twists to face me.

'Jane's away until morning,' he says.

That's it. All he's doing is stating a fact of which we are both aware – but we each know that's not what he's saying at all.

I put my glass on the table and turn to face Ben and we both know what happens next.

FORTY-SEVEN

THE NOW

Three weeks after the night that Ben rescued me from my flat, I missed my period. The thing is, even after I've told Jane, she nods only with acceptance.

'How long have you known?' I ask.

She sighs again and has another brief glance upwards towards Norah's room. 'A while,' she says. 'Ben was acting so strangely after the night he picked you up. After the night where *you called me* and asked for help.'

Jane spits the words and I don't blame her. How can I? I never said I was a nice person, because I know I'm not. I did this to my best friend and then I killed my husband.

'I thought I was being kind,' Jane says. 'I thought I was helping you – and look what you did.'

I don't know what to say. Sorry isn't enough – and nor will it ever be.

'It's not as if you hid it well,' she adds. 'You and Ben used to be decent friends and then, from nowhere, you could barely look at one another. You stopped coming over and, if ever I suggested doing something with Ben, you'd always find a reason not to. After that, you told me about your miscarriage and something clicked. I thought you were lying at first, but then I realised what the dates meant – and it wasn't hard to see why David left.' She stops, probably waiting for confirmation, before adding: 'I'm right, aren't I? This is why David left. He found out about you and my husband – and then he walked out?'

I don't answer. She's right and yet she's so, so wrong.

'How did you make him appear in the photo?' I ask.

A smirk slips onto Jane's face: 'You don't know how close I've been to asking you about that. I almost texted to ask if you'd seen anything weird in the photo. You never said a word and I wondered whether you'd missed it.'

'How did you do it?'

'Don't you know what year it is? It's easy enough to edit someone into a photo on your phone. There are YouTube videos everywhere showing how to do things far harder than this. I have to do something with my time while looking after Norah.'

She picks up her phone from the table and taps something on the screen before turning it around for me to see. There's a photo of David in a blue suit – but he's not at the awards dinner; he's at some sort of evening party.

'I took it at your engagement party,' Jane says, although, for some reason, I don't remember him wearing the suit. I suppose I've blocked much of that night from my memory. 'It wasn't hard to slice him out and paste him into the back of your picture. I thought you'd missed it.'

'I don't understand how you managed it all.'

A shrug: 'The photo editing is easy enough when you know how. You can send anonymous texts from different apps. I thought you'd like that.'

'What about my car?'

The smile disappears. 'When you texted to say you were going to drive back, I was already in your flat.'

'You don't have a key?'

'I got one when we were sorting out the cleaner. I suppose I hung onto it and then it became useful.'

'What happened to the Tigger pot?'

She blinks, somewhat surprised. 'Oh… I wondered if you'd notice that. I accidentally knocked it over when I was at yours – then I spent twenty minutes trying to make sure I'd picked up all the bits. I was only there to get your spare car keys.'

Even with this information, the truth doesn't filter through immediately. '*You* crashed into that guy?'

'I figured I'd move your car. Mess with your head a bit. I wasn't going to go far – but then that Trevor stepped out of nowhere. I didn't know his name at the time. I got the hell out of there.'

I wonder if this is how far a person has to be pushed to shrug off something like a car crash. People seem to hit and run all the time and I suppose the biggest reason is that need for self-preservation. Like that one-punch killer. Something stupid then lives change.

'He could be dead,' I say.

'And whose fault is that?'

I want to say that it's hers – and it is – but it's not *only* her fault.

'I know you're angry,' I say, 'but it took two of us that night.'

For a moment Jane glances to the stun gun and I feel certain she's going to lunge for it. I think I see her hand flinch, but then, in a blink, I'm not sure if she's moved.

'Do you know how easy it is to get a stun gun?' she asks.

'What?'

'On holiday or the internet. They're quite common in certain places. It wasn't hard to get. There are all sorts of settings. I wasn't sure if it would work properly – but then it did. I guess I got my money's worth…'

I find myself touching the double pinpricks on my neck – and then the original scar I got from David. She must have been hiding behind the front door when I stepped inside.

'Ben is Norah's father,' Jane says. 'If you were ever expecting me to choose, then it was always going to be him.'

'You used your own daughter,' I say. 'It must have been you in the park.'

'She was always safe. I didn't expect you to dump her in a toilet while you disappeared to take a phone call.'

I could argue the point – that's not how things were – but there are bigger hills. 'It shouldn't have happened,' I say. 'None of it should have happened.'

'No – but it says plenty because, after all that's gone on this week, you still couldn't tell me you thought David might be back. If you did that, you'd have to admit that he ran off because he found out you slept with my husband.' She stops and then adds: 'We're supposed to be friends.'

Jane waits for a reply but what is there to say?

Suddenly, the anger overtakes her and her voice rises to a shout: 'It's the unfairness I can't stand. You were going nowhere. You sleep with *my husband* and force your husband to run off and then, suddenly, you're a success. You've got people inviting you to conferences, to give speeches, to give you awards. You get your own studio, you hook up with the cute guy who looks after kids, and volunteers, and runs a business. The *only* reason it happens is because people feel sorry for you.'

Jane has said all this without seemingly taking a breath. She gasps and then picks up the stun gun.

'But they don't know you, do they? At the awards, when they said, "after all she's been through", I wanted to scream. To stand up and tell them who you really were. Do you think they'd be giving you awards if they knew why your husband left?'

I understand the anger. It's not only what Ben and I did, it's compounded by the jealousy that, while Jane has given up her career for a child, however willingly, I've gone from strength to strength. There's supposed to be karma in the world. Good people are supposed to win. What goes around comes around, and all that. These are the lies to get us through the days; to stop madness descending. And here I am – a person for whom none of those things apply.

'I don't understand what you want from all of this,' I say. 'I get the idea of revenge. You wanted to make me think David was back and to drive me mad. Then what?'

Jane weighs the gun in her hand before placing it back on the table. There's something about the way her shoulders slump that says she isn't going to use it a second time. I don't think she'd necessarily thought so far ahead. She was going to use David as something to hang over me for months. Something to enjoy until she eventually revealed herself.

The next time we lock eyes, it feels as if something's changed. There's a cold determination in her stare.

'I want you to go away,' she says, almost mechanically. 'That's all I want.'

I almost laugh because of the simplicity of it all. She isn't after my death or any great suffering. There's no big, grandiose gesture to bump me off or frame me for something. The car crash was an accident on her part. All she wants is for me to go away.

'I'm sick of looking at you,' Jane adds. 'Sick of hearing about your success and everyone feeling sorry for you. I want you to go and live somewhere else a long way away from here.'

Deep down, it's not even that unreasonable. Imagine someone sleeping with their best friend's husband. There's not only the betrayal – but then that person is there all the time. To disappear is the least someone who was actually sorry could do.

Jane slips down until she's sitting on the dining chair once more. I take the seat on the other side of the table from her. We sit a short distance apart while barely acknowledging the other's existence. A minute passes and neither of us says anything. Longer. I know that what happens now will shape who I am. Is the world full of good guys and bad guys, or are we all shades of grey? And, if so, how dark does my grey run? I know I should go and give us both a second chance.

Except nothing can bring David back and I already know who I am.

'What if I don't?' I say. 'What if I want to stay?'

'Then I'll tell Andy about you and David. About how you were pregnant, whose baby it was, and why David ran off.'

'Then you'd be admitting what Ben did.'

Jane nods. She suddenly seems exhausted. 'I can live with it. Norah's too young to understand if it gets out – and we'll get by anyway. You're the one whose life and career is built around, "After all she went through". You've got way more to lose than me. I'll be the one getting sympathy.'

She's probably right. Once word goes around, the conference and speaker invites probably will dry up. Membership at the studio might drop. My personal clients might look elsewhere. It's the world in which we live. Perhaps my life and career will fall apart. People will forgive all sorts – but sleeping with a best friend's husband is probably not one of them.

All of which means I have a decision to make.

Except I have already made it.

'I'm not leaving,' I say.

'Then I'll tell everyone.'

'No, you won't.'

Jane peers up, taking me in across the table. I can't tell if she's angry or resigned. 'Why do you think I won't?' she asks.

'Because you're wrong.'

Her eyes narrow: 'Come on. I know you slept together.'

'Not about that,' I say. 'We did that and I regret it. You're wrong about David. He didn't leave me.'

Jane cranes her neck backwards a little and frowns, obviously not believing me.

'So, where is he?' she asks.

This time, I don't hesitate. It's been so hard to hang onto the secret for this long and it's a relief to get the words out.

'David's dead,' I say. 'I killed him.'

FORTY-EIGHT

Jane stares at me, her mouth open and her eyebrow twitching. 'You… what?'

'I killed him,' I say, composed and calm. Perhaps I learned that from David? 'I didn't mean to – but I did get rid of the body. I did that knowing exactly what I was doing. Then I told everyone he ran away.'

Jane continues to stare, as if she's frozen. She's known me long enough to realise that I'm telling the truth – but it's only now that she must know how badly she's misjudged the situation.

'I'm not going anywhere,' I say. 'You know what I'm capable of – and you'll never be able to prove what happened to David. You can stay around if you want. I won't interfere in your life. I will never speak another word to you, if that's what you want. But you won't tell anyone about Ben and me – and you won't tell anyone about what happened to David.'

Jane slips further into the chair and the fight has left her. She thought one thing was going to happen and, instead, it's something completely different.

'If you do,' I say, 'just remember that your end game was for me to move away. Mine was to get rid of my husband's body, hide the evidence and spend two years convincing everyone that *I* was the wronged woman.'

I wait for her to look up. To make sure she is looking into my eyes when the truth is finally known. When I know she fully has my attention, I stand and move my way around to the door before speaking to her for the last time.

'I guess the question is whether I should be scared of you, Jane – or whether you should be scared of me.'

FORTY-NINE

Six weeks later

Jane and Ben moved away last night.

Nobody has told me officially because I've not spoken to either of them since that night at Jane's house. I heard through various acquaintances that Ben sorted out some sort of job transfer with his bank. Their family of three is off to London for a new life.

Good for them.

I mean that.

It's strange how we've been friends for so long and yet, in the past six weeks, I don't think I've missed Jane. I doubt that she's missed me, either. That must be who I am. Perhaps I should never have been scared of being alone because, in the end, I thrive on precisely that.

I cross to my kitchen and put the kettle on. *My* kitchen. I never did move in with Andy. I was doing it for the wrong reasons – and I've already gone through that once. It wasn't anything to do with him googling David. In the end, I figured why wouldn't he be searching for my husband's name? If roles were reversed, I probably would.

It's been a confusing few weeks trying to piece together everything that happened. I found out that Mum got her Lennon autograph from one of the other residents who lives on her row. Veronica called me the morning after everything happened at

Jane's. It's not a massive surprise because, as I already knew, she's spent a lifetime telling anyone who'll listen about the time she saw him on the street. The last time I saw her, she still claimed she'd always had it.

As for Yasmine, I don't know what to think. She never showed up for another class and the 'really got it coming to her' that I overheard must have meant someone else. She could have been talking about that night's *EastEnders* for all I know.

Trevor, who Jane hit in my car, is out of intensive care. He's conscious but still in hospital. I suppose that's one thing. Mr Patrick tells me there was a sighting of a young man running in the centre of Gradingham at roughly the time of the crash. It's a new line of enquiry that is, apparently, still open – even if it is nonsense. Whoever they're looking for didn't steal my car and didn't hit Trevor. I can hardly tell the police that – but I'm in the clear anyway. My insurance company are even paying out – and it'll be more money than my car was worth. What goes around definitely does not come around. I can promise people that.

So it's over.

I win.

Hurray for me.

Life goes on.

I'm pouring hot water into a mug when the letter box clinks. I pop in a teabag and then cross to where the mail has hit the welcome mat.

There is an IKEA catalogue, something from a bank – and then one letter with my name and address handwritten on the front.

I recognise Jane's writing immediately. It's not changed since school and we sat together for long enough. There was a time when actual, real letters used to mean joy. It would be something from a friend or a penpal. A mate from camp who we'd never see again. Now it's only bills and adverts.

Except for this.

The pages inside have been torn from a notebook, with the scrambled spiral holes along the left side. The letter doesn't say much – but it says enough.

Why did 'you know where' mean the lake at Little Bush Woods?

Jane hasn't signed it – but she doesn't need to. I'd somehow missed that. In believing it was David who was texting me, I'd led the real messenger directly to the place where my greatest secret is hidden. Jane must have followed me. I suppose it would be a fun game with most people to tell them to meet 'you knew where' – and then see where they go. How many long buried stories would emerge?

And so she knows.

I'd already led her to the lake and, when I told Jane that I'd killed David, it wouldn't take much for someone to figure out that the two things are intrinsically connected.

There is no further threat, but I suppose it is implied. Jane knows my secrets – all of them. I suppose this is her way of saying that, if I go for her, then she'll come for me. That, perhaps, she has already set things in motion. Perhaps an anonymous tip to the police that they should check the lake? Even with that, there would be no proof that I put David there. That's if he's still there anyway. He could be bones by now.

But Jane knows – and she's saying that it's not only her who is going to spend a life looking over her shoulder. We all lash out when we feel under threat.

I finish making my tea and then take the lighter from the cutlery drawer. I burn the letter in the sink, watching the embers crisp black before I run the tap to wash it all away.

Who's good and who's bad?

Everyone might be the hero of their own stories and, whatever others may think, I'm the hero of mine.

A LETTER FROM KERRY

Around five or six years ago, one of my good friends, an ex-work colleague, put up a photo of himself on Twitter. He was entertaining his kids and, in the process of this, was wearing a full-body fox onesie.

Little did either of us know that one photo would start a chain reaction that would one day lead to this book.

I downloaded that picture, did a quick Photoshop cut-out around him and have spent the entire time in between dropping him into various photographs, before posting it on his Facebook wall.

It's more or less the only reason I go on Facebook nowadays.

Remember the photo of Theresa May at her election count, with Lord Buckethead at her side? I dropped my friend into that. How about the staged picture of Boris Johnson making up with his girlfriend in a field? Yep, he's in there. Or the background of JFK in that car in Dallas, 1963? Or numerous Donald Trump images? Or the back of mutual mates' wedding pics? Or *Avengers* posters?

I essentially do this to amuse an audience of one (me) or, at best, two (him). It's been going on for so long now, that any major news image that doesn't include him somehow feels wrong.

Anyway… this is a long-winded way of explaining that my quick two-minute Photoshops of him gave me the idea for this book. If someone was to use this ability for nefarious purposes, where could it lead?

I should also point out that I don't actually use Photoshop itself – but that I've adopted it as a verb for this book in order to hopefully make it a bit more universal. An in-depth explanation of how Pixelmator works doesn't feel like good material for a novel.

The question authors get asked the most is always: 'Where do you get your ideas from?' – and I can now reveal that, for this book at least, the answer is: 'Immature, long-running jokes with former work colleagues.'

After hearing that, I'm sure everyone reading this must now realise they have a book within them.

If you did enjoy it, and want to keep up to date with all my latest releases, just sign up at the following link. Your email address will never be shared and you can unsubscribe at any time.

www.bookouture.com/kerry-wilkinson

Thanks for reading.
Kerry

kerrywilkinson.com

@kerrywk

Lightning Source UK Ltd.
Milton Keynes UK
UKHW012231240220
359233UK00005B/1565